Lili is a Mesopotamian siren, and life as an immortal being is hard enough as it is. She's asexual (which is incredibly difficult to reconcile if your entire point as a mythical being is to seduce people to death). She's also struggling with depression from being alive for so long.

Lili is an absolutely shoddy improv-detective trying to track down a serial killer so ruthless that it makes even her murderous soul uneasy. However, there's something larger at work than just one serial killer. A small town is hiding an even deadlier, global-scale secret. Forget Area 51 conspiracies. This one beats them all. With magic.

So, what better way to spice up her eternal life than being hired as a vigilante detective to stop a serial killer? Anything, literally anything. She'd trade her left lung to get out of this. Or, perhaps, somebody else's.

I0583727

CATCH LILI TOO

Gamin Immortals, Book One

Sophie Whittemore

A NineStar Press Publication

www.ninestarpress.com

Catch Lili Too

Printed in the USA

ISBN: 978-1-64890-143-0

First Edition, November, 2020

Also available in eBook, ISBN: 978-1-64890-142-3

WARNING:
This book contains graphic violence, the death of a secondary character, suicide, murder, cancer, references to mental illness.

To those who taught me how to love—
both internally and externally.

To those who have magic in their veins
and stories in their blood.

You're all stars.

Chapter One

A Scandal in Gamin

The first killing had been easy. A little girl wandering the woods with a storybook under her arm. She hardly looked up; why would she? There were no tales of the killer in the wood.

Not unless you count fairy tales, that is. And who believes in those until it is too late?

She had books about fantastical heroes who go on quests to fight Evil that had a very purposeful capital E. She had colored in the pages of the black-and-white line drawings with pencils, with sweeping trains and glittering scales of armor. The pencils scattered on the ground, pages torn up and trampled underfoot. A halo around her perfect, little angelic head.

For that alone, the killer decided, she deserved to die. She was simply too good for this world. She would never have made it anyway. It was a mercy.

The second killing was more difficult. The killer, a little dirtier with a couple of claw marks on their face that would need to be fixed with a potion later, dragged their feet in the mud. The river was close; they could feel it. The sheer power emanating from it.

Their tongue darted out between their lips, tasting it. Death. Destruction.

Power. How long had it been since they'd felt it?

The killer scaled the little inn while everyone was sleeping. The owners had tried to modernize the inn to become an unremarkable hotel, the kind with a front desk and plastic keycards, and a swimming pool with far too much chlorine. Unremarkable except for one guest they had staying there. A guest who would check out and be replaced by someone far more powerful than he. Not that he knew it yet. Who would know if they were in the presence of a god, anyhow?

He wouldn't, surely. He'd be dead before she arrived.

The killer knocked on the door of room 217. They hadn't forgotten their manners in all their years of living. A curious figure came to the doorway, pressing their bespectacled face to it. They were a poet, fingers stained with ink and mind humming with words. Black hair swept through like a Romantic in the eye of the storm.

That's the trouble with this town, the killer decided. Everyone believes in stories. That someone will try to save them.

"Are you all right?" the poet asked. "If you're looking for the receptionist, everyone's already gone home..."

The killer knocked the poet into the room and slammed the door shut behind them. A length of rope fell from their jacket.

"*Come mierda*, you're crazy! What do you want with me? I don't have any money. I'm a writer. I'm broke."

The killer put their boot on the poet's throat, uncoiling the length of rope. The poet choked and gargled and gasped in agony.

"I don't want your money," the killer cooed. "I want your room. At first, I thought I would just leave a note for the next guest. A little calling card to say I'm here. But I found something better than paper." They leaned down and traced the poet's jaw with a gloved finger. "Blood and flesh, for example."

The poet died an unremarkable death for an unremarkable life. He'd most likely come back as a ghost, the killer decided. Violent deaths always got sentimental. But that would suit the killer just fine. He wouldn't remember a thing, not in life or in death. The killer's power made sure of that. Anonymity was annoying most of the time, but sometimes it was useful.

"A very powerful immortal will be the first to find you. You're my welcome gift to her. No other will find you until then..." The killer pressed upon the body, sealing the contract in blood, flesh, and skin.

The killer yearned to look upon the immortal themselves, but that would ruin the ultimate plan. The immortal was so remarkable they might have been called a god if humans took kindly to that sort of thing. And nobody knew it yet, not even the immortal in question. That was why the killer did what they did. Killed anyone at all who might strike the immortal's fancy. It was unusual, but that's what the killer wanted.

The killer, strangely enough, wanted to get caught.

Just not yet.

*

The Sweeney Inn

"My name is Lili."

"Patty," she answers, pressing a lock of red hair behind her ear. Square-framed glasses slide down her freckled nose. Nervous, she takes my hand as I extend it over the front desk. The lobby door swings slowly shut. Yellow-white light spills out over us both as I take her in. The door slams when she finally ends the lingering handshake. "Patty Sweeney."

I raise an eyebrow at the surname.

"Yes, *Sweeney*. Like the name of the hotel we're staying at. The Sweeney Inn."

"Ah," I grin, taking my dear, sweet time since the place is fairly empty. "I didn't realize I was speaking to a famous hotel heiress."

"Coheir. But currently, I'm the concierge." She replies with a purr, leaving me wondering if the aphrodisiac worked. It's supposed to work right on contact with my skin, but I'm not certain if she's fallen for me just yet. I hope so.

She smells delicious.

I wonder how long it would take for her to die.

"You're going to have to wait to check in," she continues, going back to sorting through envelopes on the tabletop. "Jason's playing bartender. He has your room key on him, but he should be right back. You'll know when you see him. He's like me, but a guy. And unfairly buff." She rolls her eyes at that. "We're twins. Kind of like *The Shining* but without the bloody elevators bit. He's the other coheir and concierge."

"He can take his time." I allow my eyes to linger on her lips and then flick my gaze back up to her face. She blushes, and that's when I know I have her. "A long, long time."

Gods, she almost makes me forget myself with this rush of power...

Almost.

Patty has it all. Perfect smile. Cute eyes. Belly ring and septum piercing. With all the piercings, she probably isn't afraid of needles (or unnaturally long incisors.) Lesbian flag pin on her vest, so I know she's into women. The crop top she wears says FAT GIRLS RULE WORLDS. Exposing her skin and veins. And her heart. Her heart... I can *hear* her heart.

I haven't had human heart in so long.

I think my stomach's growling.

"What are your plans for the weekend, cutie?" I drawl, touching her hand a bit, fingertips against fingertips. My Siren powers call to her, that magic aphrodisiac.

She pauses, looks me dead (or rather, living) in the eye and says, "I have a girlfriend." Even against my aphrodisiac, her willpower's too strong. She must *really* love this girl.

Girlfriend 1. Lili 0.

I lean back, dropping the smirk set on my lips. "Ah. Lucky her."

Really lucky...

Fortunately, Jason finally arrives to hand me my key (and spare me any more awkwardness). I consider flirting with him, just for a nice appetizer. But then he moves closer to shake my hand. And the closer he gets, the more the distinct smell of potato chips envelops my senses.

Maybe I'll try fasting.

Failing to corrupt and devour two siblings in a single day. I've hit a horrible low as a monster. I won't last while I'm this hungry.

I might even do something I regret.

When Jason pulls away from our awkward handshake, his eyes still haven't left my face. *What's he searching for?*

"Sorry, you arrived a bit earlier than I expected. I'm going to need some coffee. Want me to grab you anything?"

"No." I force an equally uncomfortable grin on my face. "I'm good."

"How did you find travel to Gamin?"

"I forgot most of it." *Mercifully.*

"Funny." Jason turns to face me halfway. "Most people who arrive in Gamin never want to leave it. Who'd want to? Except for the...well, never mind that."

With that cryptic remark, he leaves me alone with Patty (mercifully on her cell phone, ignoring me). If I were petty, I'd be on my cell phone, too, giving the service in this place a one-star review. But I'm not petty. I'm nosy. Blame it on the whole "is an immortal and nothing is new anymore so now I have to stir up trouble" instinct, but there's something about Jason I don't like.

All of him, for example.

And then there's the way he keeps staring at me. Not a hint of fear in his eyes. Only curiosity. Only troublemakers have that much curiosity.

Troublemakers like me.

When Jason goes to fetch his coffee, I sneak a peek at his ledger. He's left it at the hotel desk, expensive with a nice marble finish. I glance over at Patty, but she's so absorbed texting (most likely her pesky girlfriend) she won't be a problem. The Sweeneys' hotel isn't doing great if both its owners can be off duty at once. And the ease with which I acquired a room last second tells me it won't be doing better anytime soon. So, I slide the ledger over to me in one sweep of my hand. I drag a box of tissues beside it as a cover.

Jason's ledger, to say the least, is concerning. It features a full-page portrait sketch of me, for one thing. Something glowing in my eyes, something markedly monstrous.

> *Lili. Age: ??? Late teens or early twenties. Gray eyes. Brown skin. Dark hair in a tight braid. Cannot place the accent, but not from Minnesota. Definitely not Gamin.*

> *Is she one of them?*

Interesting. This Jason isn't what he appeared to be. *Them.* Like he knew something he shouldn't have. Or rather...

Jason isn't human either. Not quite.

"Hey, Jason was it? I'm sure I can find my own room!" I shout toward the break room where he went to fetch coffee. "I'll just go and let myself up."

"Oh, your room hasn't been cleaned yet. Nobody's been up there since we left last night." Here, he gets sheepish. "It's just me and Patty. Sorry."

"I don't mind a messy room, really. I just need a place to sit for a while."

He peeks around the corner, but I'm already heading for the stairs. "All right, enjoy your stay," he concedes, a paper cup in hand. "Anything else I can help you with before you go?"

"Yeah, actually. How big is Gamin?"

"Well"—he scratches the back of his neck as he sets the cup down—"last I drove past the welcome sign, we were at 13,013 for population. But every person counts, you know."

"I'll keep that in mind."

No hunting for me. Too small a town. They'll remember faces.

I don't want to be remembered as a monster. But it's so hard to remember what I'd rather be. My memory, it's been slipping the longer I stay in this small town. Trapped. Caged by some horrible fear.

But before any of that. Before I came to Gamin...

Why can't I remember?

I go up the steps, swinging my old-fashioned silver key around its lanyard, and open the door to my Sweeney Inn room. (Room 217). The place reeks of loneliness, like too much bleach and fabric softener. Remnants of past guests stay in the corners of the room. A Bible with the pages hastily dog-eared. A child's stuffed toy, most likely gotten with a fast-food order, tossed beneath the bed. Only its head remains in the plastic-wrap. Gray comforters (smarter to hide the stains) with the pillows pressed in the indentation of a human head. An unplugged alarm clock with the cord snaking back to a forgotten battery. A silver-backed TV still tuned onto a countdown show, icons of the past decade or something like that.

It's a tidy room, for the most part, if unloved. Still, tidy as it is, there's no worse feeling than feeling confined in here. A monster in a zoo. Like the time when I went to a freakshow at a fair a century ago. I paid to feel something, anything. Instead, I only felt that I should be the one in their places. I freed them, the "freaks," and I ate the circus master. The one who had done the horrible deed to them. Made them feel like less than nothing.

Made me feel like less than even that.

But that's another tale.

What else to say about this sad little room? A mug stained with coffee at the absolute bottom that just couldn't get scrubbed out. I use the mug to store my medicine kit.

Or rather, my various tangerine bottles with the condescending childproof cap on them.

Or rather, just a singular tangerine bottle. The latest in a glorious lineage.

It's a bottle of antidepressants. Antidepressant brand fifty-eight, to be exact, procured from a nice young man on a street corner in New York. Per usual, it didn't work. Human medicine cannot suffice for Siren needs even if Sirens, like humans, might suffer from similar afflictions. I tried therapy, the kind where you text your therapist. But then the lies became too much, getting my story mixed up about what cities I lived in. How old I was. Also, I made a bad deal with a *garuda*, an anthropomorphic eagle warrior who flew over from Jakarta to party in Manhattan on a whim. Long story short, I lost my cellphone, my cellphone therapist, and a couple of teeth. I only replaced one of those things.

Vampires make great dentists, but horrible therapists.

We are immortal but not invincible.

As I walk further into the space, I see two young men are waiting for me in my room. One is transparent, and the other is a corpse with a rope around his neck, swinging from the rafters and smelling of rot and mildew.

"Hello there," says the ghost. "My name is Byron López. I hate to be a bother, but could you cut my body down from there?"

Chapter Two

Room 217

"Pleasure to meet you, I'm Byron the poet. The—" The spirit grimaces at his corpse. "—the less famous Byron." The ghost's body swings from the ceiling fan, spinning slowly and gathering dust. A short stool lies on its side on the floor, initials of two lovers (*B + T*) scratched into one of its legs, the edges all faded from how often people have run their fingers against the marks. I move the stool and prop it back up near the vanity mirror before stepping closer to the swinging body on the ceiling fan. I examine the scene, crossing my arms and stifling a yawn. I like looking over humans, marking them for the best meat. Suicides aren't that fresh anymore though; the meat tastes like despair.

"Byron. I met him. Mad. Bad. Dangerous to know." I grin at that. "I taught him well."

"*You* met Byron?" The ghost looks me over, looking as skeptical as a ghost can. "You're like, what, twentysomething?"

"Thank you." I wave the statement away. "Oh, darling, no! I just age really, really well."

Byron looks at me, so I take the time to look at him. The ghost has a haircut like a British schoolboy's during World War II, just brushing against his shoulders and parted in the middle. Thick metal rims cover his face in the shape of the gaudiest pair of spectacles I've ever seen with how the dense lenses scoop outwards like spoons. A long, sweeping overcoat dangles from his skeletal frame. Six feet tall at best and resembles a poetic pirate with a duster jacket and distressed jeans. His eyes are black as belladonna, and his ghostly lips are twisted into either a false smile or a very real scowl of annoyance.

"Interesting work you did here. Did you hang yourself, or did you have help?" I ask Byron's corpse even as his ghost taps his ethereal foot impatiently behind me. I make no move to cut him down, counting the number of times his body takes a lap from that ceiling fan. It's oddly hypnotic.

"Details. I believe I am past the point of caring now. Could you please cut me down?" He has a bit of an accent. Being a Siren, I can appreciate his fashion sense (we live for the drama). His patience, on the other hand, is sorely lacking.

"I don't have to help you. I'm probably the only one who can see you since most humans can't." (Except for necromancers, but who would *ever* want to meet one of those?)

Byron's ghost runs his fingers through his hair, his crescent fingertips passing basically through air for all the action's worth. "Y-you—" He pauses, trembles like the snowfall, and then starts again. "—you aren't a human?"

I look over at his spirit form and wait for my eyes to shift color. They stay stubbornly gray as I look past him at my room's vanity mirror. This makes my skin prickle slightly. My eyes refusing to change usually doesn't happen. Perhaps it's because he's dead. Maybe it's because I'm weak and hungry. I'll have to resort to a different sort of persuasion. I sigh and steel myself for the biting cold as I force my hand to break through the spirit layer.

My strength drains immediately as I grip his ethereal flesh, as much of a sense of physical touch as he's ever going to have at this stage of un-death. My hand grows cold from crossing the barrier that feels as though it's on fire. His eyes widen as he glides away from me, eluding my torturous grasp. "How many humans you know that can do this?"

He crosses himself. *"Diablo...mierda, una bruja está aquí ahora..."* He places his hand over the spot where I touched him. I see my Siren handprint marked like ash into his noncorporeal form. It fades when he removes his palm. "Don't do that again."

I shake out my hand. My horribly blistered palm knits itself slowly back together. "Trust me. That was about as pleasant for me as it was for you." I wait another moment for my skin's aphrodisiac to set in, for the moment Byron inevitably falls.

Another agonizing minute ticks by. Byron just continues to glare. I raise an eyebrow at that. "I know you're dead, but how the hell did that not work either?"

He narrows his eyes at me suspiciously. His corpse whips around, still dangling from the fan, and passes directly through his sternum as he scowls. "What didn't work?"

"Are you not attracted to me?"

"Are you crazy? I'm gay! And you still haven't cut my body down from that damned ceiling fan." Byron crosses his arms, his eyes burning with hatred instead of the lust most have for the Siren. "Besides...I didn't kill myself."

"What the hell are you talking about?"

"You asked me if I committed suicide." Byron pauses a moment before continuing. "I didn't. I tried to stop it last second. I changed my mind, but the fan swung at the last second and kicked the stool out from under me. Or at least, I think so." He pauses, staring at his feet. "I can't remember properly. Why can't I remember?"

I waver, uncertain just what to say. How does one who never dies console someone who just did? "I'm sorry for your loss."

When Byron answers me, sorrow and disappointment mingle in his voice. "That's really all you're going to say?"

I stop pacing dazedly and turn around to face him. Byron's floating over his corpse, attempting pathetically to close its eyelids. I stretch upward and close his glassy eyes for him. "Some luck I have, getting help from an aloof vampire," he mumbles, looking miserably at his ghostly hands.

"Seirína. Siren. Succubus. I'm no *vampire*. And my kind don't do much of this, not unless one of us is stupid enough to get beheaded or the like. Dying is more of a human pastime." I shrug, putting my hands into the pockets of my peacoat. "Well, do you want me to report downstairs that I found you or what? Don't tell me you're one of those vengeful hauntings." I scratch at the back of my neck awkwardly as Byron sobs. No tears flow down his cheeks, obviously. He's dead. His form just shimmers a bit as he hovers over the floor on bent knees, his hands in the air, folded in supplication, crying dry. Gasping for air for his nonexistent lungs.

Byron sobs for so long that I wonder if I should throw his body out of the window, crawl into bed, and just get something that passes as sleep while I have the chance. (Not that we immortals really need sleep. Not one of our top priorities).

I have my hands under his corpse's armpits and am dragging it toward the window when Byron floats in my way again. "Can you bring me back to life?"

I laugh, baring my pearly-white teeth at him. "Why should I care?"

"I don't need you to care. I just want what I want. Are you one of those magical creatures that does trades? If you find a way to bring me back to life"—Byron improvises, gliding so that his face is planted directly in front of mine and our noses almost touch—"I can give you all my money. It's not like I need it anymore."

"You really think the measly amount of money your broke ass had is worth anything to me? All I want is to be left to rot in this godforsaken inn. I don't want sex, riches, or fame. I just want my immortality to be spent here. *Alone.*"

Byron's face lights up with an impish glee as he claps his hands together. "I'll haunt you forever if you don't find a way to bring me back. I'll nag you until the end of time." He falls to his knees, or what passes now for them, clasping his hands. "Please. I never meant to commit suicide. I still have so much poetry left to create. I have a purpose, unfinished business."

"You and every other ghost." I consider this new proposition, nudging his corpse with my toe. "Your old body's going to rot before I find a way to put you back in it. It'd honestly be more economical if I just ate the whole thing now and saved the Earth the hassle of decomposing it."

Byron reaches out to grasp at my shoulders, but he stops himself at the last moment as he remembers my burning handprint. "I wasn't much for being the religious ashes-to-ashes type anyways. Devour my body for all I care. Just give me a second chance."

I laugh, yanking my fingers angrily through my hair, letting it all loosen from my braids. The stringy locks float up around my face, carried upward like I'm swimming underwater. The air is tense with my magic as I pull out all stops to scare this stupid, whiny ghost away from me. Byron, to his credit, only cowers a little bit. I sigh. "You'd really do anything to come back to life?"

Byron falls to his knees as my skin glimmers. I reach out to throttle him. He can't die twice, but the blisters on my palms will be worth all the pain I can cause him. "Please." He backs away, his voice warbling in fear. "Take me with you, and I will be your loyal servant."

I scratch my chin and yawn. "Servant? Sweetie, the only thing you're serving is looks in that *Matrix* jacket."

Byron chuckles at that, and I smile despite myself at his audacity. Damn. I'd forgotten what it felt like to make somebody laugh. It makes you more present like you're *somebody* instead of *nobody*. You don't get a chance to laugh much as a Siren, not with all the bloodshed and fleeing from town to town. I stop with my parlor trick magic. The air falls flat again like a lute gone all out of tune. "I'm tired of these silly games. Leave me be, ghost, before I grab a priestess or a monk to exorcise you."

"You sound like me back when I was living. Cynical." Byron deflates as he hovers by the window. He holds out a single, slender hand to feel the mist outside roll off his ghostly skin. There's something melancholy about it, to see the dead poet as he grabs futilely at the moon outside, letting the night air slip through his translucent fingers, losing his ability simply to exist. "Are you depressed, *bruja*?"

I glance over at his corpse, rubbing my own neck as I see the swollen outline surrounding his. "Who heard of an immortal Siren being depressed?" Byron stays silent, and the longer he stays silent, the more I feel judged within that silence.

What are you thinking of me, you pesky poltergeist?

He points to the empty bottle of antidepressants.

"Nosy ghost, aren't you?" Finally, breaking beneath the pressure, I grumble, "Yes, I'm depressed. I'm... I...it's none of your business now, is it?"

"If I were you," Byron amends, "I'd make every day as a Siren count."

"If I were you," I reply coolly, "I'd kick over my stool without hesitation." I run my fingers over the noose around the bloated corpse's neck, itching to throw the remaining rope over my own collar, to end my immortal imprisonment and finally rest in peace. "How ironic. I want an end to my life, and you want a do-over. It's not like either of us can get that, can we?"

Byron and I laugh as one. There's no humor in that laughter. It's as empty as the shell of an ethereal man trying to touch the moon and letting only moonbeams fall through the gaps.

"Can you give me back my life?" Byron asks with a crackle of nervous energy in his voice, placing his cold hand upon my shoulder, his fingers poking through me.

"And what will you give me in return?"

The ghost flickers uncertainly in the pale shutters of light. "Do you accept souls as payment?"

"I'm a Siren, not *the* Satan." I lean in close to Byron's corpse, but then a glimmer of light catches on an object in his hands, gone stiff from rigor mortis. I pry a tiny black book, lovingly protected with a sleeve of plastic, from his grip. Ignoring Byron's complaints, I whisper a simple cantrip that most immortals can use soon after their making, and then hand the finished product back to him with little flourish. "There, I enchanted your journal so you can write in it from the spirit world. I haven't done anything particularly narcissistic lately. How about you write a poem about me? You can even call it *Lili* just to make it extra egotistical."

"Lili. Beowulf. Odysseus. Same thing."

"You're not one to talk, *Byron.*" We both go to the window, our shaking bouts of nervous laughter made worse as we laugh at each other, succumbing to the all-too-familiar apathy I know too well. "I somehow resurrect you in exchange for a book of poems and peace of mind. That's more than fair."

I attempt to cover his eyes with one hand, but he glides past my arm in defiance.

"Look away while I destroy what's left of your body. I'm, well, I'm not proud to say it. But I wasn't able to hunt last night. So, since your body's just lying there... Do you mind?"

"Not at all. Well, no. I do mind, but I'm not going to be snobby about it." He raises an eyebrow, not attempting to peek. "Tell me, does my flesh taste more like five-star Michelin or trucker diner?"

Bite your tongue, poet.

I stand on an unsteady chair, ready to cut the poet down. To my astonishment, it takes little maneuvering. Byron's body falls face-first on the floor.

"Why have you stopped? What's wrong?"

I point to the dead poet's back as I lift his trench coat up with my shoe.

A letter's been carved into him. A message in blood and flesh.

Catch me if you can, Lili.

Or I'll catch you.

Chapter Three

Taking Care of Business, Getting Out of Garmin

Jason Sweeney, twin brother of Patty Sweeney and co-owner of the Sweeney Inn, has the most incredulous look on his face as he stands with his hands in his apron, staring up at the room.

My room, to be precise.

The only room in the inn, both miraculously and hellishly, to be on fire.

Fire is easy. You give fire life, and it destroys all it can. Living. Dead. Mortal or immortal. It doesn't choose, doesn't care. Fire's the great equalizer of destruction. I had that once, fire in me. Destroying everything I touched simply because I could.

But who needs to think on the past when you have ghosts to do that for you?

"What possessed you to set your own room on fire?" Byron watches, hovering steadily beside me. "Whoever did, it certainly wasn't me."

"You saw that note that was *written* into you, didn't you? Some creep is after me, and I'm not going to stay here a second longer. I might be immortal, but eternal life becomes finite if you get decapitated." I wave for him to follow me as we slink away from the inn, keeping to shadows. "And besides. You *just* died there. You're a new ghost. If you get too attached to the dwelling you died in, it's like opium. You go back to it, over and over again. I freed you, ripped any attachment off like a fiery Band-Aid." I nod as he raises an eyebrow at that confused comparison. "You can thank me now, you know."

"Thank you, I think," Byron replies, watching poor Jason and Patty Sweeney as they converse beside the fire truck. "You know. I think you *liked* setting that room on fire. No, not just liked it. You enjoyed it." He pauses, tilting his head at the thought. "Are all Sirens this vindictive?"

"No. Not all of them. I was different. Once."

Was I always this way? I seem to remember...

I've done worse things than this.

The firefighters shake their heads, pointing at the singular-room-blaze. Their words drift by me, floating on a breeze carrying autumn and smolder. Their suspicion. Smoke-tinged dread.

"Won't they suspect you started the fire in your room, Lili?"

"No," I chuckle at that. "Jason and Patty Sweeney have been absentminded about their electrical inspections. That room, especially, was only a misplaced match or circuit away from going ablaze. They're lucky I did the job for them. At least I contained the damage, and it'll force them to fix the wiring for good. They should be thanking me."

"Do you always make people thank you for their misfortune?"

"Only when they ask nicely."

There's also the business of Jason's ledger. Anyone writing such detailed observations about their nonhuman guests... Jason's hiding secrets.

Maybe he knew about the poltergeist in my room.

Someone with so many secrets cannot speak. And I don't want to be hanging around somebody scribbling such detailed descriptions about their guests any longer than I have to.

I stuff my hands into my pockets, weaving past the tiny crowd of drunks shuffling out of the bar area while the firefighters evacuate it. "Don't worry, I paid for any damages. I left a present at the front desk. A ring from the Edwardian era. An antique dealer traded his life for it." Byron writes this down in his journal as I go over my less-than-brilliant plan. "And as for my pyromania, I contained the fire so that it only affects the one room. Come now, I wouldn't be cruel enough to burn it *all* to ash."

I *could* burn the whole village in a single, delectable heartbeat, but I'd rather Byron didn't know that. I'd rather he thought me mostly harmless.

And I'm nervous. Nervous about this Jason Sweeney. But I don't want Byron to know that either. I don't fear Jason, but he makes me nervous in the same way an angry mob or whispers of monsters does.

I am a walking secret, and I don't want Jason to find me out.

"Hey, Lili, how does one make a Siren? Like, do you get a birthday and stuff?"

We're walking with the "electrical fire" at our backs, pushing against a crowd of people drawn toward the bright, pulsating colors like sheep in a herd. I don't slow as we walk along the cracked cement, our feet against the road. The road stretches out for so long that it's almost like this miserable town wants to imprison us here. This is what I deserve for going so far inland. "I was born beneath the sun, my skin baked like clay, and soulless for all I know. We aren't born. We simply appear. We seduce. We eat. And we exist until the universe decides that we shouldn't."

Byron glides to my left, putting his pen behind his ear like a journalist and biting at his nails distractedly. "Huh. And you call *me* the poet." He floats directly in front of me, and I nearly trip because the action is so disconcerting, causing shivers to run all along my spine. I wave my hand to swat at him, but my skin passes right through. I'm about to add a magical dose of energy so I can flick him on the nose, but then sigh and decide it isn't worth it.

"Just haunt me in silence, pesky poltergeist."

We are making decent headway away from the inn and down an empty row of shops and a vacated arcade when Byron decides to speak again.

Halfway through this town, and he makes the trip seem ten times longer.

"Shit!"

"What'd I just tell you, Byron?"

I'm about to throw every Siren trick at him and send him back to the spirit world, but I stop as I see the whiny ghost has wandered toward the town hall.

The seat of government (i.e. "town hall") for Gamin looks much like the Sweeney Inn. The town hall is vaguely modernized, vacant, and at the same time, thought-provoking. It's provoking and, like a politician, it has thoughts. The building possesses a gothic façade that hasn't been replaced since the town was founded, and a yellowing front door held together by splinters of wood and squeaky hinges. The message board is covered with multiple black-and-white, pencil-scratch sketches of young people. They stare gloomily out at us, the label MISSING hanging over their heads. When I join Byron, I see he's shaking.

Didn't know ghosts still shook.

"I knew that girl." He points to one of them, a sixteen-year-old round face smiling crookedly. "I read her books at the local library. She was in the special education group. Anna Snow. She liked the high fantasy stories the best. *Lord of the Rings*. Narnia. All that."

"If you were at the local library, why were you staying at a room at the inn? Don't you live here?"

Byron stares, enraptured, by poor Anna Snow's face. "I got this job from a college program for the summer. Ended up staying out here for longer than I planned and didn't return to college. Or home." He places his hand against the poster, but it drifts right through. "Didn't want to go back, but maybe...maybe I should have."

A few of the posters, including Anna's, have a despondent *X* crossed over their faces. There're a couple of sketches of a face hidden in the shadow of a hood with glowing eyes.

Bodies of some of the missing victims were found half-buried in the ground, all in various states of every kind of murder possible. It's nasty work, rivalling some of the horrors I committed when I was younger, horrors I swallow entire bottles of sleeping pills to forget.

I look at all the eerie faces, the eldest being high-school seniors and the youngest an infant of three. "Probably one of us, or some monster. Looks like they're targeting virgins. Most monsters go for virgins. Sense of tradition, a nod to our lurid history."

"How do you know it's a monster and not a human?" Byron gives me the side-eye. "Did you do this, or was it one of your friends? Wanted a snack, did you?"

I refuse to answer his question, seeing as I nearly murdered the Sweeney family because I was hungry. "I'm getting better at managing my hunger. And besides, I hate small towns."

"I hate the movie trailers that spoil the end of the movie and franchises that go on until you wish they had never been made at all. Why is that random fact important?"

I look at the image of Anna Snow, her wide eyes so innocent. I know a lot of monsters who crave innocence like it's a drug. "I was drawn to this town even though I prefer cities. I sensed something in this place. You, you're a sentient ghost that appeared directly after your death. Usually ghosts take a full year to materialize as anything more than a disembodied voice or a gust of wind." I crumple up the paper and shove it into Byron's chest, muttering a cantrip so he can take it in his hands in the spiritual plane. He tucks it away in his journal, frowning at poor Anna's picture. "There's something about this place. And if I was drawn to it, who says more lethal monsters won't do the same? It's too dangerous in Gamin, so best if we leave now."

Byron turns to me then, eyes gone wide. "What if the person killing these people is the same one who left a note on my corpse?"

"Don't be ridiculous."

But he's not being ridiculous. In fact, the more I dwell on it, the more it starts to make sense. A killer who left a note in my room.

What does he want with me?

"Is it ridiculous?" Byron floats forward, peering into my eyes.

I turn away so he can't see my face. I don't want to reveal my nervousness, not to him. *Looking weak in front of a young ghost. What an all-time low.* "Ridiculous. Of course. I've seen better murderers before, or rather, worse. And if they want to catch me or me to catch them, then that just means we have to get out of Gamin. Now."

I go back toward the main cobblestone road. "Come on, the exit's up ahead." I stand near the cheery sign of a smiley face flipping griddle cakes at the town's outer border. "Welcome to Gamin." The billboard looks as enthusiastic as a mental hospital receptionist insisting you're going to be just fine as they check you in for fifteen different medications. Byron hasn't moved. I put my hands into my pockets, refusing to turn around.

"You'll leave knowing that a monster is terrorizing these people?" His words cut into me despite myself. I must be out of practice in dealing with angry ghosts.

I stare at my hands, imagining blood trickling down them, staining my skin so that it would turn obsidian in the moon's shadow. "You seem to forget that we're monsters, too, that I'm only taking you on because you promised me something. Only the devil and Sirens can make bargains like that, kid."

"Don't patronize me." Byron spits. For a dead man, he's suddenly become passionate again. "You aren't as demonic as you think, Lili. You could've burned that whole inn down, but you only burned the room so that I could have a fresh start and not have people think poorly of me for being a suicide. You gave them a priceless ring to ensure their losses were covered. You agreed to help me in return for me writing you a measly poem. And lastly, you didn't have to stop at that town border sign to ensure I was following you."

"Do you ever wonder whether those are just your romantic notions of me, poet?" I want, so badly, to prove him wrong. I want to become a monster in his eyes if only to make me feel less powerless. I hate being told what to do. I want this stupid, feeble depression to stop. I want to do something right for once instead of being weak like some human. "You're projecting. I'm not the kind of person who stops serial killers out of the goodness of my heart."

"I'm not a coward like you," he shouts.

Laughing to myself, I fire one last parting shot at the newly dead idealist. "How can you save the world if you couldn't even save yourself?"

So, just to prove him wrong, I keep on walking past the town's border.

And I refuse to check behind me as I go.

*

Gamin's Town Border

Unfortunately, he follows me. One mile turns to two. Then two shifts, somehow, to six.

And still, he doesn't tire. Of course not. He's dead.

"Listen up, witch. Remember that second part of the bargain?" Byron's lower lip juts out as he pouts like a child at me. A ghost throwing a temper tantrum and a Siren giving him the silent treatment. No wonder humans want to kill and exorcise us. "I'm going to nag you for an eternity if you don't turn back and stop that murderer."

"Go ahead."

As we keep walking, he attempts to pick up rods made of dried-up, yellowed roots. His brow is furrowed in concentration as he tries to lift the comically light object from the ground. I turn away from the cement highway, Byron still trying to pick up physical objects without much success. We walk on dirt roads that run alongside a pen of fat sheep, the animals toddling along like dirtied clouds of wool and sweat. These are probably shepherd back roads, and the mud soaks into my nice leather boots. The slopping sound fades into the background as I watch Byron with some interest. He tries to pick up a dandelion, but only succeeds in creating a feeble gust of wind that knocks a single petal loose.

"It takes most ghosts a decade to figure out how to lift objects."

Byron narrows his dark eyes at me. "*Bruja...*" he mutters, alongside some meatier insults. Maybe he really was a decent poet in life with vocabulary like that. His pirate-captain coat floats up behind him like the sail of a ghost ship, his longer hair creating a thorny halo around his head. I snort and continue walking along the shepherd's path, leaving the serial-killer-infested Minnesotan town of Gamin behind me in the distance.

A moment later, a tiny piece of gravel hits me squarely on the neck. I rub the spot and turn around, narrowly missing a clod of dirt flung at my face. Byron stands there grinning like the devil, tossing tiny pebbles in his off hand, exerting the same amount of force a living human would if they chucked a weighted basketball up into the air.

"Mature."

I take another step and cry out in pain, falling to the ground. I pull at my boot and see red seeping out from my wool socks. A tiny nail is embedded into my heel. Eyes flashing, I turn back to Byron who's whistling and looking quite pleased with himself. How'd he even put that through my boot? "Bastard!" I rage, hobbling on one foot and swiping at him, trying to grab him through the spirit plane. He's grown wiser, though, since last time I throttled him, weaving out of the way like a will-o'-the-wisp or a bit of dandelion fluff. Sweating and bleeding from my gash, I swipe at my brow and sit in the dirt.

He glides over as I pick tiny shards of metal from my skin with my fingernail, hissing as my skin knits itself up slowly over the affected area. "Son of a bitch."

"I warned you." Byron struts around, his chest puffed out like the pompous, perfidious peacock he is. "Hell hath no fury like a spirit scorned."

With a roar, I scare at least five of the sheep into rolling over and fainting on the spot as I dive to attack the ghost. He's unprepared for the fury of my attack as I fall upon him and throttle him from above. "If I could kill you twice, I would, you insufferable ghost!"

With each word, I slam him against the ground again. He growls at me and grabs for my wrist and there's a sizzling sound as his fingers burn through my skin. I don't relent, holding my hands around his throat and watching as his skin bruises violet beneath my attack.

I'm satisfied to see his discomfort despite my own burns. "I can't kill you again, but I can make your un-life hell, ghost."

"You can put me through hell as often as you like, *bruja*. We can play this game for eternity." He glowers back at me, the words a harsh whisper as he chokes them out. "But do you think Anna Snow or that three-year-old baby deserve hell too?"

I scream and throw him so hard into the dirt that a piece of his skull cracks and takes time to mend its ghostly form again. I examine the damage done to my wrist and grimace to see the white of bone beneath scarlet-stained, charred skin. I can hardly hold it upright because the muscles are so scorched. I pull a handkerchief from my peacoat pocket to tie up the grisly mass of shredded tissue and skin. Aside from my wallet, that handkerchief was one of my last possessions in this world. I'd destroyed everything else, or my enemies had before I destroyed them in return. "Damn you, I just had to find a ghost with a conscience. I traveled the *entire* world, and I've been lucky enough never to meet an asshole ghost."

"*Bienvenida a los Estados Unidos.*" Byron smirks as I flick some droplets of blood in his direction. "We're in this together, *bruja.*"

Chapter Four

Why the Hell Are We Back in Gamin?

When we trudge back to Gamin, the sky's gotten damper and darker, and the entire landscape's colored like a bruise. The inn's still dark (even a single-room, electrical circuit fire failed to drum up any business), and I'm stuck standing there with an antsy, eternally energized phantom bobbing cheerfully beside me.

"Tough luck, *bruja*." Byron shrugs and fakes a yawn. "Maybe you could be like Waldo and just sit by a pond all day."

"Thoreau sat by Walden Pond. Waldo is from a children's book discussing finding him as its main exercise." Tired and tapping my foot as the crowds empty out of the main square, my skin gets all clammy as night sets its hold. "Are you even a poet?"

Byron attempts a chivalrous gesture of putting his pirate jacket over my shoulders. Naturally, the gesture has about as much success as if I tried hiding behind a clear windowpane in a game of hide-and-seek, but it is a nice thought. "Are you even a Siren?" Byron asks me, watching me shiver as I loiter in the darkening town square of

Gamin. "Shouldn't you have seduced your way into someone's room by now?"

"I can't get too close to anyone while I'm here. I'm an immortal, for gods' sakes. I'd prefer to ghost as soon as my business is finished—if you'll pardon my expression."

Byron cocks an eyebrow at me. "The serial killer's out here, and I know you're tough and all, but I don't know how you'd fare against a child-killing monster, *bruja*."

I snap at him, a dog on too short a leash, "So what do you suggest, poet?"

"You're not going to like it, but between getting accused of arson or *actually* having your body burned by a deranged serial killer..."

We both turn toward the Sweeney Inn at the same time.

"No." My eyes widen as I stare at the lair of Patricia and Jason Sweeney. The unfortunate owners of the inn I fled from because of Byron. "A Siren never begs for scraps."

*

The Sweeney Inn (unfortunately)
I'm Begging for Scraps.

The door swings open to a hungover freckled Patricia Sweeney's face. Her neck and cheeks are glowing red with the afterglow of a person in love.

Must be her girlfriend, Alice.

The rest of her throat is covered in a thick anti-acne solution. She scratches her silk-robe-clad thigh as I stand there, a none-too-mighty immortal. Begging.

"Well, well, look what the cat dragged in." Patricia bats her eyelashes at me, blowing a stubborn wisp of red hair out of her face. "If it isn't Lil, just the woman I was waiting to see, standing wrapped up like a present on my doorstep. Come back from a hike recently?" She huffs. "Don't bother. The place is closed indefinitely for repairs. A fire, not that you were there for it."

Can't really expect a warm welcome after the fire.

Maybe if we tap into those Siren powers...

I try to move closer, but Patricia pulls back, wary. Then I see the bronze, fishhook earrings dangling from her ears. Those weren't there before. Curious.

I change tactics. "I forgot to return my key." And that's the truth: the toothy bugger was still fishing around in my peacoat pocket when I left. I hold it up to the light, the key's teeth glinting dangerously like a nice set of chompers. "Here you are."

Patricia snorts. "Won't be needing that, Lil. Not with the freak electrical fire that took down your whole damn room, and *only* your room. Lucky you left when you did." Her round eyes narrow at this, and I can feel the suspicion radiating off her, poking toothpick-sized holes into my skin. "Conveniently lucky."

"Oh, it was?" I retaliate, widening my eyes, playing ignorant. "I saw the firetrucks, but I assumed it was somebody else's problem. But now that you mention it, I *did* see a lot of loose wires hanging about in my room. And the power outlets were really shaky. Electrical fire, was it?" And here, I lean in closer with a slight twitch. "I heard the same thing happened to a hotel in New York. Owners got sued for a million dollars and had to hand over two by the end of the court case. Tried to blame the innocent victim, can you believe it? For their own negligence."

Patty swallows, spitting out, "You played us."

"I—"

A large male shadow appears behind her. My stomach does a violent loop-de-loop as I meet the gaze of Jason Sweeney, who's astutely avoiding staring at me this time around. "If it isn't the savior of our little inn." He crosses his arms, and the disheartening vibe I'd been receiving from Patricia is quickly replaced by one of sheer confusion.

"Savior?" Patricia rolls the word on her tongue, her face going sour. "What are you on about, calling Lil the inn's savior?"

"Did you read that in your ledger?" I retort, satisfied to see his face drop for a brief moment before he moves forward again.

Jason takes my hand in his, a tight, businesslike grip.

The Siren's magic seeps, the strong alcoholic odor of antiseptic and potato chips. I tilt a little, the earth swaying beneath me at the power transference.

Yet Jason looks unchanged, and he grins triumphantly at that.

Triumphant or no, he still avoids staring at my face for too long, being extra careful to spend time shifting his gaze to Patricia's too. "Lil's been hiding a secret from us. That ring we sold for the damages." Jason takes extra care to look over at me this time, his eyes still not quite focused, almost fearful. "Lil saved our asses by giving that precious little gem to us, inherited from one of our relatives. She's our long-lost cousin, Patty." Jason ruffles his sister's hair, pulling entire chunks of it out from her red elastic ponytail holder. "Be grateful she came back so we can properly thank her."

Patricia sniffs. "It seems some of our relatives ended up somewhere where the sun actually shines from the looks of her." Jason jabs his sister with his elbow at that comment.

"Don't be rude to our new cousin," he mumbles, blushing slightly.

"I'll leave you two weirdos to reunite. What a shame we ended up related. I thought you were so cute when I first saw you, Lil. We could've had some *real* fun." With this final, snarky statement, Patricia yawns and saunters back into the inn. Jason leans against the doorway, his discomfort heightened now that his sister's left him.

I raise an eyebrow. Byron hovers past Jason and maturely decides to make some silly faces, occasionally scrawling some stuff across the pages of his damned poetry book. Is he taking notes on us? He really is trying to write an Odysseus-length story about me from the looks of it. "No room in the inn for your cousin?" I ask him, hopeful.

"Get in then." Jason waves me in. He continues talking as we cross the lobby floor. "Your room's out of commission for the moment, obviously. How's about I get you a drink at the bar?"

"Just water would be fine."

"On me." He watches my eyes as he says this. What does he hope to see there? If he's searching for my soul, he'll be horribly disappointed. "I owe you one. So, please, follow me."

We walk past a twist of boring corridors with cramped gray walls and horrible gold-triangle-print carpeting. When the space finally reopens into the scene of a rustic bar, it feels like I've climbed out of a linoleum-tile labyrinth and stepped out onto a pirate ship. Wood panel floors and high-back chairs. Carefully curated art pieces hang over a giant fireplace, like soldiers with pistols at their hips are going to tell tales around it. The place is filled with ghosts of voices past. (At this point, both literally and figuratively.)

Noticing my bemusement, Jason clarifies, "My dad was really into the idea of European pubs or brown bars. You know, speakeasy affairs. Instruments playing on the stage. He liked to make the inn more than it was. Into art."

Jason positions himself seven or so steps away from me. Far enough to flee or close enough to attack? I haven't seen him fight, so I wouldn't know.

I wouldn't mind finding out. It's been a while since I've had a chance to test my fighting skills. The thrill of it.

I move closer while Jason, yet again, dances away.

"Business doing any better?" He turns his back to me. Well-muscled. A former athlete from the looks of him.

"It's a…recent acquisition. That is to say. Patty and I don't know what we're doing, but college or moving out of Gamin wasn't in the cards for us." He gnaws on his lower lip, a flicker of vulnerability before pasting a shit-eating grin on his face. "Something to drink? We got new dark beers. Or root beers. We never drink alcohol while underage, of course. You're twenty-one, right? I can't really tell how old you are."

Observant. I hate observant. Maybe he wrote that one down in his ledger.

"I haven't had a beer in a while." I smile, taking a seat. Jason's shoulders relax a bit. "In Sumer, they wrote hymns about liquor and beer. Compared it to the onrush of the Tigris and Euphrates. Sang odes to the goddess Ninkasi. No matter how long ago or how recent, people drink to forget." I run my finger along the edge of the gold-painted bar, attempting to change the conversation as I notice Justin grow quiet at my strange musings. "The bar's nice though. Bit dusty."

"Tread lightly." Byron whispers in my ear. There's no point to the whispering since he's dead, but it must be instinctive from his time in the world of the living.

"I planned on it."

I follow Jason to the bar, and he plops a plate of peas, mash, and fatty meat in front of me before pouring a healthy heaping of apple cider in a mug beside it. I poke at the steaming pile of grease with a single fork tine. "What is it?"

"Our mom calls it 'savory duck.'" He watches, eyes glinting, as I take a tentative bite. Chewing a bit, I look back up into his eyes and shove the plate away.

"That's pig heart," I inform him, enunciating the words slowly like I would to an idiot. Byron pokes at it interestedly. I down the apple cider and wipe my mouth on my sleeve.

"Oh, you can tell? My mom had some Yorkshire recipes handed down from her grandmother, along with a few other things." He drops the conversational tone as he pushes the plate back toward me. "Tell me, I was never quite a fan of pig hearts. Does it taste the same as a human heart? I went by what the magical internet told me."

Human hearts?

"Come now, I thought we were cousins." I fake-giggle, trying to get a good look at his eyes to see his motive.

I reach out to grab his wrist as he still has it on my plate, but he pulls back as though my skin was on fire. "No, I know your tricks. I knew it! I knew you were a Siren, just like from Mom's stories!" And when he spins around, I catch it. He has a bronzed fishhook laced into his previously unpierced ear. Same as his sister.

I lean back on my stool as Byron floats over the empty barstool beside me, glancing longingly at the apple cider. I wonder if ghosts ever miss being thirsty or just drinking for the hell of it. "Bronze fishhook charms. Sirens? What next, unicorns?"

I keep laughing right up until I see it.

Well, well, well. I'll be damned. I knew the ledger had to lead to something.

That's the Eye.

I haven't seen the Eye since the plague years where plague doctors did more harm than good with their bleeding techniques and dead flowers. And then, after the plague, the symbol's been scattered here and there. The Reign of Terror. The murders of Jack the Ripper. The killer in Chicago at the World Fair. The Manson Family.

Their enemies called them the Evil Eye, but that's neither here nor there. Evil is subjective, after all.

At least, I'd like to think so.

Right now, the Eye's symbol is a burn mark positioned over the portrait of the Siren. They're looming over the bar, the picture of the Eye floating right in the middle of the main model's beautiful locks, sketched in such plain beige that you wouldn't see it unless you were searching for it. "The Eye symbol. You're part of the coven, I take it?"

"Gamin has its secrets." The young warlock rubs his hands nervously against his aprons. Does he methodically clean his hands, or is it unintentional how clean he keeps the place, almost as though by rote? "You have your secrets too. You must have been powerful to have possessed such an old ring."

"It was shiny, so I took it."

"Bullshit. You're one of them, from the Summerland, aren't you? I've been keeping a field journal of local magical creatures..."

"Summerland, like the Fae? Darling, don't be stupid. I'm much older." I pause a moment, still processing his words. "And I'm sorry. There are *other* magical creatures in this town?"

"Yes. Oh, oh you haven't even met them yet! This is fascinating." Jason shakes his head in wonder, scarlet hair gleaming in the window light. "When I took that ring over to the rest of the Eye, they fell over themselves to bid the highest price for it, insisting that its previous wizarding owner was long dead." Jason's words tumble out faster and faster. "Patty doesn't have the gift, so I can't talk about it with her. Mom insists I hide everything about magic from Patty."

The Eye Coven, from what I remember of my last run-in with their brood, did a whole lot of dark magic. That might prove useful for Byron. I never liked the light magic folks. They were too clean. If there was an experienced dark magic user in this house, I wouldn't sneeze at the opportunity. "And your mother?"

Jason looks down, pain distorting his features. But it's not a physical pain. It's so much deeper than that. "She's dead. Dad too."

Still talks about his mother in the present tense though. Mustn't have been that long ago. That, or he's struggling with coping.

"Shame she died. A waste of good magic." Jason frowns, and Byron shoots a dirty look at me. Mortals, they get so touchy about the strangest things. "What? Death's natural for you humans. I wish I had it that easy. Feel lucky for it."

"Lili!" Byron scolds.

"Sorry." I turn to Jason who, understandably, refuses to look at me for a bit. "Thanks for the food though. It's delicious."

I dig into the pig heart, ravenous. The meal's almost as energizing as the real, human equivalent. I feel a bit of my fogginess clear from all my traveling on those muddied, shepherding backroads. "I suppose you did take me in, and it'd only be polite to warn you." Byron and Jason both watch me intently as I sigh and dip my finger in the pig heart's bloodier cross-section, doodling an Eye on my palm. "There's a monster on the loose in this town, and it's slaughtering innocent children." This next part I confess while looking away from them, expecting to feel disappointment like a heated sword from Byron's usually admiring gaze. "And it scares even me."

A moment of silence followed by Jason sighing into folded palms, eyes cast to the ceiling like a Renaissance painting. Then he turns to me.

No, not me.

He's facing Byron. The ghost, uncertain, glances warily over his shoulder.

"How about him? Is he scared of this monster?"

"He?"

Jason chuckles at that. "Oh, don't play dumb with me, Siren. I want to know who your ghost friend is." He points to the symbol of the Eye.

I purse my lips at that. "Right. You're a necromancer."

And who would ever want to meet one of those?

Byron floats cautiously forward. "You...you can *see* me?"

"Hello there, mystery ghost," Jason says, holding out his palm and crossing the spirit barrier effortlessly. "I'm Jason."

Byron squeals with joy as his hand doesn't pass through Jason's, and he *doesn't* erupt into blistering pain. Byron would hug Jason if he weren't too shy and socially awkward about it. "I'm Byron. Like the—"

"Poet." Jason finishes with a roguish grin.

I break up the little ghost-necro meet and greet. "I take it that your mom being dead isn't an obstacle in speaking to her." And Jason, looking like the most bland, non-gothic necromancer I've ever seen, casts a devil-may-care smile my way. What a remarkably unnoticeable face he has. "Most necromancers would've tried killing me the first night. I'm sure you could use the Siren blood for a spell. Maybe sell it on the black market."

Jason continues smiling that killer smile. Same as his sister. Charmers when they want to be. I'd assume that makes them devils otherwise. "Nonsense. Why would I kill you for your blood? You'd fetch a better price if you were living." Jason barrels onward, possessing either a large amount of bravery or a small amount of common sense considering my own evil eye. "No, I expected you'd come back, Lili. I sensed it. Hence, I prepared with the fishhook charms. Wards against Siren magic." Jason chuckles softly. "I'm a necromancer, Lili. I embrace the darkness. I don't run from it."

Byron slams his fist down on the table, and I might be imagining it, but I think I see the silverware tremble slightly beneath the weight of his ghostly fervor "Let's see you embrace the darkness when that killer comes for you." He spits the last line out miserably, holding the sketch he still has of Anna Snow. "It's *muerte, fam*. The end's finally here for all of us. Even the undead."

Chapter Five

Sweeney Inn Bar

"So, there's a monstrous serial killer on the loose, and even the biggest, baddest, and arguably most dangerous mythical being out of the three of us is afraid of it." Jason considers the both of us as he holds the third mug of apple cider. We all sit in front of an empty grate back at the wood-paneled bar area of the inn, staring at the miserable pile of cold ash that accurately sums up how Gamin feels all the time, perpetually damp and miserable. *"Muerte...death?"* Jason turns to Byron, his accent not too bad for a gringo.

The ghost nods glumly.

Jason leans back, hands behind his head as he stares blankly up at the wooden crossbeams hanging over the inn lobby, the tapestries of beer-stained unicorns swaying in the wind beside more insulting Siren paintings. "Well, guess we're damned. That's what this means, right? The killer's just going to pick us off, one by one. Well, except for Byron here. He got a head start on the whole dying thing."

Byron's glare would cause a regular human to melt into the floor, but Jason is too arrogant to notice.

I cross my legs, taking in this faux pub, this *work of art* compared to the harsher yellow-white lights of the lobby. It's softer, with the wood finishes and fireplaces. If I were sentimental or more inclined to human comforts, I might even call the space *homey*. "Mortals can be so unconcerned about their own mortality, jovial even about it. Until you have to face it." I lean closer, watching his freckled features, so like Patty but less pleasant. "Tell me, would you be so jovial if the killer had their hands around your throat?"

"I'm a necromancer." Jason sits up again, puffing his chest out and trying to be tough.

"I've seen sparkly vampires that were scarier," I shoot back, lips peeled back in disgust.

Jason swallows, massaging the back of his neck as he stares glumly into his cider. "There's really a serial killer out there targeting young people. I mean, Patty and I just turned twenty-one. And Patty has no magic, no powers... What if they get her?"

"They won't," I inform him bluntly. "They're only taking virgins."

Jason spits out what little of the cider he's sipped. Byron smirks giddily at me. I stare into the ghostly fire, feeding it some pieces of bloody cloth off my healing wrist and watching it turn to a more natural, amber hue. "Whatever the monster is, Byron seems to think I'd be better at playing detective than nursemaid. He's threatened to nag me for the rest of my immortality if I don't. Though our *original* deal only involved raising him back from the dead." Byron blows kisses at me while I flip him off.

"Bring him back, hmm." Jason rubs his smooth chin. "I think I might be able to help with that if I study more on the rituals. My mom would've done it in seconds. I'm just her sloppy protégé."

"Males are about as good at magic as they are at seduction," I inform him.

"You're the least seductive Siren I've ever met now that I'm wearing the fishhook and can judge sensibly again." Jason must mean it as a barb since I've just insulted him, but I don't take it as an insult. The necromancer's cheap shot has more truth to it than he knows.

"It only makes sense you wouldn't find me seductive, I guess." Feeling empty again, I stare into the spreading fire. Fire's so clean, so pure. It must be so much easier, then, if only I could live within the fire. "My powers might paint me one way, but I use them just to hunt or defend myself. Purely to survive, not for pleasure." I snicker at that. "An asexual Siren, so how's that for irony?"

Byron and Jason trade glances and then shrug in unison.

"Asexuality is valid." Byron perks up, cleaning his phantom glasses with his jacket pocket. "*Es una parte de vida.*"

"So are asexual Sirens," Jason adds, his bravado deflating as he twiddles his thumbs. "And I'm sorry if I judged you too quickly. I mean, I'm trans. We're in this fight together, right?" He pauses, staring down at his thumbs. "No one has the right to diminish another's existence."

They both look so sincere that it kills me. I don't deserve this. I don't deserve this sort of trust. A necromancer, a ghost, and a Siren? Please, it sounds more like the beginning of a cheap joke than it does a dysfunctional kind of family.

"Thank you. I accept your apology, and I apologize if I hurt you in return." I huff, spreading my peacoat over the inn's floor, busying my hands to avoid looking at their earnest gazes. "Can we get back to discussing the murders, please?"

They remain quiet, and right when I feel like burning down the inn again, Jason breaks the awful, pitying silence. "I knew Anna Snow. Her father drank a lot at our bar. The mom was the one who drove her to all those special ed classes. We used to carpool when I was younger and learning how to manage my ADHD. I taught her how to jump over a hurdle in track, and she taught me how to dance like there's no tomorrow. She took ballet, did you know that? Or did you just see her as part of a body count?" He sighs, his cherry-soda hair falling back in front of his face. "What tore her up? A poltergeist? A Siren?"

Now it's my and Byron's turn to exchange insulted glances. "How about a necromancer, *chico?*" Byron asks him, his nose in the air. "Ghosts have feelings, too, you know."

"We don't," I offer, "they're all faked as a baiting mechanism."

"Right, sorry." Jason sighs. "It's still surreal. I know I'm part of the Eye Coven, but I never really branched out into the world since my ma died." He squints closer at some of the aftermath corpse descriptions scrawled on the back of the sketch. "And what are they doing with all these bodies, eating them?"

I bite my lower lip, itching for some more pig heart right about now. "We could only really know if we got a closer look at the body. See what's there and what...isn't." I recover from the misstep by barreling forward. "The police have enough evidence. They're probably set to bury her by now. Is there a morgue where they'd store her before the funeral?"

Jason keeps on rubbing the back of his neck until his paler flesh turns pink from the rawness of the repetitive, circular motions. He sure enjoys fidgeting, making me suspect repetition is all that's keeping this poor mortal sane right now. "I can take you to the morgue tomorrow, and you can sleep in one of the empty, non-burned rooms. Eye's all good with the morgue people. They're magic too. But..." He winces. "I don't think you'd like them, Lil."

I put my hands on my hips before throwing my peacoat on with a flourish, Lady Macbeth ready for her monologue to invoke seeling night and seas incarnadine. "Nothing fazes an immortal."

*

The Morgue

"Hollywood has turned the terrors of the night into horrible excuses for merchandising!" the angry old Russian vampire says, shuffling down the hall. "They don't make us vampires scary like they used to." He throws a pack of dust-covered CDs in our direction. I dodge in time, Byron stands there and lets them fly right through, but Jason ends up getting hit squarely in the chest. "These young vampires wearing their tight leather disco pants and their dog collars. They either make the vampires flaunt their sexiness or they think it's funny to turn them into children's cartoons. Their irreverence makes me sick!"

The vampire throws his hands up into the air as we walk down the cold, clammy halls toward the refrigerated corpse section. "Where's the terror of the night? Where's the respect for traditions? Gone! Replaced by flashy makeup and designer clothing." He waves a taloned claw in front of our noses. "Hollywood is killing the vampires, I tell you." He moans, dragging the skin beneath his eyeballs until it nearly touches his nose and then bounces back up with all the elasticity of a newborn baby. Jason flinches, but Byron just looks intrigued.

"Hollywood hasn't left its mark on you." I compliment him, warming up to the crotchety vampiric undertaker, despite my best efforts to hate him for being vampiric. Byron, since he has no blood left to give, is amused by this man. Jason's just appalled, clutching his neck possessively and looking the most miserable out of the three of us.

"Thank you. I take blood baths in roadkill I drag out from the side of the highway." The vampire waggles his thick, silver eyebrows. He must have been turned when he was in his late fifties though immortality suits him as well as a plaid suit fits an old country gentleman. "It was the great Blood Countess's beauty secret. She was also a vampire, you know."

When we reach the end of the morgue tour, Anatol the crotchety, traditional vampire has warmed up figuratively to my haughty heart. Aside from vampires being inferior ghouls compared to the complex, raw beauty of the Siren, I find that Anatol isn't quite as unbearable as the others. His rudeness endears me to him. Rude people are always far more honest than those who engage in flattery. It's the silver-tongued you must watch out for.

The undertaker must put on gloves before he can touch the door. He wedges his gloved hand, incredibly strong if still wrinkled due to his late turning, beneath the iron and silver embedded door. "It's reinforced with iron for the Fae and silver for the lycanthropes."

"Why are you still wearing gloves then?" Byron plunges his hand through the door to show off his intangibility. Jason scowls at the dead poet.

"I just sharpened my nails, and I want to keep them looking nice for when I go on a date with Jo later." He whispers conspiratorially with me, "Don't tell the fleshy one that Jo's a *jiangshi,* or he might report me to the Eye for harboring an undead without a license."

I wink at him. "Reanimating someone for a date? Mr. Anatol, how scandalous."

"Necromancy licenses, another reason for the decay of vampire youth! Nothing spontaneous anymore. It's ruining the necromantic economy." Anatol scoffs as he walks into the refrigerated room. I give an involuntary shiver. I prefer my immortal, woe-is-me life spent on warm sandy beaches. Damn this magical town for pulling me into its temperate climate grip!

When the iron-silver door creaks shut behind us, cold comes upon us with a vengeance. My breath fogs out into the dimly lit expanse, mingling with Jason's breath as he gapes at the corpses surrounding us. Goose bumps, unattractive rashes, run all along my bare arms. "I was born in a desert," I growl, "I was created to seduce, and within three days, I had the empire's greatest queen feeding me figs beneath the shade of her servants' lavender-colored canopy. I watched the mighty statues of kings in the desert rise and fall, and this is where I end up? A fridge of horrors in the American Midwest."

Jason, to his credit, looks mildly bemused by my ranting.

Byron ignores me. He looks sadly at the morgue's bodies. Occasionally, he'll lean down hopefully near one of them and wave. It's almost as though he's trying to wake another ghost up. I cannot understand this, that feeling of wanting a fellow monster as your kin. If I saw another Siren, it would be a battle. We act as great cats, jealous of each other's territory when one stumbles upon another's feeding ground. We strut around with our stripes and plumage, preening and throwing around hedonistic displays until we tire of the gory parties. At the end, we slink off to the countryside, going our separate ways to torture separate townspeople, to ruin different young lives. I wish I had Byron's empathy, if only to end the perpetual boredom of being a Siren. It must be nice, still feeling even when you're dead. I'm alive, and I feel nothing.

"Corpses," I sniff, attempting to lighten the mood, "and the hearts are frozen. I hate frozen food."

"How can you complain at so much beauty?" Jason shakes his head at me, as giddy as a tourist in a theme park. "Death is so beautiful." His skin is blue with cold, but he ignores it to poke and prod around. He gazes in awe at the array of dead people, their bodies laid neatly in rows, their faces waxen and never to awaken again. I can see it, that madness sorcerers get when they're plotting their greatest potions. He's a child in a sweet shop, drooling over the saltwater taffy, cinnamon glaze, and chocolate-covered-berries. He feasts on so much magical potential with his eyes, but he knows this is Anatol's place of business. Anatol, sensing Jason's excitement, watches the young necromancer carefully.

"Don't go picking off any ritual souvenirs," he barks, glowering as Jason pulls his hand back from one of the dead people's toenails. "Respect the dead. The undead of Gamin don't reanimate anyone unless they requested it in their wills." He turns, again, to me. "Jo requested it of our undertaker business. Wanted to be a *jiangshi,* can you imagine? I had to import the ritual equipment from abroad, but I cannot pass up the opportunity for a new undead person."

I cross my arms, inspecting my nails and imagining drawing them against the neck of Anna Snow's serial killer so I can dump Byron and live my un-life in peace. "This town, Gamin, has a booming business for death. People can't seem to want to die quickly enough. But nobody wants to go through it a second time."

The old Russian's undead eyes are sad. "Would Anna Snow have thrown away her life in Gamin so easily even if she wasn't a spoiled Siren?" I'm taken aback, scolded like a common child by this...this *ghoul.* I pout the entire time the vampire takes to get Snow's body ready, still sulking when he waves me over to join him. Anatol pauses as we gather around Snow's covered corpse in the center of the room. Byron, usually the most eager of our three-person crew, hovers nervously at my shoulder.

"Anna Snow." The Russian vampire's teasing lilt drops at that, his voice flat with a heavy sort of sorrow. "I patched up what I could of her. The monster who did this was no vampire. No vampire would waste such sweet, innocent blood as this girl owned. As sweet as the kiss of my dear *jiangshi* lover."

Damn, old man. Enough with all this lovey-dovey talk about how you want to get it on with an undead woman. Just show us the body.

When he pulls back the hospital-blue covers, Anna Snow's body appears to have been a ragdoll cut by a lethal pair of scissors and stitched back together with fishing wire. Entire swathes of skin are like fabric that's been stretched far too thin. Masses of her flesh are missing, and some of her teeth have been plucked from her mouth. I notice the sheet that covers her breastbone is sagging, the ribcage caved in on itself like a nightmarish accordion.

I lift the covers, and sure enough, her heart is gone. I try to hide the damage by lowering the covers quickly, but Byron takes this opportunity to perk up instead of being his usual, glum poetic self. "Oh, *mira*, the heart's missing. Doesn't look good for Sirens, does it, *bruja?* No, not good at all."

I grit my teeth, removing the flap entirely now that the secret's out. Sure enough, all three of us stare, captivated, at the fact that Anna Snow's heart is playing a wicked game of hide-and-seek with us. "Yes, it appears the score is Sirens with one on the murder suspect tally."

"When's the last time you fed?" Jason asks me, astutely avoiding my gaze again, fiddling with the fishhook in his ear.

It takes all my resolve not to rip the charm out of his body in disgust. "The last thing I ate was that goddamn savory duck, the pig heart." I hold my hands out as though by virtue that their copper palms appear clean of blood, my innocence will be proven. "I did not kill Anna Snow. Though I will kill you, Sweeney, if you keep up the accusations."

"I'm just trying to look out for my sister," he retaliates, staring silently at my forehead as opposed to my eyes. The Eye starts to appear on his skin. Coward, like his unpracticed, mortal magic will save him.

"Eh, children!" Byron floats between us. "We're a team, aren't we?"

Hissing, I pull back. Jason scowls, his Eye fading.

Anatol watches the entire exchange, and then calmly turns back to the hole where Anna Snow's heart used to be. "No, not the work of a vampire," he repeats. "But whatever did this—" and now he points to the rest of Anna's body. The patches of skin ripped from her flesh, the white of bone showing through in her torn knees and elbows. "Whatever did this must be sent back to whatever hole it came from. Or even the undead and the immortals will suffer."

We grow silent as the vampire covers the human girl's body and closes her frightened eyes with the pad of his thumb. "We all shall suffer greatly."

Chapter Six

Fabulous Los Angeles Nightclub (Just kidding, we're back at the Sweeney Inn bar)

When we get back to the Sweeney Inn, Patty is at the bar, sampling some of the liquor and staring desperately into a bowl of tomato soup. Its consistency almost looks like blood, and I shut my eyes to keep from getting hungry.

Jason's forehead furrows as he tries to gently wrestle the mug of beer from Patty's hands. "Whoa, slow down there, sis."

Patty slams the mug back onto the bar. "You don't control me." She hiccups, laughing with her head thrown back, her hair flat against her neck. "N-neither does Alice."

I look to Jason, who shrugs helplessly. "Her girlfriend."

Patty snorts. "Not my girlfriend anymore." She tries to get the beer back from her brother, the liquor sloshing around on the wooden floors. "She dumped me. Says she's getting out of Gamin." Her face scrunches up in frustration. "S-s-scared shitless of the murders." She slurs, red eyes turning angrily toward me. "What's *cousin* doing here? Still want to know about my weekend plans, or am I only worth something when I'm smiling and happy?"

She fumbles with her earrings, getting to her feet. Feeling reluctantly amused as she throws the bronze fishhook charm to the ground, I smile at her tantrum. Yet this only enrages her further. She stands perhaps a head or so shorter than me, so there's no use really in her mortal body taking the risk of a brawl. But that doesn't stop her, so therefore, it won't stop me. Easing into a fighting position, I am a cat stretching after a long slumber, ready for the hunt.

"No." Jason moves to step between us. "Please, she's drunk. Cut her some slack."

I sigh, disappointed as I force myself back onto the defensive instead of the attack. "Rein that human in before I get angry. I'm new at this whole mercy thing." I grin, looking at the abandoned glass mug on the floor. "We wouldn't want another stabbing, would we?"

Jason growls. "And you wonder why I don't trust you."

"Touchy." I hold my hands in the air, fingers splayed. "I was just joking, junior."

Byron scribbles some more into his notebook, hovering over Patty's vacated spot. I sidestep to avoid one of her drunken swings. "You should do something before she hurts herself, *bruja*. I don't think I could deal with her if she turned into a ghost." He winces as Patty nearly trips face-first into the orange construction canvas.

I turn to Jason. "Do you trust me enough to calm her?"

He steps away from me instinctively, so busy staring suspiciously at me that he loses sight of his sister. So much for trust. Patty, now unrestrained by her brother, runs at me.

She goes straight into my arms. She struggles to punch me again, but I only tighten my hold. That antiseptic odor burns in the air as my magic stings her skin. I hold her as she sobs, feeling awkward to see this heartbreak. I tighten my grip. Slowly, she stops crying altogether. Her breathing slows, and I'm left supporting the weight of her tearstained, beer-soaked body. I push her hair back from her face, frowning at the drool. "There." I hand her to her brother. "Put her to bed now while the magic soothes her drunken nerves. I'm uncomfortable with such displays of emotion unless I'm on the hunt."

Jason lifts his sister into his arms, bridal style, and carries her in silence to the back rooms behind the bar. I try to peek down that long stretch of hallway, that sacred space where their inn-dwelling home is located, but Jason blocks my view. Byron notices my snooping around and stops his scribbling long enough to look up at me from his journal. "You could've been gentler with them. They're still mortal."

"You were mortal too," I reply, picking up the beer glass and downing what's left in it. "You died, what, not even a week ago?"

He looks back at his work. "It's getting harder to feel things the longer I'm dead." His tone is accusatory. "The faster we find that murderer, the faster we can gain the Eye Coven's trust to get me back from this plane."

I examine Byron, his expression completely nonplussed. "That's awfully crafty, gaining Jason's trust just to use him, isn't it? What happened to catching a murderer for the noble cause of Anna Snow?"

When I get a glimpse of Byron's translucent eyes, steady as the earth yet not of this world, I see aching. It's the same expression he had that first night of his death, plunging his ghostly hand into the moonlight and unable to feel the night's icy embrace. "I'm losing myself in this form. It gets worse the more I tap into the essence of the spirit world, like summoning a fire when I got mad at you guys." He groans, putting his hand to his un-beating heart. "Looking down at all those waxen faces in the morgue, I thought that I should have joined them. I shouldn't have died at the Sweeney Inn. I never wanted to come back from what I did. Even my last thoughts were all a fluke."

Unable to handle the emotional tension, I go for the bowl of tomato soup. I take it behind the wood-polished bar to dump it into the sink. I then root around the fridge for some leftover pig hearts to curb my hunger. Busying my hands feels natural, more natural than talking to a confused ghost. "What's done is done," I tell him.

"Does it get easier?" The question falls from Byron's lips, quivering as though he's frightened of the answer. "Does forever get any easier?"

I want to tell him about the sleepless nights, of carrying lifetimes' worth of memories around in your brain. I want to tell him about how your conscience never lets you sleep, bringing up murders you committed centuries ago, as fresh as though you killed yesterday. I want to tell him about all the disgusting things I did to survive. I want to tell him the story of how centuries ago, while I was hiding out in the woods from angry humans, I seduced a young woman who was Patty's age. It was in a lakeside village beneath the full moon, and she was the daughter of the town elder who'd sent out a hunting party to kill me. I lured her to the waters of the lake and broke her heart. And then, using her salted tears as seasoning, I ate it and dumped her body, her dress weighted down with stones, at the bottom of that lake for the fish-people to pick her bones.

Instead, I remain silent and give him a weary smile.

Let him make of that what he will.

When Jason tromps back to the bar area, he goes straight for the drawers beneath the Siren painting. He carries a jar of chocolate powdered malt and a bundle of red silk bags beneath his arms. I catch a glimpse of a few of the labels: bone powder, pixie blood, and severed rat arteries.

"What are you making?" Byron asks, sliding just far enough away from me that my anxious mind believes I've frightened him away for good.

"It's to help her stay asleep long enough to forget what made her go insane in the first place." Jason's about to return to Patty when he catches my eye. "Why are you looking so judgmental, Lili?"

I stand, bearing my weight on the side of the bar. "You can't heal a broken heart with necromancy, mortal. *Amour fou,* a mad love. Death magic for a love cure, it's a cute idea. I find it funny that you try."

He narrows his eyes at me, the red silk horror concoctions slipping slightly from his grasp. Byron goes to help ease the burden, hyper-focused as he lifts the material objects. "You can try to help me ease her pain, Lil." Perhaps remembering what happened to Anna Snow, the necromancer adds, "but leave her heart well enough alone, Siren."

I brush his male aggression away, batting it like a fly, to follow him back to the Sweeneys' private apartments. The hall leading from the bar to the necromancers' quarters is decorated with old-fashioned oil paintings of sorcerers gone by, some faking battles against Fae or Siren kind, the Siren always appearing like twisted ogres or demonic temptresses in some way in contrast to the glorious, bejeweled Eye sorcerers. In the corners, I can see the mark of the Eye Coven, the glowing red pupil staring accusingly down at me, the Siren who dares occupy a necromancer's space. But the air is melancholy here, that feeling of being abandoned. Antiquated furniture, speaking of old wealth now lost, falling to disuse. Perhaps that's fitting for a necromancer. This home is a tomb.

Jason pushes a door at the end of the hall, and we walk into a room smelling suspiciously of herbs and the sour tang of alcohol. The room is plain gray, devoid of any outstanding decorations unlike the pretensions of grandeur outside. It's clear Patricia doesn't sleep in her own room much though I don't know whether it's to avoid her brother or to avoid the memory of her dead mother. As of now, she sleeps uneasily. My basic Siren cants are for initiating heartbreak, not ending it.

Jason goes to her bedside table and mixes the malt drink with the necromantic powders, shaking it all in an old sports drink canteen. And while he does so, I go near Patty, feeling Jason's suspicious eyes burning into the back of my neck. Byron continues writing in his journal, watching us with a journalist's probing eye. When I push Patty's hair back, I see the bronze fishhooks have been replaced.

"Leave the bronze in," Jason growls.

"If I use my magic on her while she has it, I'll sustain a burn."

Jason raises an eyebrow at me. Damn that trip to see Anna Snow. Now he thinks I'm some ghoul ready to rip his sister's heart out.

Ignoring his invasive stare, I close my eyes and shut them tightly. I lean closer to press my lips to Patty's forehead. My lips blister at once, the skin peeling back. I hiss, drawing away, but I must steel my resolve. I bite my tongue, switching one pain for another as I go back to search for Patty's heartache. When I press my fingers against her wrist, my skin is both aflame and frozen, and Byron looks queasy at the blood dribbling from my blistered lip. But I push away my pain and focus on the source of her heartbreak.

Jason told me to avoid touching Patricia's heart. He never said anything about her mind.

Exploring Patty's mind, I find Alice, a girl with pink hair, rhinestone earrings, and a homemade knit scarf. I see her as she hugs Patricia, holding Alice tightly like she'll fall apart if she lets go. Finally, Alice gets into a moving van, and I can feel Patty's heart ache for her lover. I can feel how her stomach drops and she wants to retch. I can feel how she wants to kiss Alice again and again. Her perfect Alice, running away because she's fearful of what goes bump in the dark in Gamin, fearful of how the town seems to be picking off its inhabitants one by one.

I reach in and steal the memory away. Slowly, I steal away all memories Patty has of Alice. It's a Siren trick, meant to wipe away memory of any rival loved ones from the victim's mind so that they won't feel guilty when the Siren lures them away. It's a mercy more than it is a nasty trick in Patty's case. I don't replace Alice's memories with false ones of me. I don't attempt to get any closer to Patty's heart than I was before. I don't want Patty's heart.

All I need are her memories.

Sweating, I look up at Jason who grimaces as he sees my skin blistering from the pain of the fishhook charm. I want to observe his eyes. I want him to see that I can get right at Patty's heart and still control myself.

The killer in this town, it's not me.

When I pull away from Patty, her breathing slows, and her entire body relaxes. I rub my hands together and wince as they're slick with my own blood. "I need a drink." I'm trembling now from the pain. "A thread and needle, too, for the bronze wounds." Everything is so cold, but I try to push the bleary vision away and stand on my own. Byron looks concernedly at me.

"And Alice?" Jason asks, moving to support me. I refuse to lean against him as I stagger to the opposite bedroom wall.

"Alice is nothing to Patty anymore. I altered her memories, to ease her broken heart." I fall to my knees, my hands leaving bloody streaks on the plain gray walls. "Why is the room spinning? Is this one of your spells, necromancer?"

"Lil..." Jason moves toward me.

"*Bruja!*" Byron calls out in alarm.

I swallow back the worst of the bile. "I hate this town."

And with that brilliant insight, I crack my skull against the carpet and fall unconscious.

Chapter Seven

The Sweeney Inn. Jason's Room. (Huh. Never thought I'd be here)

Jason runs to my side when he sees me awaken in a mess of crumpled sheets. "Lili!"

I shove him away from me, wrinkling my nose at the scent of him, like drugstore cologne and non-athletic-person-playing-sports sweat. "Jason!" I growl, shrinking away from his touch as much as possible.

"Byron!" The ghost floats into my view, shouting his own name. He gestures proudly to his journal, flipping through the ethereal pages. "*Bruja,* look. I wrote the part where you wake up after saving the barmaid's life because you're going soft."

"I'm not going soft. I just wanted to gain enough trust with Jace the mace over here so that he'd stop thinking I was going around sacrificing virgins or something." I glare pointedly at Jason, who's shuffling around and ruffling his nondescript, Midwest-boy hair.

"Don't forget you were the one peeking at ledgers that didn't belong to you. Yeah, I saw your magical fingerprints on it. But—" he coughs, offering me a cup of what smells like blended savory duck. He's avoiding my gray eyes like I'll try biting him or something. "Consider the trust gained. I... You did good, kid." He pats me on the shoulder, like a dog. I feel like a dog. The awkward practically seeps into my skin. "I believe you're not, in fact, the serial killer."

"Good," I take a large swig of savory duck. *Mm, blended pig's innards. Lovely.*

"Yes. Exactly that." He's like an echo, damn. "Good." Jason lets me relax and check to make sure my wounds are still healing properly, magical depression be damned, and then blabs after a whole five minutes. "Because we're going to need you back on your feet as soon as possible."

He doesn't even look all that guilty about making me work after nearly having died.

"Why?" I hope my brand-new baby blues appear to be scowling at him as I suck down the pig blood smoothie. I really hope he can see the scowl in my eyes, and I hope he's shaking.

"Because there's been another murder."

If this was a cartoon, I'd have spit the pig's blood all over the opposite wall to demonstrate just how shocked I was at this news. As it is, I don't stop drinking. In fact, I go on calmly until the entire blended bastardry is gone.

I muster the most concern I can in this situation.

"Oh..." I drawl, a bit over-the-top dramatically.

Byron scribbles something else down in his journal. To my immense surprise and self-loathing, I actually have a pang of concern over what he's writing about me. I'm starting to think I should've bought his soul in return for tracking down a killer and undoing his death.

"Yes, and it was someone we know."

"Oh, shoot," I sigh, "and after I spent all that time saving your sister."

"No, Patricia is still alive."

He glares at me. Byron's stopped scribbling long enough to also glare at me through his '90s rip-off Nirvana hair and dark eyes. I wave them on, lapping up the red stains on the side of the cup. Wishing I could eat a nice human steak along with the blended pig.

"It's Anatol, the vampire who runs the morgue." Byron sighs. "He's been staked."

*

The Morgue

"Shit, man, he's been messed up." Byron shakes his head as he floats closer to Anatol, who has had a stake driven so hard into his chest he's been pinned to the wooden hallway like an ant on display. "You think he ever got to go on his date with the undead chick?"

Jason shoots the ghost a glare. Byron grumbles and starts scribbling things in his journal. I, on the other hand, get closer to inspect the stake itself. "Doesn't this town have a real detective?" I growl, looking around for the characteristic flashing lights and trying to hear a Siren.

"Uh, about that." Jason awkwardly scratches at the back of his head. "I tend to sense the dead pretty quickly. Inherited necromancy ability from Mom."

I look to him with newfound respect. "So, you found a dead body, and you didn't call the cops. We're here, playing paranormal Sherlock and Watson, and you didn't do the number one smartest thing and call the cops." I sigh, running my hand along the stake. It's embedded with tiny flakes of garlic and carved through with crosses. Somebody *really* wanted this vamp dead.

Also, oddly, there's some iron and silver in it.

For Fae and lycanthropes…

"Not too surprising if the detective isn't here, considering they still haven't caught a rampant serial killer," I continue, wondering about the stake still. "If they ran altogether, I wouldn't blame them. I wouldn't want to play detective to this shithole either."

"That's Detective Ikiaq to you. And I happen to be quite fond of this shithole."

Well, speak of the devil.

A middle-aged man makes an appearance at the end of the hall. For some reason, it gives me an intense headache just to look at him full on. I catch a salt-and-pepper beard and shoulder-length hair that used to be black. Intense black eyes, and brown skin that folds over into a casual grin near his lips. Thickly muscled shoulders and a soft belly. He wears a thick black jacket with a caribou patch on the shoulder, and he's clutching a cup of hot chocolate that steams and catches on his chin. He wipes it with a rumpled napkin, looking at poor, re-dead Anatol with a sad expression in his eyes.

A little girl follows him, perhaps his daughter, with black hair cropped to her elfin ears, and a too-thin smile that disappears into her face. No matter how many times I look into her eyes, I keep forgetting what color they are. She clutches a giant spray bottle of window cleaner to her chest like a teddy bear.

"Hello, there." I go to the little girl, and she takes my hand with a smile. She tells me her name, which I promptly forget.

Detective Ikiaq crosses the floor in long strides. When he steps up close to Anatol, out of my direct line of vision, it becomes easier to look at him. For some reason, though, I keep seeing a pair of antlers sprout from his head whenever he pops up in my peripheral vision.

"Are you…?" I begin, trying to tread as delicately as I can about it.

"An *Ijiraq?*" The detective grins, taking in more hot chocolate. I'm beginning to wonder if the cup ever empties when he finally stops sipping and crumples up the papery casing in one hand. "Why, yes. Yes, I am."

Jason, noting Byron's confusion, pulls out a miniature spell book and flips through its pages. He finally stops at a diagram of a half-caribou, half-man creature with the information for an *Ijiraq* printed over it in his mother's careful scrawl. "Inuit shapeshifter. Kidnaps kids and lets them go if they have a special stone to find their way back."

Kidnaps kids… I look over to the little girl whose eyes and name I can't quite remember. *Well, aside from Anatol, that'd mean he'd fill out some of the descriptions for our killer.*

I cross my arms and lean back on one foot, my hair pulled back into a ponytail that probably wasn't the wisest decision. In the mirrored reflection of the metallic morgue door, I see my eyes shift to a hesitant hazel. It's the closest thing I can do to shapeshifting. Eyes reveal a lot about a person. It's why mine usually stay a neutral gray. "Perfect. If you can get people lost on a trail, then surely you can put those skills to use and find this murderer's trail."

"Lili…" Byron again, glaring at me from the corners of his eyes. "You're being an asshole."

Nothing new there.

Detective Ikiaq sighs and combs his hands through his beard. "Yes, well, I wish I could say the same about you, Siren. I wish you could just sing a song and lure them over here, but unfortunately, whenever I get close, they just vanish again."

I narrow my eyes at him. "How convenient."

"Look, as much as I appreciate our fine Gamin citizens helping out—" he looks pointedly at Jason, avoiding my scowling self. "and the Sweeneys have done a lot to ensure we magical citizens stay firmly out of sight of the normal populace, I'd rather not risk more lives than necessary on this case."

"I don't think we should—" Jason begins to protest, but I drag him out by the collar. He's a heavy guy, but with the pig's blood meal I had, I'm strong enough to wrestle him out of there with relative ease. Byron flutters behind us nervously.

"You know what? You're right, detective." I nod my head and wave bye with a smile. Ikiaq goes back to his sketching the crime scene and babysitting that creepy little girl. "You have a good day now, you hear? Enjoy the lovely scent of body, erm, decomposition."

When we finally slam through the front doors, Jason pulls out of my grip. Well, not really. He just unzips his jacket and wriggles out of it. "What was that for?"

"A kidnapper of kids? Doesn't our dear detective fit the regular serial killer description?"

Jason scowls down at me from his height, bland hair and eyes filled with a near-murderous fire. Not that he'd ever murder. Too boring. Too vanilla to a murderer's Chianti and fava beans. "Then why don't we march back in there and—?"

"You're both ridiculous." Byron shakes his head at the both of us. "We have a necromancer, a heart-eating Siren, and a poltergeist in this group and we're profiling the detective for *doing his job*?"

He does have a point. Monsters catching monsters, the irony speaks for itself.

"But the little girl!" I jab my finger into his chest. He grunts softly at the impact but manages to mostly stand his ground. "What about that little girl he had with him?"

Jason's expression shifts then, eyes narrowing slightly. "What little girl?"

I turn to Byron, but the ghost's face is blank. He didn't see her either.

I can't believe I'm dealing with these nonobservant idiots.

"Look." I shake my head, sighing. "We have our own leads to work with anyways. Remember what Anatol told us yesterday?"

"He had a hot date?" Jason and I swivel around to glare at Byron, who currently looks like he wishes to shrink behind his '80s/'90s overcoat and pull a John Bender and walk right out of this awkward situation. "What? She was an undead hottie, or something. I'm a sucker for romance!" He pulls out a book of Edgar Allan Poe poetry. "See? A real goth-romantic."

I fight an eye-roll. "Yes, as our paranormal pest here informs us, her name was Jo, and she's a *jiangshi* that Anatol brought back without the Eye knowing." Jason's irritation slowly disappears as he sees my plan. "Let's follow what leads we got before another mythical monster becomes dead for good."

I think back to the traditional old vampire, lamenting over the state of new vampires today. For just a moment, I fall back on the regular hopelessness I've been feeling lately. That tiny, annoying voice telling me to lie down forever. To join the ranks of the eternal dead myself. The voice telling me immortality is useless, endless, and that I'm better off in a grave.

I shove it off when I turn to the two most irritating people in the world. A wannabe jock necromancer and a poetic ghost who was too sarcastic to stay dead for long. I look out to the classic Midwestern horizon of pine trees, fallen seeds, and bent grass with fake log cabins. I think on the creepy little girl with the spray bottle, and how her face would look on a poster next to Anna Snow's.

I wonder why I can't remember what the little girl's face looked like.

And why, for some reason, I'm starting to doubt I ever saw her at all in the first place.

"Maybe we should go back and help..."

Byron and Jason look at me like I'm crazy.

"Help..."

I can't remember what I was saying. I put a hand to my face, and it comes away damp, smelling faintly of salt, earth, and unspeakable things.

Jason puts a hand softly on my shoulder. Byron sympathetically floats down to my level and peers anxiously into my face. "Hey, Lil. You doing all right?"

Jason pulls his hand away, sighing as my vision comes slowly back into focus. "When you go to that other place..." For some reason, I feel like he's referring to those moments when I zone out and feel like life's ending. Like there's no purpose to going on. "When you go to that other place, don't stay long. Come back, okay?"

Jason nods enthusiastically, bringing a pang to my heart. And he's the dead one, damn it all, he shouldn't be feeling worse than me about my struggles.

"Yeah." I shake off the unease, the little voices in my head. "Let's get to Jo the hot undead woman's house." I think back to Anatol, his booming voice and proud vampiric vigor. "No more deaths unless I kill someone myself."

Chapter Eight

The First Suspect's House

"How did you even find out where she lived?" Jason looks at the ranch house in front of us as though we just found the entrance to an ancient tomb. He plunges one of his hands into his hoodie to keep warm. The other, he's using to desperately tap at his cell phone. "I've been searching her up for a half hour, and I can't even begin to—"

I hold up an old address book I found at the back of the bar. It was being used as a stepladder next to the pantry. "Damn, you make me feel old sometimes. You see, back before they invented tiny metal internet devices, we used something called books. Phones. Addresses. Little containers of knowledge made of paper and ink."

Jason flips me off. Byron very intently writes this down in his journal.

I sigh, going back to knock on the front door. It swings open and I'm staring down the barrel of a shotgun.

Click-click.

"Who the hell are you?"

I raise my hands slowly above my head. I've been shot before because, obviously, people don't take too kindly to having their hearts torn out and eaten. It wasn't pleasant, even with fast healing.

The woman before us has shaved half of her gray hair, a tattoo of wings decorating the balding side. It doesn't take away from the striking quality of her black eyes and high cheekbones, defying gravity and fighting the wrinkles at the corners of her eyes and lips. She's skeletal, looking extremely ill with gaunt cheeks and a tank top that hangs like a dress over her, pants swinging from a chained belt loop.

She has a smoker's voice, and her eyes drift over to face Jason for a second. Knowing that our necromancer can't exactly bring *himself* back from the dead, I shove my chest forward to press the barrel further into my own body.

Jason raises an eyebrow, the action not going unnoticed on him. *What the hell?*

I communicate something resembling *I got this*.

"We needed to speak to you about Anatol from—"

Boom.

I look down at the gold-flecked blood oozing from my chest wound. It's never pleasant looking at your own insides, and the pieces of flesh littering the cement garden path behind us. I sigh and, shoving the rifle further into the crevice where my ribcage used to be, slam my way into the house. Unbalanced from losing the rifle, the *jiangshi* stumbles backward. I dig my knee into her stomach and pin her skinny arms above her head.

She hisses at me, the lower half of her jaw unhinging. I see a rotted mouth beneath her black lipstick, the forked tongue.

"Nice to meet you," I gasp, slamming her again into the ground. "My name is Lili. And I could rip your head from your body if I really wanted to. But seeing as you shot me, and I still haven't decapitated you, I'd say that gives me some leeway for a nice chat, doesn't it?"

Jason throws up into the shrubs nearby. Byron pokes interestedly at the new hole in my torso. The *jiangshi* spins away, spitting up black gunk.

"My name's Jo." She shrugs as I pull myself off her and help her up. "Jo Kim."

She rips up some of her black tank top and hands it to me. I pack the wound, wincing as it's been a while since someone actually wounded me.

"I'll get you some liquor for that."

I swallow back the pain, fighting to turn a grimace into a neighborly grin. "And a packet of meat, raw, if you have it."

*

Jo Kim's Living Room

Jason dips a needle into some vodka and starts patching up my wound.

"Get the bullet first, dumbass." I rummage in the makeshift medical kit Jo gave me and hand him the smallest pair of tweezers I can find.

Jason pales a little. *How amusing. Necromancer's nervous of blood.*

He obligingly picks out the pieces of bullet and then goes on to sew me up. I look at the amusing setup of the raw meat over a coffee dripper, waiting for the blood to drain and picking at little bits of congealed blood while I wait.

"You have two first names," Byron mumbles.

Jo glares up at him. "Like you're one to talk. You're just another ghost named after a dead poet." She kicks her skeletal legs up to the coffee table. I look to the corners of the room, note how she has a tank of oxygen and an IV set next to the TV and a dusty wheelchair.

"Cancer," she says, noticing my shifty gaze. "It's why I act like an angsty twenty-year-old instead of a sixty-five-year-old like I am. Was. Damn, being dead's hard to get used to."

I nod to the bullet holes in the wall, positioned right behind Jo's head right now where she sits on the sofa. The wallpaper stained a dry red. "It's the reason why you had Anatol turn you into a *jiangshi,* isn't it?"

Jo shrugs, drinking the unused vodka straight from the bottle. "Well, my brother would've called me a gangshi." She drinks, grimaces. "He was into all that stuff, the bedtime stories that made you check all the closets and lock all the windows at night."

"You don't drink blood too?" Jason eyes my coffee-dripper-meat setup nervously as he sews my wounds, pinning back my skin with his fingers as my body tries to heal itself faster than he stitches.

"I eat, well, souls I'd suppose you call it." Jo sighs and sips some more from her glass. "And vodka. Anatol was gonna teach me some more about what it's like being a sort-of vampire. He never showed up to our date though."

"Anatol got staked," Byron replies, quite simply.

Jason and I both glare at him at the same time, wishing he'd stuck to his scribbling.

"Sorry..." he mumbles.

Jo finally breaks her hard-ass mask for a second to swear beneath her breath. No, not swearing. She's praying.

Dammit, she doesn't know any more about Anatol's death than we do. She didn't even know he was dead until now.

Then why pull the rifle on me? There's something here still.

After another moment of silence, I surprise everyone by apologizing.

She grunts.

"You spoke about your brother in the past tense," I start, hoping she'll speak further. When she doesn't, I press. "Why?"

She grunts again, but this time, she gives herself away by glancing nervously at Jason. *Looks like the boring Minnesotan necromancer's making her nervous. Better check out why.*

"Jason, leave the room after you're done."

"Why?"

I glare at him, and he sighs and finishes stitching me up.

"Bathroom's down the hall, to the left," Jo calls out after him. He waves his thanks, his blue jeans and blond hair fading out of sight.

I look at her, and she looks at me. This awkwardness goes on for a few more seconds, only Byron still dares to bustle around and scribble his poetry as we wait. But, being a ghost, he doesn't really make much noise. Just flutters around a lot.

Finally, she speaks to end the silence. It's a common knowledge thing, really. Silence makes many people uncomfortable. Only the really old immortals will feel one with the silence. Humans? They're suckers for filling the air with useless words.

"My brother moved to Singapore with my parents. He struck it rich as an investor while I struggled by, teaching kids for a crap salary because I was convinced I was changing the world. I'm the only one who stayed behind in Gamin. But then, he came back to Gamin a few years after I was diagnosed." She leans back in the chair, obvious pain contorting her features. Old wounds reopened. "I should've known it was for something other than me. A new money scheme of his. He just wanted to give money to help renovate his stupid bar."

"Whose?"

I move to finish off the red meat and drink the rest of the cup, feeling a bit better even though I lost a lot of strength from the rifle attack.

"That one's father. Hollywood handsome, and as charming as a seven in a bar of twos. The kid looks a lot like him, acts like Bea, the mother though." She nods to where Jason went. "Tae always fell for pretty boys in need. And Todd was one of the only bi boys in town. My brother was always going on about how Todd Sweeney would change the world. And then Tae just went ahead and died of a heart attack anyways." She laughs. "Like brother, like sister."

She clenches her hands into fists, almost crying as she laughs and laughs. She goes on for so long even Byron looks scared.

"Could you—" she shakes her head, turning to me as the sound of her laughter turns to gasps of pain, unable to stop "—use your magic and stop this pain? You're a Siren, right? Can you do that?"

I pause a moment, see her trembling. "Of course."

I pull forward and break her fear with a kiss. When I pull away, I whisper, "Anatol seemed really eager to kiss you before he died. That one's for Anatol, yeah?"

She quiets down a whimper, wringing her hands. My magic seems to have calmed her enough that she can see clearly, wrenched from her memories. "Thank you."

I go to the vodka and wash the rest of the bottle down, hoping to sear the kiss from my memory. *God, I hate touching people.*

I go down to the bathroom door and knock on it until Jason appears, looking very bored. "It smells like undead lady in here."

I reach past him for the roll of toilet paper so I can rub Jo's black lipstick from my face. "We got what we need from here." I look to Jason's forehead, trying to envision the Eye glaring on his forehead. "And when we get back to the bar, we need to talk."

Chapter Nine

Sweeney Inn Bar. (Are we alcoholics yet?)

Jason has his hands on his hips, all *I'm serious now, look at me*. It's a tough guy act that nobody's buying. "My parents weren't evil."

Patricia is swiping through a dating app when Jason reaches over, irritated, and shuts down her phone. "Hey, I was looking for love!"

Jason pockets her phone and ignores her, glaring at me again.

"Jo said your parents stole money from her brother. Said he was obsessed with your dad. Then he dies mysteriously of a heart attack." Jason rubs at the back of his neck, face twisted in the *ew, my parents aren't even good-looking* way. "If that doesn't sound like some kind of twisted necromancy magic, then I don't know what does."

Byron nods, scratching out a sentence and rewriting it with a different adjective this time. "*Tus padres son del diablo.*"

"My parents weren't of the devil!"

Patricia sighs, trying to grab her phone while her brother's distracted. He dances back. "Would you guys stop talking about your weird Dungeons and Dragons campaign already? I just want my phone."

Right, Patty still doesn't know.

I move to jab Jason in his too-muscular chest. *Damn, the kid really could've gone pro for some sports team.* "Let's put it this way, Jason. If your necromancer doesn't decide to be a little less chaotic and little more good, then every character in the party is going to die and it'll be a TPK!"

Blinking, stunned from my usage of D and D terms, Jason just goes, "Huh?"

"Dungeons and Drago—"

I'm close to gloating about my campaigning D and D knowledge when Jason plows forward with, "Wait, so are you chaotic neutral then, or chaotic evil? Because alignments matter. And is this five E or three E? And, more importantly, do Tieflings exist in this world—?"

"Enough with the Dungeons and Dragons!" Byron shouts. We both turn around, flushing furiously. "Need I remind you that we are still very much a target in this case? *Pendejos!*"

We don't really know how to respond to the insults, but we don't have to.

Because Patty does for us.

"That was rude of him."

Jason looks to his sister, wariness in those farm boy eyes of his. "Rude of who?"

She points to Byron.

Oh shit.

Jason, gaping, stares between Byron and Patricia.

"Yup." I shuffle my feet awkwardly against the ground. "It seems she sees dead people."

"How did you—?" Jason strides over to his sister, but at the last second, his foot catches on a board. His sister's cell phone slips from his pocket and both he and the precious screen are about to get shattered on the ground.

"My phone!" Patty gets up, throwing her hands up into the air.

And everything just...stops.

Jason and the phone pause a couple of inches from the ground, hovering and turning in midair. Patricia, on the other hand, stares at her hands in wonderment, turning them over and over. Her brown eyes gleam until they're amber, like fire. Her freckled neck seems to elongate as her brown hair rolls past her shoulders. Power suits her, her eyes burning behind those rimmed glasses of hers. Making her look like a killer librarian.

"An actual *bruja*," Byron laughs. "*¡No manches!*"

I reach over and hand her the floating cell phone. Jason is left twirling helplessly on the ground. "Patty." I take her hand in mine. She turns up to me, trembling from a mixture of excitement and awe. "We need to talk."

*

Still the Sweeney Inn's bar (We aren't addicted. We can quit anytime)

"So, you're a ghost poet." She points to Byron. "A fairly wimpy necromancer." That's her brother. "A pretty cute witch." To herself. "And you're...you." Here she stares straight at me.

I exhale, wondering why I even bother to breathe as an immortal. I guess it's comforting. Makes me feel like I'm blending in with the humans. "What a scintillating observation."

But Patricia bravely plows onwards. "And something is out to kill our entire town, and you suspect it has to do with our parents. *Evil* parents."

"Allegedly evil." Jason huffs at that, avoiding my sharp glare in his direction.

Patty goes over and shoves her brother. "You big, macho doofus!" She shoves him again, and it's quite amusing to see how she and Jason get along. Humans are so young compared to me, but these two siblings act particularly like troublesome toddlers together. "Why'd you decide to keep this a secret from me? Misplaced acts of chivalry?"

"No!" Jason splutters.

"Don't you dare say it was to *protect* me when there's a serial killer on the loose!"

Jason goes silent.

"Whatever is happening, I won't stand for others dying. I happen to love this town, and if my parents were evil..." She crosses her arms and pushes her brown hair off her neck. "Then all the more reason to help out because karma. And all that."

I really want to correct her randomly throwing karma into the mix, but I decide against it. Byron reacts, though, much to his regret.

He starts to applaud her heartfelt speech, but his enthusiasm cuts short when Patricia shoots him a nasty glare. Sighing, I pull the two siblings apart from one other.

"Enough with the declarations and sweet human mish-mash. Remember, this is a real killer we're trying to stop here. And we should follow the leads we have. Most logically, the next person to be questioned is Tae Kim."

Byron hovers at my shoulder, black bangs falling all wispy over his ghostly eyes. "But, *bruja,* he's dead."

Jason and Patty scrunch their noses up when I turn to their direction, all smug. "Since when was that a problem for necromancers?"

I clap my hands together when nobody reacts. "Great, I'll take that as your overwhelming agreement with this plan. We'll rest up tonight and bring Tae back when we're all fresh as daisies tomorrow morning." I wave at them, not daring to look back to one of the spare empty guest rooms on the charred second floor of the inn.

Chapter Ten

I Don't Care Much

Today's the day we bring Tae Kim back from the dead.

I don't feel like getting up today.

I don't feel like very much at all.

"Lili?" It's a freckled nose beneath the gleam of glasses. Mousy hair and a scowl. "Won't you get up? We gathered all the weird chant things and herbs we needed and..." She stops and the door hinges squeak as she takes me in, peering out blearily at her from the covers. My peacoat and brown pack linger, untouched, in the corner. "Oh. You're still there. I see."

She nervously wavers between walking the rest of the way in or not, but then does nothing instead. Byron arrogantly floats right through her, and Patty's teeth chatter in shock. "*Bruja, vamos*. We have things to do, dead to raise, and—"

"Oh." Patty agrees.

"Yes, oh." Byron nods, crossing his arms, his ghostly overcoat and journal fluttering in a nonexistent breeze.

Patty's gaze shifts to my things in the corner. I don't have enough in me to stop her. Her eyes drift to the empty bottle of antidepressants peeking out from one of my peacoat pockets. Number forty-nine. That bottle failed too. She walks over to my bedside. "May I take your hand?"

I shrug. "Sure," I mumble.

She smiles. "It's okay if you're feeling a bit, well, sick today. I understand episodes. I have them myself." She pulls my covers up to my chin. "Get some rest there, love. I'll have Jason make you some blood-soup or whatever you Sirens eat."

"I don't need to be coddled, I—!" I snap, suddenly defensive. Then I soften, see the understanding in her eyes. "I'm sorry. Thank you, Patricia."

She beams at me, dimples partly showing. "Any time, dear. Just shout if you want to talk."

"We're here for you, *bruja*." Byron agrees. "We'll kill this demon today, then more tomorrow. Does that sound okay?"

I nod.

One demon at a time.

*

Sweeney Inn bar (We have problems. Many)

I go downstairs, the steps old and rickety, ignoring the scent of ash and smoke still heavy in the air. Patricia's poking through her cereal, and Byron is making some dramatic edits in his journal. Jason leans against the bar, twitching over a cup of coffee. He has a college boy backpack filled with scrolls and herbs. Patricia's clutching a tote with a jar of salt and summoning powder.

I wave to Jason. He doesn't move, staring at me with those pale eyes of his. His hair's a wreck. Gel couldn't hold much of it down. Bedhead's strong with this one.

"Are you feeling better?" he ventures, careful. Always careful.

I shrug.

Jason crosses his arms, waits.

"Yes." I grit my teeth together, hissing out the answer. "Yes, I'm feeling well enough." I button up my peacoat over a pair of rolled jeans and a black tank I borrowed from Patricia. My brown pack carries some old pig's blood in a thermos. Some of my cards and a beaten wallet that used to be new back in 1902. I had all my bank accounts memorized after the first couple of decades or so. You can only come up with so many different passcodes over the course of the centuries. And social security numbers can be easily fixed.

"Then let's reanimate a corpse." Jason shrugs his backpack over one shoulder and hands me a warmed canteen of pig's heart, a worn smile tugging at his lips.

"You're still evil," I tell him.

He shrugs. "I'll let you have that one."

*

Where the Dead Things Are

We cut upwards through the cemetery. For a small town, Gamin has an impressive collection of wrought-iron gates and ominous mausoleums. Some of the headstones are so old that you can't even read the inscriptions anymore, not even with my eyesight. Some graves are so rotted that the headstones are just a memory—if they ever existed at all. Just bones beneath overturned earth. A weeping willow and an oak tree lean against one another, defying nature and gravity in their gnarled embrace.

"Do weeping willows even grow in this kind of soil?" I pause, hands stuffed into my peacoat where there's a wrapper from a candy that went out of production sometime in the 1800s. My procrastination impresses me sometimes.

"Lots of things in Gamin exist that shouldn't." Jason points to a root that reaches upwards, almost shaped like a human hand. "Watch out for that." Patricia nearly trips over it anyway. "It doesn't stop them from existing."

"*Pero,* like, how do you know where Tae's grave is, Harry Potter?" Sometimes, I really don't mind having Byron's sense of humor around. Now is definitely one of those times. I sip on my pig's heart mash and wait for Jason's reaction.

Growling, he points to Patricia, who takes the responsibility of explaining away from her brother before he implodes. She waves a bundle of printed-out papers. "It's a copy of our parents' database. Jason showed me this morning."

"Necromancers. We always find the dead," Jason mumbles, still red in the face. Amusing, just how red he can turn. "Or they find us."

Jason pauses at the crest. Patty, of course, skips right by his human barrier. I humor him and stand back from the scene. A slight dip in the ground. An array of trees, a particularly tall one settled in the midst of the orchard.

I look around, trying to find a grave. Instead, we just stare at the towering maple with prettily groomed flowers around it. "Was Tae a tree?"

"No," Jason grunts, bending on one knee. "But he had one implanted in his corpse. Thought it'd keep him from being reanimated by our family if he went au naturel."

I whistle, long and low. "So, he knew you guys were a part of the coven?"

Jason shrugs, sprinkling some purple root on the base of the tree. Patricia rifles through some spell books until she finds one that's highlighted in neon pink with tiny, demonic unicorns scribbled through the margins. She lowers her own tote and starts arranging jars. "Mom and Dad supported an open relationship. They both got together with whoever they liked. Dad was never good at keeping secrets during, um, certain points."

Byron goes wide-eyed and then hurries to take notes. Patricia has the good humor to start humming as she works while her brother just scowls, burning up to his ears in embarrassment at revealing the nature of his parents' relationship. Amusing, his ascribing a human morality to me. Like Sirens are the prudes of the immortal world. A thin line of sweat trickles down Jason's forehead as he places his palms against the roots of the tree.

Patty takes out a canteen similar to the one that held my pig's blood. It contains a soupy, violet-tinted mess smelling of iron and pretentiousness. "Vampire blood," she whispers.

I really hope that's not Anatol.

I try my best to stifle my unease. *He's dead for good, get over it.*

"Poured over the roots of a plant, it forms a mandrake," Jason murmurs. "Patty, help me."

Patricia bends down toward her brother and places her freckled palm over his. Her hair is pulled back from her face with a butterfly clip. As they both murmur the words beneath their breath, Jason first, then Patricia repeating, a red indent starts forming on their foreheads. The Eye slowly burns into their flesh, fire without fire's bite, and Patty tries to pull away, nervous.

"Don't break the summoning spell, or there really *will* be consequences." He holds his sister firmly to him. "It'll only *feel* hot, Pats, but it won't burn you. Okay?"

She nods, biting her lower lip before she finds the courage to continue the incantation.

Byron hovers a little bit behind me. I continue watching it all with some interest. Witches always tend to have a flair for the dramatic. Everyone who occupies this world does, in some sense. What can I say? My kin don't shy away from bringing down entire ships if they can, or seducing kings away from their beautiful queens if it so suits them. Sometimes, both king and queen at once. We all want to be remembered.

The immortals and the undead are just a tad bit more, well, conspicuous.

Another few moments, and the vampire blood soaks into the tree's roots. The bark at the front of it starts twisting and contorting. One knob starts falling inward, forming a nostril. The whorls above it turn to eyes. A split and crack shatters the silent cemetery like thunder. A gaping maw, the mandrake's mouth, shudders open with a scream. Somewhere, far-off, a murder of crows caws and screeches in fright. But I'm still watching, impressed, as the mandrake shudders to life. The thin leaves over its "eyes," if one could call them that, snap open.

Then it starts shouting at all of us, Jason in particular.

"Todd!" the mandrake shouts, in a voice much like Jo's, except somewhat clearer. The creature's eyes fixate on Jason, who's stumbling back with his hand still firmly on his sister's. He moves to step in front of her, but Patty still steps around him to get a full view. "Todd, you..." The mandrake looks at its own trunk, another horrid scream. "Todd, you sick bastard, what did you do to me? I don't have a body. I don't have legs!"

I step in front of the Sweeney siblings, hands set firmly on my hips. I snap my fingers in front of the mandrake's wood-knotted eyes. "Hey there, that's because you decided to have a maple tree planted over your body. If you weren't so stubborn, you'd get a corpse reanimated instead of a trunk." The mandrake glares at me, but I don't shy away. "Don't look at me like that. Jo sent us here."

The tree laughs, some of its loose leaves and branches scattering around us. Patty dodges a particularly wicked-looking stub. "My sister and I were never the closest. She always said I was stupid for chasing after fairy stories. Now she sends a filthy Siren and some necromancers to twist my words for her."

"How does everyone know I'm a Siren?" I throw my hands up in the air in disgust. "Do I have a certain scent or something? Do I glitter in the sun?"

The others ignore my exasperated outburst. "Well—" Jason clears his throat. "Your sister's actually a *gangshi* now."

The mandrake pauses and turns back to Jason. "Ah," the creature rumbles, gurgling from its very roots, "how strange that my sister's now forced to believe in the things in the dark. Many things have changed since I've been dead or sleeping. One really can't tell which until they can't wake up." The mandrake looks around it, to the sky, to the earth. "Sleeping. So tired..."

I snap my fingers again. The creature's lidded eyes come to focus. "No sleepy time until you give us some answers. There's a serial killer in this town, and you might have some knowledge to save it."

"I didn't like Gamin. Let it rot." The mandrake laughs. *Typical, selfish creatures,* I think and then correct myself, reminding myself that I was one of those typical, selfish creatures before Byron coerced me into helping him.

"You'd let Todd and his children die?"

Jason opens his mouth, probably to correct that he's not his father since he's Mr. All-American, but Patty elbows him to shut up.

"Ah, Todd!" The mandrake rouses again with glee, looking longingly at Jason. Jason, per usual, turns tomato-soup red. "I suppose I could tell you what little I know. I could tell you how I was murdered, for instance. But I don't think that'd be very useful, seeing as I'm now dead. No changing the ultimate tragedy. Like that story Jo loved as a little girl, the Fox Sister. In hindsight, the sister in that tale devoured her entire family, that's probably why..."

"No!" Patty volunteers, stepping in front of her blushing brother. "That would help us immensely, Mr. Kim! Tell us all about your murder." She blushes, too, now, the blush of having to pull the parent card. "For, um, dad. Todd."

"Well..." Tae takes in a deep breath, or more the mockery of one. His tree roots glisten with the purple-black hues of the vampire's blood. The liquid is trickling dry. The mandrake will sleep soon without any more vampire blood to awaken it. "Parents were dead already and buried at home. Sister resenting my love, growing distant that I'd passed over her for my lover. I had my fortune at Todd's disposal. My love. But curiosity got to me. Todd was becoming distant. He and his wife were fighting over something. Todd wouldn't let me help. Said I'd helped enough in renovating that rickety inn for their family's future."

The mandrake looks off, the blood trickling down into the earth, absorbed and hissing. It shifts with a groan, weakening. "Then I found the book. I was wondering if there had been a clerical error. Families often fight over money, right? And Beatrice had never seemed jealous of me. Had welcomed me, even. I found where the money went."

"Where'd it go?" I place both palms on the tree's trunk, desperate now. "Where was the excess money going?"

"Leaf," the mandrake mumbles, lips stiffening as the last of the vampire blood dries up. "It. Was. Leaf."

What the actual fu—?

"Stop there!"

The mandrake shudders with its last, false attempt at a breath. Then it fades back into being nothing more than a tree, the last of the vampire blood soaked into its roots. Tae Kim is back to sleeping. A rattling groan. Could be mistaken for the wind, but we know better.

But I can smell something. Humans. Beating hearts, beating fast.

Humans in pursuit.

"Stay back," I growl. Patty's about to ask why, but we're cut off by the intruders.

We turn around to face a group of seven angry-looking sorcerers with the Eye burned into their foreheads.

Of course, more meddling necromancers.

"Illegal magic, property seventy-six B of the new mandates of the Eye Coven." The woman at the front, muscular legs set in sneakers and a pair of comfy jeans, sighs. She dresses young for her age, looking to be about thirty with a black bob and fake lashes. Lots of makeup to remain forever young. *Not everyone can be immortal, though humans often try to be.* And, by the looks of her, she's a lover of cross-training and bodybuilding.

Wasn't aware you had to be so fit to wave a wand.

"Reanimating mandrakes without a permit." She sighs, pointing to a buff man at her side who looks like he hasn't missed leg day in his whole life and lives on protein shakes and magic alone. He's dressed in an ill-fitting suit with a pair of glasses over a square nose. "The Sweeney children too. What a shame that this would be coming out of you."

Jason and Patricia share a look. "Who the hell are you?" Patty asks, crossing her arms and glowering at the buff dude and the thirty-year-old in teenage clothes.

"Sabrina." *Oh, that's precious.* "And you two are facing a very hefty fine."

She then turns around to me, and scans me with something that looks like, and here I have to take a second glance because I can't believe it, a price-tag scanner. Like the kind you see at supermarkets. Nonetheless, it burns through my retinas with its demonic red laser. Luckily, I blink away the pain.

"A Siren." She chews on her lower lip, eyebrows raised and wrinkling up her forehead. "Your kind don't really pass through Gamin, do they? Too busy sinking ships and wrecking marriages, aren't you?"

I scowl right back. "I could say the same for you necromancers, Sabrina the teenage witch. At least my relations are with the living. Then you can have your fun with the leftovers."

"It's necromancer, not necrophilia!" Sabrina all but screeches. "Like I could expect one of *yours* to tell the difference. Now, Sweeneys, come along. We'll have to fill out your lifetime membership forms, and your fine for the mandrake. Bring your ghost and your—" She looks me up and down, peacoat and all. "Bring your pet with you."

Bristling at being called a pet, I know very well that these sorcerers mistakenly believe they're the top of the food chain. Like humans believe they're above animals, except sorcerers are worse because they believe they're above humans too. Salem had the right idea, in my personal opinion. "I'm not an animal!"

Patricia fights snickering, even as Jason looks worried. "Here, Lil. Good girl!"

Jason hugs close to my other side, Byron fluttering beside him. "I don't like this," Jason murmurs. "There's a reason my parents didn't trust these people."

I grunt in acknowledgment. I don't usually like to agree with jock necromancers from Minnesota, but I'll have to agree with this one. Something very rotten is going on in Gamin, and it's not the undead.

Chapter Eleven

Just Outside the Cemetery

We walk in peace for approximately twenty seconds toward the mysterious caravan of shiny, black vehicles parked next to the graveyard.

Then I go for an escape.

I hook my arm around the neck of Sabrina's male bodyguard, pressing as much exposed flesh as possible against him. *Ugh. Ugh. Ugh.* Since he's so much taller, I have to lift myself off the ground to properly choke him, like wriggling up a tree. I kick, hard, at the back of his knee, waiting to hear his neck crack.

It does.

"Run!" I scream to Jason and Patty. Byron's just following for shits and giggles, I guess.

He stays standing, his head bent at an irregular angle.

"Siren!" Sabrina calls my name like one would a disobedient dog. "Would you stop damaging Frank #575? Your charms won't work on a dead person." She smirks, proud of herself. "Unless *you've* taken to necrophilia."

Frank takes my moment of stunned silence to lift me by the back of my neck. If you're not a dog, this hurts immensely as the skin of one's neck is most definitely not meant to stretch that far. I take the pain bravely for a few moments before screaming. My body, not knowing any better, futilely keeps healing itself as Frank tears chunks out of it.

Jason steps forward, anger flashing in those baby blues of his. "Let her go!"

Patty steps on Frank #575's foot. The giant, undead creation grunts.

"Frank," Sabrina practically cackles, "drop."

He throws me, a bruised and slashed pulp of flesh, to the ground. The Sweeneys move to help me out. Spitting blood and broken bits of my dignity, I wave them away. "Leave me."

"Control your pets better." Sabrina sniffs. "It's probably because you gave her a unique name. Made her think she's important. No discipline at all. All our summoned or undead minions are assigned Frank and a number. Get it? Like Frankenstein?" The Sweeneys stare hollowly on. Byron claps, but being a ghost, doesn't make much impact except on a bunch of floating leaves surrounding him. "Ah, well. Humor wasted. This will make the next moment quite unpleasant."

She pulls a gun from her pocket and shoots Frank #575 in the head. The bullets behave differently, speaking as someone who's been shot a fair many times, and the resulting gore of the scene is most definitely not what a normal piece of mortal weaponry would do. I pocket one of the bullets, still covered in formaldehyde-scented gray matter, before Sabrina notices. It helps that part of my spinal cord had been damaged and is still in the process of healing, so I can fake having bad balance to crawl over to the bullet. Patricia pats Jason soothingly as he retches. Frank #575 fell, as luck would have it, directly on Jason's athletic sneakers. Jason currently has an unfortunately detailed view of the inside of a brain cavity, and scattered pieces of dislocated jaw.

"Can't have damaged goods. Business." Sabrina shrugs casually for re-murdering somebody.

She smiles, smoothing unseen wrinkles down on her outfit. Waving the gun as coolly as one might wave a pencil, she urges us toward the funeral caravan waiting for us. Another Frank picks me up, not exactly like the last one except for being dressed the same, and places me in the back of the vehicle. He folds down the seats so I sit there, on the floor. Byron hovers to join me in my humiliation while Jason sits next to the driver and Patricia takes the back seat to sympathetically check up on me.

"Don't touch me," I growl, snapping like I really am a dog.

Patricia respects my wishes and smiles softly. "Thank you for trying to get us out of this." I soften at her gratitude.

"I'm sorry I couldn't do better." I turn to stare out of the rear window of the vehicle as the graveyard and Tae's maple tree fade out of view behind us. The rest of the cars circle around and follow in pursuit. It smells like hearse and body rot in here.

I prefer not to think of what's been here before me.

I prefer not to think I failed these magical humans and one dead ghost at all.

*

A Coven with a Company

"Welcome to the Eye Coven Corporation." Two more Franks, a bodybuilding man-woman duo, lift me from the back of the car. My injuries have mostly healed by now. My pride still stings. Jason and Patricia are offered water and snacks, both of which they decline.

They smell delicious.

No, don't, Lili. If I could just reach into my pack and pick out my thermos, there'd be no problem. But the Franks have too good a grip on me. Half dragged and half walking, I'm led to what resembles an unremarkable, one-floor office building decked out in steel-framed windows and sliding automatic doors, two exits. Byron takes some excited-sounding scribbling notes on my oh-so-heroic defeat. Jason and Patricia share a pack of trail mix they brought from the inn between them.

"Necromancy not pay well? Maybe you got competition from Hogwash?" I ask, regretting it as female Frank breaks my nose. It heals. I don't regret the taunt or my never-shutting mouth.

"Hogwarts, *bruja*," Byron corrects. I repeat his words, so Sabrina hears.

"Cute ghost." *Of course, necromancer. Can see ghosts. Idiot.* "We prefer building down instead of up." Sabrina flashes her prize-winning smile at me. "Closer to our clients that way."

As we go through the front doors, the only thing there is a perky receptionist, a former intern according to Sabrina's explanation. He wears a headset and closes all his internet tabs as we walk in. Umber skin, and an Eye that looks warped, like it was modified.

"Broken eye?" Jason asks, smiling back at the pretty former intern and then blushing his usual tomato-soup red.

"I changed it a little for my favorite anime. Purely aesthetics, of course," the young man answers, in a timbre that's trying to mimic an adult. He can't be far out of college, or perhaps high school. Mortals age so quickly. It gets difficult to tell. "My name's Erik. Used to be an intern. I used to pick up phones and watch the magickers do their work. Now I pick up phones and watch...the elevator."

He nods halfheartedly to the glass elevator with the digital display out front. The glass is irregularly thick. Perhaps magic-proofed.

Or sound, for the screams.

"No chatting with our...clients. This isn't lunch hour, Mr. Borden," Sabrina snaps, and Erik jumps up, nearly choking himself on the headphones wrapped around his neck. He goes to the elevator's digital display and taps in a quick passcode before the doors beep and hiss open.

"Sorry." He grins, going back to his computer at the front. Byron can't take his eyes off him, his ethereal gaze fixated on Erik's hunched-over figure.

"Locs, a side fade, and a passion for the art of anime." Byron sighs. "I'm in love."

Sabrina glances back. "You'll have to fill out a permit form for your chattering ghost, Sweeneys." She waves us all into the elevator. Noticeably, she's positioned closest to the emergency buttons, watching all of us.

She taps in another digital code, and the elevator descends into darkness. Turns out the glass doesn't block out screams. We zoom past a floor where all my eyes catch is a blur of metal and fire and horrible stains of blood. Another floor of huddled, massive figures. Corpse-like hands clawing on top of one another. Another floor, just a wall of black-and-white photographs. Another, a room full of jars, the contents floating in what appears to be blood.

A man performing an exaggerated form of exorcism. The ghost in it was screaming in horrible agony. I'm not sure if I believe in a hell. Ironic, I know. But if there ever was one, an exorcism would be the closest thing for ghosts. Byron shrinks from the last scene, as scared as I've ever seen a ghost become.

"That's what happens to those without proper permits. Usually." Sabrina practically bathes in Jason's and Patty's discomfort. I clench my fists, wishing I wasn't so weak from only pig's blood. Wishing I was stronger than my setbacks, strong enough to push past and kill her right there. But, as such, I am weaker than I've ever been in all my immortality. Vulnerable, and ultimately imprisoned by two zombies called Frank. Sabrina reaches for a makeup compact, dabs at the mascara smudging her lower eyelid. "Lucky you're a Sweeney. You get a free pass."

"Yeah." Jason scowls. "Lucky us."

Chapter Twelve

Eye Incorporated

Turns out that we haven't plummeted to semi-hell like I expected. Instead, we file out of the elevator, or in my case, get dragged, to a tidy administration office. Interns behind cubicles. Manila folders. Seas of pens and paper, all stacked neatly and catalogued. The interns type furiously into their computers. Maybe they're trying to hack the human body with their dark web magic, or maybe they're playing Tetris. Seems they get all sorts at the Eye Coven.

Sabrina goes to one of the coffee-swilling interns and murmurs something about permits, entire strings of letters and numbers that make no sense to someone who doesn't get this jargon. After some finger-tapping, a folder's produced, with SWEENEY smeared over it in marker.

"Shall we?"

We proceed into a side corridor, a burrow that looks like a regular cubicle in a bank. Uncomfortable stuffed red chairs that are too low to the ground. A desk far too large that bumps your knees. A large computer that's been out of date for a decade. We walk across from Sabrina's high-back chair where she steeples her fingers and opens the folder to the first few papers.

"Sit."

I'm dragged to the corner where Byron sympathetically follows me. One of the Franks digs their elbow into my stomach, making sure I don't try to wriggle out. Patricia and Jason go on and sit opposite Sabrina.

Jason leans over, takes a look. His brow furrows, eyes looking devoid of any color in this harsh fluorescent lighting. Makes him look half-dead himself. "These papers are meant for our parents, Todd and Beatrice Sweeney." He pushes the papers back, frowning. "In case you haven't noticed, they're dead."

"It's not meant *for* them; it was made *by* them. Think of it as a present from beyond the grave. We get a lot of those here." Sabrina taps on the papers again. Patty leans over this time, tongue running nervously along her teeth. "You wonder why I keep bringing up the fact that you're lucky to be Sweeneys?"

Patricia smiles too sweetly at that one, batting her lashes and all. "You're fond of the Sondheim musical?"

Sabrina doesn't even grin. "It's because your parents were very high-up in the organization of the Eye. And they would've been legendary, too, if they hadn't run off to play house in that creaky inn of theirs." She taps the paper with a pen, little ink splotches spilling like new wounds over the surface. "You two could be a part of all this. Wield so much power."

Jason and Patty exchange a look and then snicker like schoolchildren caught in the act. "I saw plenty of your weird office-from-hell today." Jason takes the pen and starts chewing on its end. A nasty habit. Freud would've called it a sign that he secretly wanted to sleep with his mother. "Our parents went through a whole lot of effort for us not to get involved with you. We're not signing."

"Even if we did sign, there's no point." Sabrina latches onto Patty's every word, eager to let the mousy girl keep talking so long as there's hope. "We don't want this Evil Eye Incorporated type of lifestyle. I just found out I was a witch a day and three-quarters ago. Let me at least dance naked in the woods with Satan first before you shackle me down to a desk job."

Nice one, Patty.

"Our parents want us normal." With a look from Patty, Jason amends, "Wanted us to be as normal as we could be. We aren't signing."

Sabrina inhales and exhales. Maybe it's something she took from anger management classes. She shuffles through the papers and produces some shorter sheets with far less writing on them, just a few numbers and a date. "You don't know just how big this is yet. You will, someday. I'll ask you again, and you'll give your left hand to sign. For now, here's your damn permits. Fill out whatever you're comfortable with. That one's for the mandrake, next for the ghost. Final for the keeping of an extraordinary domestic." She glances at me, grinning in the corner. "What are you smiling about, Siren?"

Sabrina motions for the Franks to bring me to her. They force me to sit in the chair closest to hers. The fringes of her black bob tickle my nose. I lean closer, to see if I can get the Siren magic to lure her to my side. She snarls, and the Franks pull me back before I can do harm. "I was grinning about the fact that I'm an *extraordinary domestic.*"

"I know what you are, immortal." She peers closer at me, long nails drumming against the desk. Just far enough that I can't reach her, scare her with a hint of my power. Make her lose her precious control. "Imagine what we could do to a body like yours in the labs." She reaches out and her fingers trace my face without the danger of touching my skin, hovering maddeningly close. "Cut. Snip. Tear. It'd just heal. Makes me shudder, to imagine what you were like in your prime."

"Stop it." I shake my head, not wanting Jason or Patty to hear this. They know part of what I am. Lucky for me, they were too lazy to study anything past their mother's handy creatures one-page guidebook. But, with Sabrina, I don't have that luxury. Evil witch has done her research well.

"You must've been something like a god in your heyday." She's taken notice of Patty and Jason's distraction; their pens cease writing. They turn to me with wide eyes, eager to peer past my façade. "You see, children, there are the *true immortals,* then there are the mere *reanimated.* Reanimated is what the Eye deals with, obviously. From death, comes new life. A better life. Vampires. Ghosts. The boar demon of Indonesia. Skinwalkers. The list goes on and on."

She points to me, and the young Sweeneys' eyes bore expectantly into me. *What do they see, and what don't they want to?*

"But your Lili is one of the *true immortals.* And they differ because they never had to die or sell their souls or do much of anything to gain some immortality with all the strings attached. They simply are and will continue to be until the universe itself ends." She laughs. "We could use her blood to try and find eternal youth, so our clients never have to die to regain a perversion of life. Wouldn't that be something? To dissect a god?"

"I'm not a god." I refrain from outright spitting at the concept.

"Tell me then." Sabrina steeples her fingers once more and rests her sharp chin on the makeshift cradle. "You think one made you? The Greco-Roman Siren myths always feature your kind in some sort of disgrace for not being perfect. Godly rejects if you will. Like fallen angels."

"Now you're just mixing different traditions together. If the deity of the Abrahamic religions made me, then surely, I am a demon and not an angel."

"Yes." She winks conspiratorially at the siblings. "That's not even your true form. It's why you're weak enough for the Franks to hold you back now. Tell them where you got your face, Lil."

"I scavenged."

"How?"

"I took the parts I liked off the corpses of those I *seduced*, for lack of a better word in my profession."

"How did you do it? Use daggers? Your nails?"

I spit on the desk. Get smacked by the Franks, but don't regret it as my bruises heal. "Want me to show you how?"

Jason turns away while Patricia inches herself in front of me as though to physically shield me from Sabrina's interrogation. "Whoever Lili was, that's not who she is now. She's our friend."

"You don't know what she did, Patty," Jason murmurs, his voice low, torn out of him.

Sabrina takes out some hand sanitizer and a tissue box to clean off my saliva from the desk. "Give her to me, and you won't have to."

Patty leans back, eyes shifting between Jason and Sabrina. She runs her hands over her freckled arms as though to scratch the freckles away. "She's not for sale." She shoves the filled-out permits across the desk. "Too much paperwork as is."

Thank you, Patty.

I think.

Sabrina takes the papers and shuffles them together. They disappear back into the marker-smeared manila envelope. "The Franks will see you home. Shouldn't be running around unsupervised. There's a killer on the loose, you know."

"Must drive up profits. All this death," I drawl. Sabrina doesn't order the Franks to smack me this time. I lift my chin, a challenge.

"Our eternal life insurance policies are selling like hotcakes." She nods, and the Franks lift me up again. They carry me toward the elevator. Patty, Jason, and Byron follow. "You're always welcome back, Sweeneys. If normalcy ever gets to be too much for you..."

Patricia smiles sweetly and flips her off as the elevator doors close.

Byron howls with laughter and even steadfast Jason snickers as we catch the last glimpses of rage on the businesswoman-necromancer's face. The Franks, per usual, stay silent.

Chapter Thirteen

The London Underground, About to See David Bowie's Ghost Perform. (Just kidding. We're back at the Sweeney Inn)

Patricia rubs a witch hazel bark poultice into the back of my neck, taking away the sting of having my flesh torn out by the Franks' meaty, undead hands. "And they didn't even appear slightly suspicious to you?" I mutter between moments of intense pain.

Patty rubs her elbows into my neck, piling my braids atop my head to keep from getting the slimy poultice in it. Slowly, some sensation returns there. It still feels grimy. Probably Sabrina's influence. "Of course, they did. But I've only known the truth for a few days. And our parents isolated us from the rest of them, so we don't know how they act usually. Maybe that stuff's normal."

Byron sits, or rather, has half his ass floating through a bar stool. "She gave me the creeps." He holds up his arm. "See, gooseflesh. And I'm dead."

"Erik liked you." Patricia throws side-eye at the phantom.

"Some evil's worth sinning for," he replies, fanning himself. "Ah, Erik the former intern. Take my word for it, we're going places." He looks off into the distance. "*Que guapo.*"

I try to steer the conversation back to where it started. "But it'd make sense. Killing people to sell their eternal life insurance policies. Driving up fear." I grunt as she starts rolling a large, medical wrap over my skin, the adhesive irritating and itching. "Nobody has to fear death with a necromancer at your side. Become one of the reanimated, and never fear death again if you can pay for it..."

Patty rubs the poultice over my nose where the Franks got a few good jabs in. Jason wanders in from the bar, paging through his parents' old spell books. Reciting incantations into his cell phone's voice recorder.

"Jason," Patty calls, and he looks up with his eyebrows drawn tight, lips thin and thoroughly irritated. "What do you think?"

He pauses in the act of tapping a few instructions onto his cell phone screen. "I think we should disband the Scooby gang and go see Detective Ikiaq. We got called in for not having a mandrake permit. I hesitate to overstep any more magical boundaries without a weird paranormal lawyer involved. Maybe let some stuff die down first, so the Eye stops watching us so closely."

Let things die down first. What a clever pun for a such a boring necromancer boy.

"Paranormal detectives are one thing, but paranormal lawyers are just ridiculous. Unless you count the Sphinx." I leap off the barstool, rolling my shoulders a couple of times to check the damage. I have to push my shoulder in a little farther with a grunt. One hand is still in my peacoat pocket, feeling for the strange, overpowered bullet that Sabrina killed Frank #575 with. "But there's no harm in seeing Detective Ikiaq anyways. Maybe we can bribe him to keep any illegal happenings on the down low for a while." Jason and Patty's eyebrows rise at that. Byron doesn't even blink, still dreaming about Erik. I shift the bullet between my fingers, grimacing as my fingernails scrape against old gore. "On our side, anyways."

The Sweeney siblings cast each other a dubious look. Byron floats to my side, holding a piece of ghostly paper in front of my eyes. I catch smidgens of a haiku, and a few lines of blank verse. "It's coming along nicely. If anyone alive reads it, you might even have a bestseller."

"Sell my memoir to the dead. There's more of them. We'll make a killing."

Byron has the good graces to laugh at my jokes. The others continue whispering amongst themselves and ignore my pun. The heathens.

"All right." Patty tugs a jacket on, to step back out into the uncertainty of Midwestern weather. Jason fills a coffee mug with pig heart for me, and packs sandwiches for the others. "Let's bribe the detective." She proudly holds up her hand, showing off that Edwardian ring I'd originally given them. To pay them back for burning down their inn. "Think this will do?"

"I thought you sold it to Sabrina. You took the cash, didn't you?"

"You thought many things," Jason replies drily, all of us watching as Patty shows off her ring. "But you underestimated Patty's ability for being petty."

*

The Detective's Office

"Absolutely not." Detective Ikiaq snorts, taking a sip of hot chocolate. He slides the ring back across the table, not even taking a proper look at it.

"Why? That's a valuable ring in wizarding circles!" Jason splutters.

The detective only sniffs. "Yeah, it's also a fake."

Everyone turns to glare at me accusatorily. "Mimicking cantrip." I shrug. "It worked well enough to fool Sabrina, didn't it? Think of its resale value."

"No deal." The detective repeats, crossing his arms.

I reply by sipping my blended pig heart and not breaking eye contact. It'd be easier not to break eye contact if he didn't have that strange illusion thing going on where his side profile turns into an antlered creature. He brushes dark hair behind his ears, taking a bite of oily bread before going back to his hot beverage.

He sniffs the air, lowering his cup. "Savory duck?"

"I couldn't eat them." I growl, nodding to the Sweeneys and Byron, who's examining some of the papers plastered over the detective's claustrophobic office space. "And I just got thrown around by dumb and dumber over at the Eye Coven. Give me a break."

"The reanimated can be a sonuvabitch." He laughs a little. Something even resembling sympathy enters those dark-brown eyes of his. He's well-adjusted for being a true immortal like myself. Not quite dead, but never quite living either. Who am I kidding? Everyone's well-adjusted compared to me. I'm a wreck. "I can't just keep calling you Siren after learning you escaped a scrape like that and gave them some hell over there. Those necromantic capitalists."

"Lili, Mr. Ikiaq." I observe his outstretched hand for a bit, the worn lines and carefully molded fingerprints. It's good work, for a shapeshifter. One would almost think human if you didn't look too closely.

"Lili." He folds his hand back. "Don't trust people, our kind, do we?" There's something then in his eyes that shifts from deadbeat small-town detective to ancient being. Just a faint glimmer that isn't quite right, that makes you nervous down to your stomach.

I think back on the Sweeneys and Byron, how that damned poetic ghost got me roped into this scheme in the first place. I wonder why the detective feels so strongly about serving Gamin in the first place. Why he wears a human mask at all.

"You're loyal to them," he remarks, leaning back as though we're at lunch and not separated by a desk. Not separated like two beasts set to heel by their owners. Two powerhouses restricted by the humans beside us. "I'm loyal too. But not to people. To the town itself."

"Why, did you fall in love with Todd Sweeney too? He seems more of a legend than a person." I take a seat across from him, disliking having anything but a clear view of him. All the better to keep the shapeshifting vertigo away.

He sips his hot chocolate and wipes the grease from his hands with a napkin. "No, Lili, I'm loyal to this town because it drew me in, same as all the others. Same, even as you." He looks me in the eyes, and for once, I feel hunted. It's a tingling feeling on the back of your neck, one that never quite fades. It's very rare to happen to me. I usually always feel in control. But with the detective, there's something about him.

Like a wolf getting too close to a mountain lion, I can sense the other predator packs a bite worse than mine.

And I'm not eager to face another true immortal alone. Not weak as I am. Not having deprived myself of human hearts since coming here. But we're on the same side...for now. "You've sensed the energy here, haven't you? Haven't you wondered why more people aren't reporting ghoul or zombie or vampire attacks every week, why normal humans mingle so easily with us? Maybe thought, 'hm, I wonder how that detective hid an entire vampire's body and stake and kept the other local cops from sniffing around too long?'"

"I mean...no," I admit, itching at the bandages on the back of my neck, my hair all tied back. The bullet still burning in my peacoat pocket. "A lot's been going on, what with the possible serial killer and all."

He harrumphs and then goes back to his hot chocolate, dark eyebrows pulled low over his eyes. I pretend to examine something on the wall, just to get a glimpse of his true nature and alleviate the budding headache I'm getting from staring at his shapeshifted form too long. From the corner of my eyes, I see a creature, half caribou and half man, with red eyes and nostrils that are steaming, fur matted with snow that never melts. When I look back, he looks slightly bemused, a quirk to his lips and some chocolate foam at the edge of his mouth. "Those necromancer-wannabes and that young ghost over there are good kids. But you and I, Lili, we're too old for banter. Let's cut the fat. You show me what you want to show me, and I'll tell you what you need."

"You don't mind we're chasing after a killer?"

He snorts again. He must have allergies or something. "Two necromancers, a ghost, and a Siren? It sounds like the beginning of a bad joke."

Scowling, I fish out the bullet and slide it across the table, simultaneously slipping the ring onto my thumb. No use in having it wasted. I'd give it to Patty if she asked for it.

The detective fishes out a pair of reading glasses and balances them on his nose. He turns the bullet over, scraping off some blood with his nail, and the clearing shows the Eye pattern engraved on the bullet. "Iron. Silver. A crucifix tip. Rowan trees." He hisses, dropping the bullet. A burn blister forming on his skin. "A bit of sand from the shore, some charmed afterbirth, and who knows what else they packed down to a molecular size to place in that bullet. Damn those witches! Always out to kill us folk with their chanting and wand work."

I smirk as Patty and Jason appear particularly offended.

"This thing"—he shoves it back across the table—"was made to kill almost every single true immortal, reanimated, or otherwise magically inclined creature in sight. Makes sense the Eye would have it, flashy as they are."

"So, it could've been made by the same people who killed Anatol, the vampire who ran the morgue?"

Detective Ikiaq chews on his lower lip, scratching absentmindedly at the stubble on his chin. "I hope you're not implying what you're implying, Lili. But if you are, I wouldn't blame you. Eye's become awfully bossy for such a small town, especially one like Gamin. Maybe they wanted their enemies kept dead instead of close."

Necromancers are evil. I knew it.

Patty narrows her eyes at me as I'm all but rejoicing and rubbing Jason's evil heritage in his face. "Why can you hold that bullet just fine if it's supposed to kill all of you?"

I shrug, placing it gently back inside my peacoat pocket. I show her the angry red welts that are already healing on my fingertips. "I'm used to pain." I take another sip from my coffee mug filled with blended heart, waiting for my body to knit itself together like it usually does. "I think that'll be all, detective. Thank you for bring us into your office."

"Thank you, Lili." He stands up, leaning against the desk, wiping the crumbs from his lips. "*Ajunngigiarlutit.* Good luck out there."

"Say hi to your daughter for me!" I call.

He looks confused for a split second. "I don't have a daughter."

"Oh, I'm sorry. I just thought...never mind then." A faded memory in my mind, of a little girl hiding behind Anatol's murdered body. A faded memory of a girl whose eyes and face I can't remember, no matter how hard I try. A girl forgotten.

I must have imagined it. I struggle to move past the awkwardness, recovering before the air grows stale. "*Ajunngigiarlutit,* detective."

Of course, the Ijiraq doesn't have a daughter. Why the hell did I say that?

Why the hell can't I remember her face?

I wave at him as the door closes. I secure it behind me before we crunch our way back out through the gravel path, toward the main road we walked down to get here from the inn. I'm starting to wonder more about things I never questioned here in Gamin. Like why the weather is permanently caught between mud-spring and fog-fall. Why everyone seems so moody and dramatic. Why nobody seems to drive cars out here. Or why everything is within a reasonable walking distance. Maybe there really is something to Gamin. Something that drew me here.

That won't let me leave.

The walking might be relatively comfortable for me, having walked half the world over in my long, endless life. Must suck for the humans. In fact, Jason's looking a bit queasy from the exertion. And Patty's sweating buckets.

Jason gags, looking paler than usual. "Does something feel *wrong* to any of you? Something feels wrong to me." He shivers in the breeze.

Patty places her hand against his forehead. "Are you getting sick?"

"Come on." I wave for them to follow me. "Let's get back if you're feeling ill."

"No, not ill, more..." Jason shakes his head. "*Wrong*."

Byron floats through the wall after us, looking a bit shaken. "I'll never get used to going through walls like that. Like seeing the inside of an egg before it's cracked. It's all wrong." He shudders. "Anyways, *bruja*, I got some good notes down while you were out there. I think you'll want to take a look at—"

I hold out a hand, stopping the Sweeneys behind me. They bump into me and are about to start yelling when I point to what lies ahead. They have the good manners not to make a sound.

Blood soaking into the earth. A young man with long hair and fragile features. Cords of muscle hidden beneath the angelic façade. Turned inside out, skin to bone. Fingers turned to claws, frozen as the body stiffens in rigor mortis. Reaching. Reaching.

And beyond it all, a scent. Familiar. Sickly sweet.

It's not the first dead body I've seen. I shouldn't be scared.

But it is the first Siren's corpse I've laid eyes on in a damned long time.

And that alone is enough.

Chapter Fourteen

Just Outside the Detective's Office

I bend down over the other Siren's body. I plug my nose and start sorting through the poor man's guts. The squishing alone is far from pleasant. Jason, ever the trouper, gags. Patty squeaks and mumbles something about how "it's far more purple than it should be." Byron sighs and clucks his tongue, looking over my shoulder as I sort through the guts.

Byron moans loudly, as only ghosts and red-light dancers can, when I don't move fast enough. "*Bruja*, I still have to tell you what I found in the detective's office." I glare back at him, wishing I could easily swat him away.

"I'm a bit busy right now, Byron." I glower as I go elbows-deep into the torn-up sludge. "Looking for this Siren's heart. We all have one. Even me."

"Sort of," Jason grumbles.

"Lili's heart is getting better," Patty amends, readjusting her glasses to keep them from slipping down her nose. "You're like the Grinch, and we're the Whos. And your heart's getting bigger, but it—"

I lift up my prize as she releases another squeak akin to a deflating balloon. Jason faints, and Patty has to catch him before he gets a concussion.

"What?" I ask innocently, picking through the murdered Siren's heart with my fingernails as Patty mumbles some incantations to set Jason's nausea right. I twist my thumbnail beneath a cavity, like separating fruit from seeds, and a bullet pops out like a cherry pit. I dig into my pocket for the one the detective monitored, and it comes as no surprise to me that they match. "Can't handle that your parents worked for evil?"

Patty looks between the two bullets, leaning Jason against the trunk of a nearby tree as he slowly comes to. Byron goes and places a permanently freezing hand against Jason's bare skin to speed the process up a little bit. I pocket the bullets and drop my kin's heart back into his emptied chest cavity. I wouldn't feel right eating it. "Eye Coven bullets. Our serial killer is killing for a company. Just a paranormal, corporate conspiracy. No shock there."

I turn around to go back to Detective Ikiaq and present the evidence, but Patty places a hand on my shoulder. I stop. A century ago, I'd have bitten a girl's hand off for trying to make me wait for her. I have so little patience for mortals. With the case closed, I can resurrect a poetic poltergeist with the necromancers' help and skip out on this town so I can find a way to die for good and end my reign of boring immortality.

Yet still, the detective's words ring in my ear, making me question myself.

You're loyal to them.

I'm not a werewolf or a vampire. I don't need packs or covens to be protected or protector. I have myself. I need nobody.

So, then, why do I still pause?

"Lili..."

I turn around, counting silently beneath my breath in every language I can remember, some long turned to dust. Like I should've if I'd known what was good for me. I open my mouth to reply, but Patty places her whole hand over it, so I taste nothing but the sugary cereal she had for breakfast, and the tang of dried toothpaste. "I was just getting your attention because Byron really wanted you to listen to what he found in that office."

Byron is, indeed, fluctuating up and down, creating a vortex of angry leaves and crunching twigs. He holds his journal before my face, showing something he'd scribbled down in a smear of what appears to be nasty ectoplasm. The substance just kind of *seeped* into the paper to maintain a corporeal form when it came into contact with the physical realm.

In normal vernacular, he spat on the paper, so his ghost-spit would stick against the wall and trace what he found there.

I run my fingers along the markings. The brittle indentations are simplistic. Like a game of tic-tac-toe. Five lines, some shorter, others longer. The pattern is random.

Like someone keeping count.

I glance back at the Siren. Patty points to a mark near his ear, or where his ear *used* to be. Five identical slash marks. Random lines.

Definitely keeping count.

"A penny for your thoughts?" Patty asks, crossing her arms in a very self-satisfied manner. I snort, getting to my feet and brushing a soup of blood-and-mud off my knees.

"The detective is somehow connected to this." I chew on my lower lip, knowing how wrong that answer tastes, resting in my mouth like bile. "Or someone's trying to frame him."

I hide the Siren's body under some leaves, and Patty and Jason chant a cloaking spell. We make quick time back to the detective's office. My knuckles rap against the detective's door, so hard that the entire doorframe shakes.

"Lili." Jason's turn this time. The strapping Midwestern boy shakes me by my shoulder. I hold in my temper, feeling very much like a wolf these kids decided to tame like a puppy. "Lili, look."

He points to where the main highway winds behind some trees. The outline of a low-riding car, complete with a sputtering, smoking engine.

"The detective's car. The sonuvabitch left without us." Byron harrumphs, all self-righteous all of a sudden. Such a paradox. A ghost being the holier-than-thou one. "That settles it, doesn't it? Proves the guy has it out for Sirens."

"Just because he's an immortal, doesn't mean he's the murderer."

"Oh yeah? You're an immortal, aren't you?" Jason peers closer at me, even as he leans farther away. I can practically *feel* how his whole body turns away from me. Disgusted. Just a hop and a skip away from being part of a pitchfork-bearing mob. "Suddenly defensive about immortals, aren't you?"

"Don't be ridiculous, blondie." If I barked anymore, I'd basically be a werewolf. "Why would I kill my own kind?"

"Guys, enough!" Patty shoves us apart and plucks at a note that fell with a pin still attached to it. "It's from Mr. Ikiaq. He says we should meet him at the river. He found a lead. Also, another thing..." She squints at it, adjusting her glasses as they slip down her nose. "No, this can't be right..."

"Hurry up! Ah, forget it. Lemme see..." Byron rolls his eyes, hovering in a half-crouch to try to peer over her shoulder. "Huh. The detective says we ought to trust the Eye."

Patty crumples the note up and shoves it in a pocket that she DIY-ed onto a patchwork dress.

Jason throws his hands up into the air, stomping off. "That's it. I'm done."

"Wait, Jay..." Patty pleads, grabbing his elbow. "Come on, we can't let Lil and By face whatever this is alone."

"Trust the Eye. Don't trust the Eye. The detective might be in on it. Hell, Lil might be in on it at this point." Jason grabs Patty's arm in return and twists her so she follows him. "Come on, Pats. Don't be naïve. Mom and Dad weren't perfect people, not even *good* people. You don't think I know that?" His voice drops as he shuffles his feet, a pained expression in those baby blues. "But I do know one thing. They did right in giving me you. And you're all I got, Pats." Patty softens at that as Jason loosens his grip, his eyes brimming. "I can't lose you to whatever strange immortal murder-fetish is going on in this place. Maybe it's time we sold the inn, packed up, and just left town."

I pause, taking it in. Patty opens her mouth, ready to reply.

"No, Jason's right this time, Pats...erm, Patty." I nod my head, even as Byron gapes at me. I gently pry Detective Ikiaq's note from her freckled fist. "Whatever mess this is, it doesn't involve two teenagers. This mess is for the dead, the reanimated, and immortals to handle." I take them in, the blond farm boy with baby blues, and the girl with hair tied back into a librarian bun, a patchwork dress like a living ragdoll, and soulful eyes. "My kind's been dead on the inside for a long time, sweetheart. You two are human. Weak without a spell book." I smile wryly at her. "Not much of a fair fight, is it?"

Patty wrenches her arm out of Jason's grip and stomps right up to me. She shakes one finger, imperious as a queen, in my face. Hell, Queen Victoria would be shaking in her boots to see Patty stare her down with all the might of the eternal flame in her eyes. And I *met* Queen Victoria... Tried to get her to leave Albert; she was damned well in love with him. But that's another story.

Patty's lower lip trembles as she cries out, "Lili, don't you *dare* think you're going to leave me behind like some weak little kid."

"I never called you a weak—"

"No, don't you start." She shouts even louder. "I know how you see me. Jason's the *real* necromancer, right? He's known he's had magic for longer. Shit, he's known about your kind since my parents trusted him with that information. I didn't know you existed outside of the cartoons with the singing fish until a few days ago!" She mumbles something unintelligible under her breath before continuing. "But if you *think* that I'm going to pack up and leave after everything I've seen, then you give me more credit than I deserve!"

I wrinkle my brow at that. "I'm sorry, I'm giving you *more* credit than you deserve?"

"Yes!" She "harrumphs" at that. Harrumphs! Again with that Queen Victoria attitude! "You seem to think I'm reasonable, or wise, or freaking possessing some semblance of self-preservation instinct. But, boy, you're wrong!" She shakes her head again, frizzy hair spilling from its ties and flying everywhere. "If you think I'm going to run away from certain death because I'm sensible, then don't worry, I'm completely *not*."

I pinch the bridge of my nose. "Hold on, I'm getting a headache with this lack of reasoning."

"Well, I'm not finished!" She throws her arms around me, and I want to draw back.

"Touch aversion," I squeak.

"Sorry, I just thought a hug was appropriate at that time." She drops her arms immediately. "But know this, Lili. I happened to read tons of mystery stories and watched the specials where towns like this go *very* bad *very* quick. I know that I'm a pretty sorry excuse for Sherlock Holmes, Nancy Drew, or that French guy Agatha Christie wrote about. And I know my brother has a decent hold on magic but is pretty freaking stupid..."

"Hey!" Jason protests, but Patty keeps on chugging.

"We probably won't help you that much in a fight. Maybe Jason can throw a few magical firecrackers, and I can scream pretty loud." She jabs a finger at my heart, or where it should reasonably be if it even is anymore, and she starts to enunciate every word like she's crossing the t's and dotting the i's as she goes. "But, at the very least, let us be meat shields. Let us be *your* meat shields, Lili." She sighs, finally inhaling and exhaling for the first time I've seen since she's started this rant. "Because when I'm old and wrinkly someday, and I survive this hellhole, I want to tell the Grim Reaper, who I'm assuming is a decent enough fellow after all the other magical creatures I met, to tell them: *I saved Gamin.*"

"See, I don't really have a regular, human moral conscience..." I glance over her shoulder at Jason, raising a single eyebrow. "So, whatever you just said is a good enough reason for me. How about you, Jay?"

He holds up his cell phone, an icon of a car glowing on its surface. "I don't know, man. Patty's pretty determined, and I can't let my kid sister die without me. Think of how badly she'd rat me out to my ghost-parents." He shrugs. "So, I already ordered a digital ride-share to get us to the river while she was ranting. You know, the place the detective told us to meet at."

Byron makes a quick, dare I say it, nearly ritualistic gesture. His eyes drift first heavenward and then cautiously toward our feet. "May God have mercy on our souls."

Chapter Fifteen

The Gamin River

The trees are bare even if it's too early in the year for the leaves to change color yet. They line a river crackling with ice. Frothy water trickles downstream, dragging along shriveled twigs and pebbles with it.

"There's ice on that river already... That's odd." I snap a branch beneath my shoes, noting how eerily similar it sounds to bones. "Does Gamin even have seasons?"

"Damp season," Jason replies. "Frigid season."

"Wet season." Patty elaborates. "Hoary season. Nippy and chilly and brine."

Byron perks up from behind me. "They're right. It only ever seems to have one season here. Cold and miserable. You're lucky if you see the sun once a month."

"Ice all year round." I snort, my breath coming out in icy puffs. "And nobody thought to question that?"

"No, we just take things for granted here. Those who question get lost, that's what Mom and Dad used to say." Jason shrugs, coming up alongside my left to pass me when I slow to a stop. Something's between the trees, lying by the river. The others' eyesight is too weak to notice it, but I'm sure...

Yes, yes, it is.

"Stop." I hold out my arm to stop Patty. Byron floats calmly past, and Jason pauses a few steps down. "Stay here."

"Why?" Jason starts toward me, refusing my order to stay still.

The thing below shifts, dead foliage crackling beneath its body.

"Because I'm trying to protect you, you idiot!" I snap.

I slide down the riverbank, mud slick against my waist and shoulder. I don't bother trying to scramble tenderly past rocks or balance myself with trees. It's faster just falling. Hell, I'd heal fast anyway.

When my fall finally slows, I stagger through the trees. My gaze rests on the heap of arms and legs. The massive antlers, the yellowed eyes and fanged snout. Split eyes and a tongue carved down the middle, a jaw slack. A torso that's not quite a man's and not quite a caribou. A monstrosity between the two, a half-baked transformation. Spidery thin neck, and a large skeletal head resting on it. A barrel chest on the hind legs of a predator. Eyes with three pupils, squat like a feline, holding the symbol of the moon. White dusts his thick, dark coat, like perpetual, unmelting snow from the arctic.

He's in Ijiraq form.

"Detective Ikiaq!" I shout, trying to get his true form's attention.

Blood, purple blood oozes all over his chest. He still wears his detective clothing, the button-down and trousers. But they're all torn up from where his true form broke through. The shirt's in tatters and soaked through with blood. I turn him around, see the bullet that burned clean through. The same bullet as all the rest.

The Eye Coven.

I press my ear to his chest, hear nothing at all. No semblance of living.

"No, they can't have gotten to another immortal..." I hear crashing behind me. Patty and Jason following, slowly.

"The detective, oh my God." Patty places her hand to her lips. Jason looks horribly worn from all the dead bodies we've seen today.

"I told you to stay back!" I snarl, holding him protectively to me.

"Much good that did." Jason swallows, fighting his nausea reflex.

I turn his wrist, a curved claw, over. See five indentations slashed into his vein. "The five marks are on him too." I go through the motions, numbly, examining the rest of his body. On his other hand, there's cloth dug into his fingernails. Tiny pieces of fabric from where he clawed at somebody. But there's no blood, only cloth.

The detective was an Ijiraq, a legendary hunter. How could he have missed?

Or is he dealing with something that...doesn't bleed?

I pick out the pieces of thread, and Patty holds out a tiny plastic bag. She empties out some of the ashes from the earlier mandrake ritual into a separate bag, making room for the mysterious threads. I turn the body over, kneeling at his side in shock.

"Shit, we'll have to cart both these bodies to the morgue." I turn to Jason. "Is it even staffed after Anatol's death or...?"

"Um, Lili." Jason points past my shoulder. I turn around and see the shadow of the Ijiraq rising behind me. Standing at nearly nine feet in height, still in his true form.

His giant caribou antlers rise even higher above that, at least another five feet. "Detective?"

"Get out of the way; he doesn't recognize us!" Patty shrieks, running back. Jason tackles me to the ground with a thud as the detective swings a claw at us.

"*TuKuk!*" He snarls. "Die!"

"*Ijiraq!*" I cry in response, rolling hard on my shoulder. I leap back up, popping the bone back in with a groan. "*Kujanâlunguna!* Leave it alone."

"We aren't your enemies," Jason cries, the Eye carved into his flesh with fire. His eyes are bright with his magic's inner flame. "We aren't the ones who hurt you."

"*TuKuk!*" he repeats, slashing at my chest. I dodge back before launching myself forward again with a snarl. I twist toward his back and wrap my legs around his body. I dig my hand into his bullet wound.

"Jason!" I hold on tighter as he howls in pain, his entire frame shaking. I steer clear from his poisoned antlers, rising another three feet above his head. "You and Patty need to calm him down."

Jason goes to Patty, who's somehow found a tree branch to protect herself. "Pats, grab my hand."

Patty nods, winding her fingers through her brother's. Her Eye sparks, slowly, on her freckled skin, etching a pattern that spreads through the veins on her neck.

My grip slips slightly, my skin sizzling with the strong, familiar scent of antiseptic. "Easy there, detective," I coo, but the Ijiraq's in too much pain for my usual seduction to work. He howls, and when he swipes at me, I dig my nails into his bullet wound. A raw scream tears itself from his throat. Byron spits ectoplasm in the creature's eyes, blinding him.

"Enough!" Jason and Patty speak as one, their combined powers glowing from their skin, their eyes. Wind lifts the fallen leaves around them, entangling in Jason's clothes, Patty's hair. They each lift their hand, an eye glowing, a magical etching protruding from the magic from their palms. "By the power of the realm of the dead, we demand you kneel."

Their voices as one, a legion of the dead realms, the Ijiraq falls to one knee with a low gurgle in its throat. The Eye burns over his chest, melting into his skin. Another moan, the bellow of a defeated animal, and he drops to hands and knees. I roll off his back, gasping from the pain of having slammed my ribs on impact, held onto his true form for so long.

I hold my palm over his lower back, whisper, "Change him back," to Patty and Jason.

They murmur another incantation, followed by a command. "Denounce your true form."

The Ijiraq fades away, back to the regular form of the detective, sweat and blood on his skin. His hair plasters over the back of his spine, the bruised bones on his skin. The bullet wound in his back remains, healing slowly.

He won't return to full strength until he eats...

"Fuck!" He screams, eyes wide with fear and pain. "Lili...?"

"Stay here." I urge him to rest. Patty and Jason, exhausted, return to normal. Jason gives the detective his jacket while Patty murmurs comforting words to him. The detective focuses, his human eyes still glowing faintly with the Ijiraq crescents, the ghost of antlers still rising above him if you glance at him from the corner of your eye.

I go to my jacket, which had fallen off during the fight, and search through my pockets. I finally find a flask of lukewarm blended heart, a quarter remaining. I uncork it and pass it over to the detective, who drinks it gratefully. A line of red dribbles down his chin, mingling with the mess of purple already on his chest.

"Someone shot me," he remarks blankly, eyes angry. Eyes burning in agony. "But they were aiming for my human form. The bullet was too far north to damage anything vital in my true form." He spits out more strange, purplish blood. "Bastards."

I hold up the bullet I'd found earlier, tossed to the side during the fight. "Eye Coven. Our friends had a pattern." I lean back, wincing from my injuries. It will take a lot of rest back at the inn and more savory duck for my own wounds to heal, but the detective needs it far more than I do. I wasn't the one impaled by a magical bullet. "They shot a Siren outside your office. Maybe they were trying to get to you?" I gently take his wrist and turn it around to show him the five lines. I drop his hand just as quickly. "Or were you just another mark out of five?"

Patty takes out the folded, yellow note he'd left on his office door. She passes it over with a grimace, her glasses resting crooked on her mud-splattered face. "You said you found a lead. Tell us what it was before you forget."

"Patty, the man was just shot," Jason warns, but Patty remains firm.

The detective winces again, pressing his fingers to the wound. It's healing better now with the bloody meal, but still imperfect. "No, it's okay." He sighs. "I thought it'd be good to get out of the office. I feel stronger near the ice." He nods at the river, already covered over in that strange, out-of-season layer of frost.

He struggles to stand, and I let him lean on me. He's a tall man, but nowhere near the insane height of his Ijiraq form. "You're right, Lili. I called the Eye while I was in my office. I wanted to see who was buying these so-called monster-killing weapons. I wanted their commerce records, on behalf of the investigation, but they refused." He looks meaningfully to Patty and Jason. "They only give the information to necromancers, it seems."

Patty and Jason exchange a look, and Jason eventually braves the implication. "You want us to get those records."

"Yes." He holds his hand protectively to his still-healing wound. "Call me petty, but I want to find out who put a bullet in me." His lips peel back in a near-animal snarl. For a moment, I think he'll turn again, but he stays firmly shapeshifted.

I nod to Patty, who pulls out the makeshift evidence bags with the mysterious thread. "We found this under your nails. Did you scratch at your attacker?"

He winces, placing a hand to his eyes. "Damn, I can't remember. Must've hit my head during the fall." A low growl from his throat as he spits back the information. "I smelled them, though. I can't forget how they reeked. They weren't human, Lili."

"So, either they're reanimated, or immortal." I stare evenly back at him. "If it's the latter, then they're killing their own immortal kind."

"Or the coven built a murder-machine in those Frankenstein laboratories of theirs." Byron huffs, floating down by us. "Sorry about the ghost spit by the way, detective."

Detective Ikiaq raises an eyebrow at the ghost, but otherwise seems to reluctantly accept his apology.

Patty chews on her lower lip, all thoughtful. "It *could be* that the Eye Coven is behind all this. It'd make sense, the evil corporation out to eliminate anyone who threatens their business. Sell some eternal life insurance. Fear death, no problem, turn into a vampire!" She sighs. "Or it could be something worse." For the first time since I met her, I see darkness in her eyes. The shadow of true, thrilling fear. Fear that forces you from your body, to enter an inhuman state, assuming you were human to begin with. "Far, far worse."

A rustle of talons against the leaves. A gray-white shape blurs, exploding in a burst of speed toward the sky. It arcs overhead, unleashing a battle cry.

"Only an owl," Jason remarks.

"Yes, some say that it brings death." I shade my eyes with my hand, staring at the creature as it stares back at us. It scouts the forest floor for its prey. A predator animal, just like myself. Except I've trained myself not to eat the mice.

"Birds can just mean messengers. Messages don't always have to be so grim," the detective replies, wincing as he staggers forward. He leans his weight against a tree. "I need liquor, lots of it." He looks pleadingly at the Sweeney siblings. "Don't you two own a stocked bar?"

Patty sighs, shoulders slumped and lower lip pouting. "Dammit, guess I'm back on bartending duty. Well, let's go. You mystical misfits."

Chapter Sixteen

The Sweeney Inn bar (We're not even pretending now)

Not to pigeonhole witches, but damn if they don't all fix amazing drinks. It must be all the potion brewing because honestly, they're the best! I know liquor doesn't much affect our kind, but witches are *born* bartenders. Chocolate liquor, sour-sweet wines, champagne that leaves kisses on the insides of your cheeks, and an array of fruity, tangy, and burning to suit your needs.

Also, witches know what herbs successfully simulate intoxication in certain magical species. Even if Patty never *knew* of her preternatural abilities, she'd still have this gift inherent within her. Only unnamed.

"This is your sixth." Patty frowns, handing me and the good detective another mix. "Ginger beer and a snap of lime."

"It's only my sixth drink?" I ask, chuckling as I toast Detective Ikiaq. Jason's busy sewing him up as Patty lets him drink them all into bankruptcy.

"Your sixth *bottle*," she corrects, her fingernails drumming against the table, bitten to the quick. "If you weren't so cute, Lil, I'd be angrier."

I consider the offer for a moment and then stick out my tongue. "Patty, are you a gambler?"

"Why?"

I point to myself with a wink. "Because it's all aces up in here."

"Ace is short for asexual." Byron clarifies for the baffled detective, pretending to sip daintily from a glass of red wine that Patty set out just to humor the ghost.

"Hey!" The detective's grip tightens on the glass, and I wince at seeing it crack at the edges. "Watch the knives, kid."

Jason scowls, pulling up the pair of plastic gloves he'd borrowed from Patty's hair-dye kit. A bloody scalpel gleams in his hand, a pair of thick twine and needles between his teeth. He speaks around the obstruction with a slight lisp. "You heal too damn fast. Have to cut you open to remove all the shards."

Another pinch of the twine and the detective slumps over, beating his fist against the bar and howling. I'm still sober enough to pull him back and stuff a cloth napkin in his mouth. "Hush up. You want that *thing* to come back and shoot you full of magical bullets?"

The detective's eyes shift to the telltale Ijiraq gleam, the soul of the world and a legend held within them. His soul-blood thrumming with stories and magic, not mortality. Just as quickly, he calms himself. "There was a time we were feared, Siren. We were the largest immortals in our homes. No human creations, no reanimated, no human conjurers could defeat us. Then the people whose belief created me were subjected to colonizers on stolen land. I was drawn here to Gamin when the fear took me. Once, we were untouchable. Now, because of this killer, the immortals have changed. We *fear* even as we have to fight."

He turns to me and I stare back with a certain measure, trying my hardest not to let that selfsame fear seep in, growing with the intensity of it all. To run if only to avoid admitting that I'm also afraid. Before I know it, the silence has ended and it's my turn to speak. "When I first met the ghost, Byron, I told him something in Gamin drew me to it. I usually choose cities—so much easier to take and disappear that way. But *something* drew me here, some energy. It drew me here to you. For once, I wished to stay instead of fleeing all over again."

The detective looks at me, and I can't help but feel a flood of shame at it, at admitting it. *Even with the power I have, I still want to flee. Selfish really is a synonym for coward...* "My people fight to live every day. Missing indigenous women are murdered. Rights are trampled. Treaties are broken..." He drums his fingers against his thigh, shaking his head at it. "And they call *us* the monsters. But those monsters, the ones I named? Those are human."

I down the rest of my drink, the ginger burning its way down my throat, sloshing around with the warmed, soupy heart mash I ate earlier. "Detective, there was a time when neither humans nor their creations nor their reanimated could harm us. No one could strike fear in our beings." I stand with a flourish, the barstool toppling behind me. "I propose a new promise, then—to fearing no longer!"

*

We Haven't Changed Locations

I blacked out. When I awake the next day, I assume I gave quite a rousing speech because everybody is shouting at me to hurry up. Apparently, we are going on an adventure. Byron holds back, floating about my room while I endure the worst of the witch's brew haze. He nods to the drawstring bag that holds Patty's homemade lunch for me, just like an enchantress mother.

"That was quite a speech you gave," Byron informs me. "You got everybody ready to storm the Eye Coven Corporation today."

"Huh?" I grab woozily for the bag, miss, right myself, and then stagger to my feet.

"Yup. Detective Ikiaq guards the spare getaway car he had stored in his office's garage. You guard Patty while she pretends to negotiate for the whole 'you-too-can-own-our-evil-corporation' contract. Jason will search the place for information about hired undead assassins. And *I*—" Here he blushes, if ghosts can blush, and glances away, his once-dark eyelashes fluttering over ashen cheeks. "I will distract the receptionist, Erik."

"Or will Erik be the one distracting you?"

"*Cállate, pendeja.*"

I slump over to the door and take the vial that says DRINK ME, YOU DRUNKEN MERMAID IDIOT. Most likely Patty's special touch. I down the potion, which tastes suspiciously of sea salt and crushed gravel, and immediately feel my head clear.

"A heist," I tell him. "We're insane enough to do a moony misfortunates' heist."

"Mystical misfits' heist," Patty calls out, pulling me by the arm to the detective's getaway car. "And, yes Lil, we're going to do a heist."

*

Eye Incorporated

We don't get to do a heist, but not for lack of trying.

We drive up to a face-off. None other than *gangshi* Jo Kim is pouring gasoline all over the Eye Coven Corporation's front. She brandishes a water gun filled with more gasoline in her other hand, screaming at corporation ice-queen Sabrina, decked out in an all-white suit that's now covered in piss-yellow stains. In this moment, I have no greater pleasure than seeing Sabrina with her pristine coif all in disarray. A scowl on smudged lipstick. And Jo Kim, bless her, raining down fire and fury upon the Eye. A lone *gangshi* in a ripped-up black tank top and jeans with silver hair, a cancer patient turned reanimated, all ready to start a one-woman revolution.

My hero.

"Sabrina! What seems to be the problem?" Patricia calls from right outside Ikiaq's car, all fake nice and a vision in curves and freckles. Jason waves and runs his hands through his strangely stiff hair. *My gods, is that gel he's wearing?*

Close to the gas-stained building, Jo shoves the nozzle of the gas gun beneath Sabrina's chin. Two hefty Franks lurch to help her. Well, more like one and a half. One of the Franks has lost their arms, and the telltale stains on Jo's fanged mouth and clawed hands explain it. "Because of them, my brother haunts my dreams. I did my part. I *gave* them the message. Still, they refuse to confess their crimes! And I'm going to bring their building down…"

"For the last time," Sabrina spits. "I have no idea who your brother is!"

"Tae Kim. The mandrake. Don't lie to me, he told me he saw you in his graveyard!"

Sabrina pauses, a sour note of recognition passing over her face. "The one always hanging around Todd?"

"He was the Sweeneys' business partner, dipshit! I've had nightmares of Tae's face, begging me to get to you. So just do it already! Confess your crimes!"

Hold on, nightmare visions. Confess? Crimes?

"Lil, stick to the plan..." Jason warns.

"In case you didn't notice, Jay, that plan's been terminated."

I rush forward and go straight for Sabrina and Jo. Detective Ikiaq's my backup, shoving the two Franks out of the way to give me a direct path to them.

I push Sabrina and Jo apart. Jo growls and I flinch a little at the sight of her teeth, but I stay firm. Sabrina scrunches her nose up like I'm diseased.

I whip my head around to glare at them both. "Start talking. What crimes?"

Sabrina crosses her arms, silent, with her eyebrows arched scornfully.

Jo hammers ahead, pushing against me until I shove her back. She blinks at the force, clearly unused to being matched in strength in a while. The mutilated Frank seems to be evidence of her wrath and the machete in the dirt beside her. I'm impressed. Those Franks take a long time to wound. She must've been extra persistent.

"Tell them, Sabrina. Tell them what the Eye Coven's done to the Sweeneys."

Jason and Patty creep up cautiously behind Detective Ikiaq, who's still flexing his claws in his half-turned form and intimidating the Franks with his unnatural size.

"You bitch," I spit at Sabrina. She squeals at the germs. "Did you try to have these kids killed too?"

"What are you, stupid?" Sabrina rolls her eyes at me and the detective shifts a little closer to me, a preemptive warning to keep my cool. "You think I'd kill my greatest assets?"

They're Sabrina's greatest assets?

"Don't lie." Jason scowls, looking like a washed-up rocker as his gelled hair falls out of place and his somewhat ill-fitting shirt sags at his waist and tightens at his shoulders. "You sent your gun-wielding assassin after Ikiaq in the forest. You left a dead Siren outside his door."

Patty pipes up beside her brother. "But we didn't think you were aiming for *us*."

Sabrina pinches the bridge of her nose, closing her eyes as though hoping we'd all disappear. "Again, I honestly have no idea what any of you are talking about. Why would I want to kill Detective Ikiaq? It'd be a waste of a perfectly *dazzling* specimen." Here, she pauses to wink at the detective, who morphs back to his human form and waves sheepishly back to her. With a come-hither smile on her face, she continues, "But fine, I'll admit to the crimes this crazy woman keeps yammering on about."

She leans in closer to Patty. I move to guard her, but the freckled witch just swats me out of the way. *Right, she can take care of herself, but I'll prepare myself just in case.*

Jo flicks a lighter open, holding it threateningly to the corporation building and all the spilled gas. "Talk faster, witch."

Sabrina waves frantically against it. "Fine! Jason, Patty, the corporation was supposed to pay you an allowance every year after your parents' passing. But business has been bad, so instead of handing the allowance to you... I've been taking it."

"How much?" Jason asks.

"You dick!" Patty screams.

"It could be a huge chunk of cash!" Jason whines.

Sabrina sighs. "Let's put it this way. It's enough to keep you comfortable for the rest of your lives."

Jason and Patty have murder in their eyes.

Ignoring them, I go on with, "If you can just take their money, why are the Sweeneys worth anything to you?"

"Simple." Sabrina pushes her hair back, patting it back into a coif instead of a sweaty mess. "The allowances are *nothing* compared to the lottery sums that were frozen after your parents' passing. The funds only unfreeze after you two sign a contract joining our company." She shrugs. "The necromancy business is old-fashioned like that. Rules of blood inheritance are thicker than gasoline, or...something like that."

A blur of silver hair and faded black. Jo hurls herself at Sabrina, and the detective has to rush forward and restrain her. "No, you're leaving so much out!" Jo slumps over at Ikiaq's strength. He holds her in an awkward sort of hug, hushing her as she lashes out. She doesn't fight mainly because I think she doesn't want to do serious damage to the detective, not the other way around. "Tae told me you'd have more to say. More to confess..."

Sabrina grins a little at Jo's misery, the smile fading as I continue to stare steadily at her. "Is that *all* now? Are you satisfied I'm not trying to kill any of you?"

I exchange a glance with the Sweeneys and then the detective. They all look as dumfounded as I feel. "Fine, but we'll be back." I inform her. "And we're not cleaning this up," I continue, pointing at the trickles of piss yellow.

Jo drops the lighter. Sabrina falls to her knees to catch it, staining her hands and knees in gasoline. Jo spits as we drag her away to the sound of Sabrina cursing us out.

We head back to the car, a worn-in roadster painted black and refurbished. The seats sigh a little as Jo joins us, mushing us all in the back while Patty gets shotgun.

"She's hiding something still." Patty remarks, glancing at us in the rearview mirror.

"No shit," Jason grumbles. I simply nod.

"At least we know it's not murder. I saw it in her eyes. She sees the Sweeneys as money bags, but *living* money bags, at least. She gets nothing if you're dead."

Jason leans his forehead against the glass. "How comforting."

Wait a moment...

I glance around, noticing the air is unusually lukewarm.

"Where's Byron?"

We all peer out of the window to see the specter wave cheerfully at a scowling Sabrina and Frank crew. He passes right through Jason, who shudders audibly, and then drifts halfway through the bottom of the car.

"Where in the nine hells were you?" I grouch.

He starts to whistle. *Whistle,* of all things, like he's suddenly turned from *Poltergeist* into more *Casper the Friendly Ghost* kinda territory.

Byron holds out his ghostly notebook in explanation. Ten digits are scrawled in glittery ink, sealed with a wizard stamp of the Eye. Magic glittery ink. From a necromancer...a necromancer with headphones slung around his neck, a devil-may-care smile, metallic-tipped locs, and melt-your-heart eyes.

Patty and I exchange a look.

"Erik," we reply in unison.

Jason glances over at Byron's notebook. Byron holds his undead breath.

"Nice." Jason nods. Approving. "Get those digits, you sly dog, you."

Byron holds his arms around us, his fingers passing through our shoulders. "Aw shucks, I'm glad you agree, *cuerpo*." He leans his head against Jason. "Because now you have to enchant a ghostly cell phone into my realm, so I can call him."

Jason deflates, no longer flexing so much as he did before. I'd argue the farm boy was going through puberty if he wasn't so well defined with that timbre in his voice and everything. Working out and wearing gel in his hair. I wonder if that was his way of trying to gain control over a seemingly incontrollable circumstance. If he truly looks anything like his father, it's no wonder Tae was so infatuated with Todd.

We all need some sort of coping mechanism with the world we live in.

Chapter Seventeen

Jo Kim's Dwelling

We pull up in front of Jo's house. I hold her elbow before she leaves the vehicle. She turns back to me like she'll bite me.

"They cut down Tae's tree, you know." She spits on the ground, wrath incarnate in the set of her jaw. The cords of muscle. "Those whatever Eye Coven bastards. They cut down his tree because Tae had helped you. He's in the spirit worlds now. Can only come to me in dreams…"

"You think you're next?" I watch her, wary.

She shrugs. "Covens or something else. It's nothing I can't handle."

"Be careful." I tell her. "The bodies outside Ikiaq's office, the murders. Anatol." Jo grimaces at the mention of the vampire. "We need you, you know. You could always come with us…"

"I want to stay in my home. Your lot is nice and all, but I don't belong with you. I want to wait here. Closer to Tae's memory." Jo pulls out a gun, grinning at us. "Silver rounds. Bought it off a monster hunter. Tae kept all this shit lying around his old room. I'll be fine." She leans forward. "May I? It's good luck to kiss a Siren."

"Go ahead."

I kiss her because I think she's sick of death and needs the comfort. Curling my fingers around the wiry hairs at the nape of her neck. Smelling cigarettes and blood and fight on her.

"You're a good kisser," she informs me.

I laugh, throwing my head back. "Wait till you get older, Jo. It takes more than one lifetime to get this experience."

She shakes her head, closing the car door with a thwack. "Funny. I forget sometimes that you're not as young as the kids. You're even older than me." She nods to the Sweeneys. "You're really something else, aren't you, Lili? Entire centuries, hell, even *eras* wrapped in a young kid's body."

The car drives off then, and I twist around to wave at her as she recedes. A monster hunter's shotgun at her hip. A jaunty sway to her gait.

I can't help feeling like a wife seeing her sailor off to war.

"Will she make it?" Ikiaq asks me, just low enough that only immortals can hear.

"Nothing's sacred in Gamin," I reply.

He nods as though that solves everything.

*

Meanwhile, at the Sweeney Inn…

We file into the inn's lobby and then filter off into the halls. There was a sort of silent agreement that Detective Ikiaq stays here until the case was officially closed. Two immortals are better than one, and all that. A while back, he went out with a shovel and Jason. Presumably, they dug a grave for the dead Siren outside. Ikiaq said he would help run Anatol's morgue until he could find another vampire to run the place. Somebody who "respected the old vampire ways," as Anatol would've liked.

Jason goes back for a pack of cream biscuits and hard mints. Patty pours mugs of tea. It all tastes like ash and flavored water to me. Ikiaq, too, I'm assuming. Human food isn't to our tastes any longer, but sometimes it's nice to put forth the effort for the mortals. Makes them feel comfortable when we fake normal.

"So." Byron tries his hardest to lift a peppermint, channeling into his inner poltergeist so he can manipulate the physical realm. It hovers and spirals. He's getting better at moving things while keeping his cool. "I'm all for brooding, but now what?"

I sip at tea, stomach growling in protest at the mortal fare. The tea's mixed in with turmeric, reminding me of the old times, the first years.

Figs and dates and lounging in the sun as they worshipped...

Walking through the bustling, gritty markets where children hid behind canvassed eaves and those with diseases on their skins reached out to me, begging for mercy.

Memories of walking the streets. Hearing my old name. My true one.

"Hello, earth to Lili?" Patty waves her hand in front of my face.

"Right, sorry." I cough a bit to root myself to the moment. "Jo told me that Tae's mandrake form had been sabotaged by the Eye. Sabrina's hiding shit, obviously. But she won't tell us more—unless we torture?" The Sweeneys shake their heads vehemently at that one. "All right, no torture. In that case, Jo told us that Tae's crossed over to the Dead Realms. He can only reach his sister in dreams, but that's probably 'cause they're connected by blood."

"We're necromancers." Jason stands, his shirt shifting to reveal a ceremonial dagger he's tucked into his waistband. My eyes home in on the engravings on the handle. They read *B.T.S.*, which is either a very prominent K-pop group, or the initials of "Beatrice/Todd Sweeney," their parents. "I've been studying from our parents' journals. I might be able to cross over if we sacrifice a chicken."

"What?" Patty squeaks. "Do we have to go killing chickens just yet? Animal sacrifice sounds nauseating. And you've been reading Mom and Dad's journals?"

"Well, they trusted me first with the magic." Jason rolls his eyes. "Come on, chickens are basically dinosaurs. You used to love chicken nuggets!"

"Enough!" The detective slams his fist down on the table and the bickering ceases. "It's obvious, isn't it?" He points to Byron, who's busy sketching what appears to be Erik atop a royal steed. "We send the *dead one* over to the Dead Realms. It saves us all the hassle of dying ourselves."

We pause, turning to the introspective ghost all at once. Byron runs his thin fingers nervously through his ethereal hair. His duster jacket floats beneath him as his combat boots hover a few inches above the floor. His eyes lose focus behind his spectacles. "Alone?"

"You died alone, didn't you?" the detective continues.

I'd share the detective's deadpan humor, but I've known the ghost longest out of all of us. "It's all right, Byron. You're more poet than you are pirate." I walk up to him then. He scrambles to fix his spectacles. "But didn't you always dream of adventure?"

He stammers a bit. "I mean. I studied literature."

"Yes, and those are heroes' stories. Heroes' tales." I smile slightly, my skin itching for Siren's magic. But I let it die down. No, I can persuade him. "You fought bravely when the detective lost his wits in the wood." Ikiaq scowls deeper. "And I assume you've written down my undertakings like we promised in our original deal?"

He holds up his journal sheepishly. "There's enough material here for a novel. But Lili—" He moves closer, and the rest of the inn, the crackling fire, mugs of tea, and wooden lodge-like interior, it all drifts away. He's just a scared boy who changed his name to Byron. Standing on a stool with a rope around his neck, too scared to die, but also too scared to live. "I'd be alone in the Dead Realms. They might not let me back."

"I know," I tell him. "You might not think I do. I've lived for so long, though, and I know. What it's like to be tired of life."

"Does it get better?"

I swallow, thinking of the last episode I had where Patty and Byron watched over me. Even Jason asked for my wellbeing. "Well, people like us, Byron. We manage to find each other. Sometimes, it just takes longer. But heroes like you and me? We survive. We always survive until our stories are meant to end." I nod to everyone gathered around, nipping at cream biscuits and balancing candies next to mugs of steaming tea. "And besides, you can't leave us yet. You'll come back." He smiles as I point to the journal. "You and Erik have a date."

Byron takes my hand, and it passes through. He tries a second time, and without any help from my power, I feel a light dusting as he rests his fingers against my palm. As gentle as an embrace. "All right." His eyes have cleared, almost lively now. "I'll go to the Dead Realms."

Jason sets his empty mug down with a thud, brushes crumbs from his face. "I'll go too."

Patty rolls her eyes. "And my axe and my sword. Jason, you're a sucker for acting heroic. We need you here, not dead."

"No, I can do it." Jason struggles to keep himself calm, his nose twitching as he faces his sister. "I told you, I've been studying Mom and Dad's books. A necromancer can follow a ghost into the Dead Realms. People come back from the dead all the time."

"Like who?" Patty glares at him, smudging her red lipstick as she chews on her lower lip. "Name a couple examples, smartass."

"Wayne. Kent. Stark. Casper. Orpheus. Gandalf. Ebenezer—"

"Wayne? *Gandalf?* And you were about to say Scrooge! Those are just fiction."

"I don't know." Jason throws his hands into the air. "We're surrounded by ghouls and goblins right now. We have magic! Who's to say what isn't real?"

"Well, if everything's real, then where's my letter to Hogwarts?"

"*Quiet!*"

We all turn to face Byron, who's gone back into poltergeist mode. Teacups and biscuits float around his outstretched hands, his duster swirling about him as his boots come up to my shoulder. His spectacles are gone, replaced by the blinding light emanating from where his eyes used to be.

Detective Ikiaq and I rush to collect the teacups before they fall. Jason and Patty sit back down, staring obediently at the poetic ghost.

Byron sighs, calming down as he drifts closer to the floor. The spectacles reappear. "Enough of this. We go to the Dead Realms tonight. Discuss if you must. Jason, take whatever cursed items you need." He looks at us each in turn, pausing to stare the longest at Jason. "We leave at midnight."

With that, the ghost simply vanishes into thin air, leaving us all wondering.

"What the hell was that?" Detective Ikiaq breaks the silence.

Jason, sighing, gets up and makes for his room. His ceremonial dagger glints in the light beside him. "I'll get my things. Patty—" He turns around, swallowing to see the fear in his sister's eyes. "Patty, I'll help you make a scrying bowl. That way, you'll be able to track our movement in the Dead Realm. Lili and the detective too." He goes forward, pulls down his sleeve, and then takes off Patty's glasses to dry her eyes. "I have to see if they're there, Pats."

"I know." Patty swallows, grimacing. "I can't believe I'm crying over you, imbecile."

He smiles weakly. "I know." He ruffles her hair. "Dipshit."

They laugh together at that. Jason walks away after a quick hug, ready to gather his things. I go to Patty, reluctant to sling my arm around her just yet. "Are you all right?"

She looks up to me, throwing her arms around my shoulders and pulling me into a hug. "No. But if any idiot would survive, it's Jason."

*

Hell's Kitchen (Sweeney Inn)

"All right, so let's talk about the Dead Realm." Jason scrambles to grab more ingredients as he helps Patty prepare the scrying bowl. An obsidian bowl filled with water. A mirror placed at the bottom of the surface, poisonous and life-giving herbs at the top. Necromancers can work it only, it seems. Snobs. "It opens at midnight, then closes at twelve minutes past twelve. But time lasts longer in the Dead Realms than in the land of the living. Every minute here feels like five in the Dead Realms. That gives me and Byron an hour for, well, supernatural visiting hours." He points to a drawing on the kitchen wall. It's done in red crayon and looks like something out of a low-budget horror movie. "That's our entrance. It'll turn into a portal at midnight."

"And if you aren't out by then?"

Jason swallows. "Well. The spell book says we won't be able to find our way out again until All Hallows' Eve." He looks up, blanching, blond hair falling into his eyes. "There's no mortal food or drink in the Dead Realms. I guess... I guess that means I'm dead."

Patty moans and puts her head in her hands.

I look to the clock—11:57.

"All right." Jason steps back, hopping on his toes like a boxer. He pushes his hair back from his forehead. The Eye gleams, at first like a river of fire on his skin and then settling into a pattern like an old, reddened scar. The drawing of the door on the kitchen wall starts to bleed into blackness. Byron reappears at Jason's side, hovering a foot above the floor. He links his ghostly hand through Jason's.

"Ready, farm boy?"

Jason grins despite his nerves. "As always, Dead Poets' Society."

With that, they rush at the wall. Despite knowing what's going to happen, I still expect a crunch of bone as they make contact with it.

Instead, they go straight through.

"Like Platform Nine-and-three-quarters," mumbles Patty. We all crowd around the scrying bowl then, watching as Patty places her hands on either side. Her own Eye comes into being, her frizzy hair pulled back into a ponytail.

With that, we follow their journey into the Dead Realms.

Chapter Eighteen

The Dead Realms. Admission is Free. Leaving is Where They Get You.

"The Dead Realms look like Wonderland," Jason huffs, "if Lewis Carroll did just a little bit more drugs."

Byron yelps and Jason jumps as a spirit, little more than a bunch of mist in a vaguely human form, rushes at them. They settle when the mist-being disappears, confused and chattering off in the distance.

It's a fairly accurate assessment from what we see in the scrying bowl. A picture of an endless field of wheat where every seed is in such exquisite detail that it goes on forever. An endless symmetrical pattern of perfect fractals. A single blade of grass replicated forever and ever, where every color will mimic the color of the last. Trees break up the monotony every few feet, a magnificent oak that rises three persons in height.

The season might be the end of spring or early summer. No blade of grass holds a single drop of water. No tree bears fruit. Even the grain is too young to be anything but pretty. Even if humans somehow stomached the plants, they would fall like ash within a *mortal's mouth, killing them slowly before insanity ever did.*

Creatures like birds sing overhead, but there are no birds in sight. Something buzzes like the lazy hum of an insect, yet nothing lands. Occasionally, a purple-blue shadow rises across the blue-gray horizon. It looks like a hand, or perhaps a set of eyes. Watching. Waiting for the endless expanse to break.

"They know we don't belong here." Byron shudders, wrapping his hands around himself. "It's why they keep stretching this field. They'd take us where we liked if we were to stay."

Jason shakes his head. "We cannot stay. Keep pushing."

"Tae! Tae! Tae!" Their screams echo over the field. A sound pops up, an echo in the gray darkness. A tree comes closer, a mighty oak. A spider's web glimmers, gossamer as a fairy's hammock. No spiders in sight. Tae drinks wine and has empty bowls of pistachio shells littered behind him. He looks younger, perhaps only seventeen. His wrinkles of worry have disappeared. His hair is jet black, and eyes set above sunlit dimples. A freshly pressed white suit and a strong jaw, like Jo Kim's face, but calmer.

"Mm, hello?" Tae calls, recognition not yet dawning.

"Tae? Tae Kim?" Jason walks forward, Byron bobbing at his side. "Your sister, Jo Kim. She sent us to find you."

"Jo. Jo." Tae giggles at the name. "My foxy, foxy sister."

Byron and Jason exchange a look.

"No, she loved the story." He rolls from the hammock and lands smoothly on his feet, like a panther. "She loved the story about the Fox Sister. A childless couple, they're

always childless, aren't they? They beg for a girl. Well, a girl comes to them, but she's really a many-tailed fox in human skin. One by one, cows go missing. The farmers send their son, who came after the sister, to check on why the cows are going. Well, the son doesn't come back. Then the mother. The father sees that the girl is eating them all to become human. Each sacrifice is another one for her gain." He runs his finger along his throat, that odd, dazed smile still on his face. *"Her father kills her, of course. Humans don't play well with monsters."*

Back from the scrying bowl, I shake my head. "Monsters..."

Patty places her hand on my shoulder, and for once, I don't feel like the touch is wrong. It's comforting. They're family. "We'll never hurt you, Lil. You're not a monster to us."

I look at my hand, the copper skin stretched over seemingly human bones. "Thanks." I reply, dry as can be. I wonder if they ever see the real me.

"Enough of this, Tae." Jason takes Tae by his shoulders, hissing like the touch burns or freezes all at once. *"You came to your sister, Jo. You said you had a message to deliver about the Eye Coven. Well? Tell me."*

Tae focuses in for a second and then, to the shock of everyone, he places a kiss on Jason's cheek. Except he misses Jason's cheek as Jason's flinched. Instead, he kisses Jason's neck. "Todd, is that you? Sweeney Todd. Todd Sweeney." He pauses, staring deeply into Jason's eyes. "Gods, Todd. How I've missed you."

"The Eye!" Byron barks, repeating what Jason is too stunned to.

"Right," Tae's voice emerges like a sigh. *"The father had a little girl. Her name was Selena? No, maybe Saba?"*

"Sabrina." Jason replies. "Her name was Sabrina."

"Right." Tae continues on. "He was a single father. His name was Mr. Bender. Mr. Bender was desperate for enough money to keep her well-fed, or else, he'd lose everything. That's important to say. To explain why he wanted, so badly, to fight the Sweeneys. Todd." He points to Jason. "And his wife, Beatrice. The founders of the Eye. Bender wanted to change the business, to sell to whoever had the money to pay. To open up necromancy to those who had money, instead of those who deserved it."

Jason hisses at that. "Reckless magic. Nothing good comes from reckless magic. That's what Mother and Father always told me."

"Wait. More." Tae sways, eyes lost in a trance. His youth falls on him strangely. Like an old man wearing a young person's fashion. "When child support asked for Bender's child, Bender knew that the Sweeneys were running the business into the ground. They'd be fine. They came from an older necromancer family. Bender was spited by his family for his abilities, a curse. He had nothing. So, he wanted to steal from the Sweeneys. He turned the Eye against them, saying their rules were old-fashioned. The Eye was just a banner for the Old Ways, but Bender wanted more. A business. Modernity."

Jason falls to his knees then, hands curled into fists. "Sabrina's sonuvabitch father killed my parents to rule the Eye."

Tae kneels beside him. "Not before your parents killed him too."

Jason looks up then, confused. "No, they can't be murderers, could they?"

From behind Tae rise two figures. A woman with Patricia's frizzy hair, but Jason's leaner figure. A man with Jason's full lips and sandy-blond wisps, but Patricia's rounder jawline and heartier figure. He had laughing eyes. She had clever ones.

But murderers? Maybe.

"Mother, Father. You taught me about my magic!" Jason screams at them. Byron must drag him away. "You said that reckless magic leads to reckless mistakes!"

"Clarence Bender would have hurt you." Beatrice speaks, chin up. Unashamed. "We did what we had to in order to protect you and Patricia. We wanted to leave the Eye, and all its ill-begotten riches, to you."

"It was a violent time. A time between old ways and new. An era, as Bender put it, of biotech-sorcery," Todd amends, jovial eyes turned down to seriousness. "Come on, son. We didn't know that the spell would carry over into the real world. We just wanted to neutralize Bender and cut ties with the coven. To free us all. We had to do it. We couldn't be blamed for murdering him straightaway. We needed a third party."

"What did you do?" Jason screams. "What spell did you cast to kill Clarence Bender?"

"A summoning." Todd and Beatrice reply as one. "We're sorry for the summoning."

*

Just Your Average Minnesotan Kitchen

The bowl sloshes, water spilling from its sides as Patty screeches into it. Sweat pours down her face, the Eye burning hotly on her forehead. "*Jason, get out!*"

Jason, as though he can hear, twitches slightly. Byron moves for him. "Jason, we must go back to the land of the living. Come!"

Jason fumbles for a red crayon and drops it as he's still mesmerized by the image of his mother and father. Todd and Beatrice are gone. Their images, alongside Tae, beneath the gentle hammock of the tree, have faded.

"*Jason!*" Patty screams.

I go to the kitchen wall and draw over the door with more marks from the red crayon. "What are you doing?" the nervous detective cries.

"Panicking!" I reply.

"They're running back!" Patty moans, staring at the clock. It's hit 12:11. "Oh, fudge nuggets, I'm not sure if they'll make it!"

Byron picks up the red crayon, his form more corporeal in the Dead Realms. More solid. He reaches for a pale-white bark of a birch tree, hastily sketches a door.

Jason's still behind him, kneeling and dumbfounded, in the dirt.

"*Jason, come on!*" Patty's crying and shaking the table. The detective has to pin her arms to her sides to keep from smashing the bowl altogether. She lashes out, elbowing him. He grunts, his long, dark hair slipping from his ties, falling over his face.

"The door's working. It's—"

I turn to the door. Byron's gone through it, but back in the mortal realm, his form is ethereal. I reach for Jason's free arm, struggling to reach through.

The clock strikes 12:12. The tinny alarm that Patty set wails to high heaven like a cat in a trash can strewn alley.

"Come on!" I cry and thrust my hands into the wall. A bitter chill crawls all the way up to my elbows as I reach into the Dead Realms to pull the rest of Jason's body out. His left side is still submerged as the portal tries to pull him back through. It's like pulling him from quicksand. The harder you struggle, the faster you sink back in.

Detective Ikiaq runs over and then, finally, Patty. She grips his hand while Ikiaq and I reach for sturdier points on his body. We don't want to crush him with our strength. Patty pleads for him to snap out of it.

"You're my brother, dipshit," she sobs as Jason stares on. Pale eyes glazed. Near-unseeing. "Wake up, Jay, wake up!"

She shakes her head. "I'm sorry." Then rears back to slap him.

"Patty?"

With that, he finally moves enough for us to get him free. We all lie on the floor gasping.

It's 12:13.

It takes us another few minutes before we realize that something got left behind.

Jason's unconscious on the floor.

His entire left arm is gone.

Chapter Nineteen

He's Alive (sorta)

"Oh, my gods!" Patty falls back on her heels, at her brother's side in an instance. She can hardly look at him without retching. "Ohmigodohmigodohmigod..."

I run to him. Detective Ikiaq takes his shoulders. I lift his legs. Patty moves the scrying bowl. It's near empty anyway from all the commotion. We lay him flat on the table.

"There isn't blood," I note, seeing how his left arm just looks...empty. I pull at his sleeve, searching for a severance wound. "Byron, you're a ghost. What happened?"

He whirls around, face scrunched up. Confused. "They tell me—"

"Who tells you? Who's they?" Patty snaps, furious at the poor, dead poet.

"Patty, enough," I scold. "Continue, Byron. I don't care if you're talking to all demons or saints, what do they tell you?"

I push the sleeve back and swallow to see it.

No, to *feel* it.

That feeling, like when I was reaching into the red-crayon-door and into the Dead Realms. It's a chill all along the space where Jason's arm was. A chill even I, an immortal, can feel. The hairs on the detective's arms rise. A warning sign when even the predators feel like prey. I close my eyes and can almost physically see it.

A *nothingness* where Jason's arm was. A Dead Realm contained in that space.

"The Dead Realms claimed his arm. No—" Byron searches for the right words, bobbing up and down inconsistently as he does so. "They *became* his arm."

"A phantom arm. A literal phantom ghost cyborg arm thing." Detective Ikiaq chuckles a little at that. "Nice." He frowns at our looks of incredulity. "What? I might be immortal, but I'm a Comic-Con goer still. Just because I'm literally ancient, doesn't mean I can't appreciate pop culture."

Patty shakes her brother awake. When Jason blinks his eyes open, they've cleared somewhat. His pale eyes fix on his sister. "Huh?"

"Can you move your left arm?"

"Just fine," he replies and then pauses. "Wait, it feels...funny."

We all exchange a look.

He tries to sit up right away, but just falls back down again.

"Please don't be alarmed, but you have a ghost hand," Byron says.

"A what?" Jason turns his neck to see his left arm, and he screams and thrashes. I have to hold him down to ensure he doesn't roll right off the table.

"My arm!" he wails. "Where is it?"

"The Dead Realms claimed it!" I scream into his face, trying to plead with him to stay still. He eventually gives up, exhausted, as I keep holding him tight. Mortal strength goes easy. "It's still there. We think."

"We'll figure this out, Jay." Patty soothes him, cradling his weak body in her arms. "We'll figure this out."

He shudders, resting his head in the crook of her arm. "I saw them, Pats. I saw them."

"We know," Patty replies, pushing his blond hair from his forehead. It's grown longer since we first met, just kissing his shoulder. He even has a grazing of stubble on his chin. It's like he's left more than just his arm behind in the Dead Realms. Like a piece of himself.

We help him off the table and wrap a loose sling around his phantom arm. It seems to help Jason that it's restrained...whatever *it* is.

With that, we're all about to migrate back to the bar and common area, but an air-sucking *whump* knocks the wind out of us. Another one then, louder this time. *Whump.*

The pots and pans on the kitchen walls rattle. A glass falls off the bar behind us and shatters. Jason reaches grimly for his waistband and pulls out the dagger with a blade as long as a humerus bone. Patty reaches for the scrying bowl and the bag Jason brought in with a spell book and some sorcerer ingredients. The detective and I pull our respective teeth and claws. Byron hovers off the floor, eyes bright, duster flapping.

"Rnnnngh..." A moan as bare hands and crowbars hit against the inn walls. The inn shakes at the pressure of so many people fighting their way in. "Rnnnnnngh..."

I prop the back trash door open, the hefty metal scraping against my fingernails. I peer into the alleyway, seeing the broad shoulders and unnatural height of a Frank. The brute-force beast swivels its head toward me and charges. Two of its friends follow at a distance behind it.

I slam the door just as it reaches me, taking its hand with it. It squeals as I pull harder, sealing the metal door with a lock. Its friends bash against the door behind it.

"Sabrina's Franks," I tell the others. "It's a Franken-pocalypse."

Detective Ikiaq has the pleasure of physically recoiling at my joke.

Patty stuffs the scrying bowl into a cloth grocery bag with the rest of her scant sorcery supplies. Jason runs to his connecting room in a mad dash. Ikiaq rushes outside to the common area, teeth and claws bared, antlers rising. Still not fully shifted so that he can fit through the doorway.

Byron disappears. I'm assuming the dying squeals from outside mean he's working his poltergeist magic on the Franks and ripping them apart.

"Shit, he has the car keys." Patty grabs a very big knife and runs out.

I reach into a freezer, grab a frozen heart, and crunch my teeth into the ice like it's a bloody apple. "Waste not," I mumble, taking a few more bites before rushing out into the fray.

I have to slide beneath the bar to avoid getting decapitated by a flying Frank. Detective Ikiaq roars. Another Frank is speared on his antlers, his large frame nearly scraping the cavernous lodge-beam ceiling of the inn.

I leap over the bar and hiss as I land on my knee.

"Gods, why do superheroes make it look so easy?"

I limp up just in time to catch a Frank in my grip. My teeth extend and my muscles bulge, losing myself to my true form. I clasp my hands around its knuckles, nails extending into claws that bite into its skin.

No, keep it in. For their sake, keep it in...

But it's difficult. My skin itches like spiders are crawling all over it. I want to be free. I want to...to...

Bring the world to its knees.

"Lil!" Patty whirls round to me, her market bag still slung over her shoulders and heavy over her chest. She extends one hand toward me, Eye blazing on her forehead.

The Frank howls, its unnatural veins turning black with sickness. It falls to the ground, bleeding that disgusting bile. "Thanks..." I mutter, reverting to human form and leaping over its body.

Ikiaq shrinks to fit through the doorframe. What's left of his antlers end up taking out the top of it anyway. The door flies from its hinges.

"Shit," Patty mutters.

"Sorry," the detective replies, reaching into the tattered remnants of his jean pockets for his keys.

We rush toward his gray off-roader, the tires slunk into the mud. A Frank pounds at the driver's seat. Spiderweb cracks spread through it.

"Son of a—!" The detective rushes toward the creature, rears his fist back, and drives it full force into the Frank's nose with a crunch. It lumbers up to grab his legs when I leap onto its back and kick its head back down until it twists.

The detective nods his thanks as he opens the car doors. "Get in."

We rush into the car. He throws a duffel bag off his shoulder and into the backseat with me. It catches me in the stomach, hurtling me further into the seat covers.

Patty takes shotgun. Byron appears in the trunk, looking eerily pleased with himself.

"Where's Jason?" The car purrs to life as Patty whirls around, looking anxiously for her brother.

"Shit." I wipe mud from my brow. "The ass went back for his things."

"Hey!" Jason comes running out then, his dagger dripping and a backpack slung over his good shoulder. "Over here!"

Jason puts away the dagger to wave his good hand, running as he goes. He shoots toward the vehicle just as a Frank falls from the inn roof. More clamber over fences and walls, all either rushing toward Jason or our car.

It's a mob.

"Lili, open the back door."

I unlock the door and swing it open. "And then what?"

He reaches back and shoves me out the door. "*Get him!*"

I roll, barely missing the spinning car wheels as it jerks into reverse. I get up and kick a Frank out of my way as I scream, "*Dammit, Jason!*"

I run as fast as I can, so fast that the rest of the world dies away. I hear the pounding of my feet against the ground, feel the mud sinking in through my black boots. Jason runs, too, not nearly as fast. He keeps getting bogged down by the little things. His heartbeat. His lung capacity. All the things that make mortals so mortal...and delicious.

Focus, Lili.

I shove another Frank out of the way. I don't have to finish them, fatality and all, I just have to get Jason's ass back into the car. The detective drives in misshapen donuts, the car door flapping open and shut as Franks try to go for it and just get run over by the tires.

"Lil—"

I ignore his outstretched hand, instead picking him up by the waist and slinging him over one shoulder. He's hefty, sure, but basically weighs as much as a biology textbook would weigh for a high schooler. Manageable if you rip out all the useless pages. "Come on, dumbass."

I go back to the car. The detective has calmed down a bit now and he slows the vehicle to a regular drive away from the inn and toward the roads. There's a noticeable dent in the number of Franks from all the ones Ikiaq ran over. Patty looks mildly sick. The door opens and shuts. Opens and shuts. With another roar, I toss Jason in just as the door is opening.

It shuts behind him with a click.

"Open the door!"

Jason fumbles with the locking mechanism. "It's stuck!"

"Jason, I said—!"

I tumble as a Frank tackles me from behind. I rear an elbow back and knock out its teeth before crawling out from under it and rushing after the car. The detective's picked up speed, heading for the main highway.

The Franks slow as the car recedes. I pass by a flyer with a pentagram drawn on it, hot-glued to a tree.

A summoning spell. That's how Sabrina got so many of these assholes here at once.

The car drives toward me, and I scramble for its trunk. "Wait!" I kick my butt into gear, missing the bumper. The next time I leap, I grab onto the back-windshield wipers. I manage to kick my way up and switch my grip to the open window. Jason's sweaty palms pull at my arm. I swing my leg around, spider style, and hook my ankle and arm into the open window space. "Agh," I huff, feeling something dislocate as Jason pulls too enthusiastically.

"Sorry," he whimpers. But, through some feat of miracle strength, Jason's tugging is enough to pull me halfway into the speeding car.

Ignoring the pain, I pop my shoulder back in by throwing myself fully into the car. Jason yelps as I land on him.

"Sorry..." I mutter in a half-assed reply, panting as I roll over onto my back and stare up at him. News flash, nobody really looks good from this angle. It's like being an ant under a microscope, seeing everything at a distorted angle as you stare up at them. Not even Mr. Farm Boy Quarterback Goldilocks.

Wait a second.

Jason's arm is out of its sling. He pauses, confused. "Did I...?"

He looks to the open window. I wince, rubbing at my shoulder. "Lift me through a window like a ragdoll? I think you did." I punch at the phantom arm jokingly, suppressing a shudder as cold air runs through me. "You have a nice arm there, champ."

Jason looks to the dead spot incredulously. "I guess I do."

Chapter Twenty

On the Road Again. (See: zombies)

The driving pattern calms as we get out of range of the summoning spell. I thank the gods for small towns. The roads are empty save for one very confused trucker driving a load full of strawberry milk. I push myself up into a sitting position. Patty, Byron, Jason, and I all turn to stare at the inn. It's still getting torn up by what's left of the Franks.

"Maybe they'll clamber back to Evil Eye Incorporated with one of my sports bras in their fists. You know, the booty of war," Patty jokes.

Jason grimaces. "I don't suppose you have another really expensive Edwardian ring to sell to pay for the damages?"

I shake my head. "I have accounts stashed with contacts overseas. But nothing physical. And those accounts have been...dwindling, in recent years."

Byron swivels around at that. He's perched between me and Jason, half hovering through the seats again. "You're a broke-ass immortal?"

Detective Ikiaq chuckles at that. "Did any of you humans account for rates of inflation? And when you have to keep studying how banking and investing is changing, it's a self-study in economic idiocy. Not to mention, for the longest time, we'd be chased out of wherever we were staying. First, it was the religious calling us demons. Then, it was the conspiracy theorists calling us government pawns. No job security in that." He smiles and glances back at me in the rearview mirror, his dark eyes sparkling. "We always hire down-on-their-luck immortals at the detective agency, Lili."

I cross my arms, sticking my tongue out as the Sweeneys and Byron chuckle. "Some centuries are better than others, okay? Besides, the job market skills keep changing. And what do you think I'm going to do, enroll in *high school* once a lifetime? Doomed to repeat those four years for eternity... No thanks!" I glare at Jason. "And a 'thank you for saving my life, Lili' might be appreciated right now."

Jason turns to me then, blushing and looking into my eyes with a puppy dog plea. "I'm sorry. Thank you for running back there and saving me, Lil."

I nod, noticing how he fixes his hair, all nervous. "You're welcome," I reply, a little less sure of myself this time.

Patty, noting this uncomfortable silence, decides to break it. She throws her head back in defiance. "If we ever get the Eye business back," she says this now with a determined gleam in her eyes, "from that witch Sabrina Bender who screwed us over, then maybe we can help you out, Lil. Teach you how life goes now. Be a...a family. Of sorts."

"Thank you, Patty."

Patty twists back and holds out her freckled palm. I take it with a smile. Jason puts his human hand over ours. "I'll help too."

"Me too." Byron places his cold hand at the very top.

The detective reaches back, car swerving slightly. "Me four."

"*Eyes on the road!*" we squeal at once, all of us erupting into nervous laughter as the car rights itself.

I lean back, feeling oddly warm. And fuzzy. "Well," I growl, putting the age-old grimness in my voice. "Where to next?"

"Where does anyone go during a time of the zombie apocalypse? The neighborhood grouch with the safe house and weapons." Jason perks up.

"Jo Kim." The detective laughs, and I laugh with him. "I've been on the receiving end of her target practice for years. She doesn't like anyone snooping around her premises. Not even friendlies."

I purse my lips, remembering how she drilled a hole in me on our first encounter. "Yeah, I've been *very* well acquainted with that shotgun of hers."

"Good, you two know each other." The detective chuckles, pulling up to the Kims' house. I look to the ranch home, wondering if she's cleaned up the chunks of my flesh from the garden path. "You go first."

"What sort of misplaced chivalry," I grumble, swinging my sore legs out of the vehicle. I roll my shoulder back a few times. Speedy healing, practically good as new.

It was a good idea I ate that heart back at the inn. Who knows when I'll get fresh food now?

I stride up to the door and pound on it with my fist a couple of times. I back away quickly, holding my hands in the air. Jo swings it open, silver hair slicked back and her trusty shotgun at her hip. "Please don't shoot. Again." I fight the eye-roll.

The *gangshi* looks me over, her skin free from the blood and gasoline, flesh stretched tight over bone. She's settling into her ghoulish looks, dressed in a black bathrobe with plaid boxers. Still on the skinnier end from chemo, but now muscles building up. Changing her body chemistry to be fuller. Faster. Inhumanly strong. Her hair's going from a dull gray to bright bluish silver. She's showered recently. I can smell the floral scent of her shampoo.

"You gonna stare at me all day, Siren?" She kicks the door open with her hip.

I shake my head, dropping my hands at once. "Just trying not to get shot." I pause, looking at her skin, her hair. Revitalized. Reborn and rejuvenated like a damn shampoo commercial. "Weren't you in your sixties when you turned?"

She shrugs and holds up an unstoppered vial. "Sabrina's secretary let me snag some anti-aging potions. A way of apology. Also, it was a 'please don't burn our shit down again' kind of gift."

Damn, didn't know there was a reanimated cosmetics market. Wonder how that commercial would go? I grin. "Arson's underrated these days."

She considers me for a moment before she looks past me. "The garage is behind the house with the tool shed. I'll open the fence up and wave them on through. I don't have much food for the kids. Just powdered milk, oatmeal, cereals, and biscuits. Basically, whatever didn't expire before I turned."

"You're just going to let us in? No questions?"

She snorts. "Tae told me to expect guests."

"Ah, right. Of course."

Jo disappears to let the detective through the gate. Patty lumbers in, carrying the Sweeneys' combined things and kicking Ikiaq's duffel bag across the floor. I take in the surroundings. The old IV bag, medical wires, and tanks have all been shoved into a hall closet. Jo must've been in the middle of moving the wheelchair, too, before she let us in. I fix it for her, plopping the last remains of her sickly human days in the closet.

"She's cleaned," I inform Patty, running a finger over the coffee table. I show her the pad of my thumb. "No dust."

"I haven't been here before." She hugs her arms around herself. "Dad didn't bring us along when he went to visit Tae. Adult stuff, he said. Business stuff. He'd bring Mom, though, sometimes. She never minded. She loved Tae, too, in a different way. Knew he was hurting, and Todd was the only way he could learn to love himself."

Jason and Detective Ikiaq walk in after a few moments. Jo straggles behind. Ikiaq immediately goes around, throwing sofas in front of doors, locking windows and latching things. "More guests?" Jo drawls.

"Franken-pocalypse," the detective replies. "Where do you keep the other hunter weapons?"

"Hey, that's my made-up word!" I trail after him as he follows Jo's pointing hand to the cellar. The lightbulb swings above us as we tromp down the wooden stairs. "Why do we need weapons, anyways?"

"We don't, but the Sweeneys do. Patty and Jason's magic is fine for personal combat. But these are incoming hordes, not knights on horseback. Spells take more time than a trigger pull. They're necromancers, not Gandalf."

Again, with the Gandalf references.

We come up to a rack hidden behind bottles of liquor. Modified crossbows set up like multi-shot guns with arrows in the barrel. A vest with a front pocket shaped like a holster, holding room for tons of arrows. The arrows designed are paper-thin, but all tipped with some kind of gold substance.

"Ichor," the detective whispers.

"Food of the gods?" I venture.

"More like their blood." He tips the vest, the Eye branded in its shoulder. Another bag, this one filled with empty glass vials. I read the assigned label.

"Spell-holders." It's Patty's voice this time. She picks up one of the vials, just the size of her pinky. "Cast one spell and it multiplies amongst each touching vial. It's high-tech magic."

"How do you know? I thought Jason studied the spell books, not you."

Patty snorts. "Oh, the spell books filled with thousands of pages of subpar diagrams? Typical of Jason to geek out over it but end up working twice as hard. I used to use my parents' computer. They had, well, I suppose now thinking on it, they were digital test simulations of magical weapons. When I was little, I just thought they had coded a video game in their spare time." She laughs, twisting the vial round. "How'd Jo get her hands on this stuff?"

"Tae used to work closely with your parents. He must have gotten the prototypes."

"Right, my parents." I can't really detect what I'm hearing in her voice when she mentions her parents. Is that disdain? Hurt? She reaches past me for the modified crossbow. "I'll take the ichor-tipped arrows."

I raise an eyebrow at that. "You took archery too?"

"No! What am I, Katniss? *But* I'm a prodigy at heavy-duty paintball and laser tag." She beams at that. "First place captain for five years running."

"Well then." I pick up the bag of instant spells. "Let's prep for the Franks."

Chapter Twenty-One

Jo Kim's Living Room

I envy zombie movies. They never linger long on the boring parts.

This isn't a movie.

"Are the Franks *ever* going to get here?"

"I don't know," Jo replies, setting down steaming mugs of tomato soup and plates piled high with grilled cheese in the center of the table. Raw meat assortments for me and Ikiaq. She heads back to the kitchen, scooting plates aside. When she comes back, she brings a potted plant that's just beginning to show green.

Then she takes out a flask and dumps, yes, I can smell it...

Animal blood.

She's watering the plant with animal blood.

I gaze steadily at Jo, waiting for an explanation.

"I took a clipping from what was left of the ashes on Tae's tree. Or rather, Tae's tree trunk after what the Eye did to him." She runs a hand down the tree clipping, sighing.

"It might not even bring him back, Jo," Jason warns her. We've all changed into clothes that Jo had around the house. Our old ones were covered in blood and dirt from our last Franken-fight. It's why I have to keep from snickering as I look at Jason in a proper button-down and trousers, like he's headed to service. Patty and I lounge in some of Jo's many flannels and stretch shorts. Ikiaq's too large to fit into Tae's clothes, so he had to settle for a pair of oversized swim shorts and a dark-washed pajama muscle tee reading "I LOVE GAMIN."

Byron, being a ghost, still wears the duster and jeans he died in.

"I know it might not work," Jo replies, sprinkling the last of her animal blood on the plant. "I don't care."

"Jo, one question." I lean forward, glancing at her newly blue-silver hair. "How have you been feeding yourself since you turned? Don't you eat souls?"

She turns to me, smiles. "A lady never tells."

I back off at that. There's many things I won't find out about Jo.

Even though I want to.

"Lili, a word?" Byron drifts off near the kitchens. I follow him, leaving the Sweeneys to devour their grilled cheese, and Ikiaq to nibble at a ham hock.

We enter the kitchen. A sunroom tapers off the back porch, and Byron rests, cross-legged, on the table, sitting on a pile of empty cans. I lean against the kitchen island, noting how the cupboards are growing significantly bare.

No canned souls, huh?

"Your story's coming along nicely," Byron tells me, smiling that awkward grin. "A real heroic tale with blood and guts and glory. Everything."

"Thanks. Yours isn't so bad either."

"You're writing it?"

"Remembering it." I press a forefinger to my head. "That's all you can ask of an immortal. To remember when everything else has gone to dust."

"Thank you." Byron opens his notebook and flips to a few empty pages. "I just need to fill in the details about the beginning."

"You met me. There's your beginning."

"No, not ours." He's adamant this time, eyes staring into me. He's changed since the Dead Realm, become more and less real all at once. "*Your* beginning."

I know what he's saying. I might not have done the immortal-goes-back-to-high-school thing in a while, but I know. You're forced to remember some things you'd rather forget. That's how memory works, isn't it? You remember more bad times than good.

"Why, Byron? I thought we were friends." I try to pass it off as a joke, but Byron only frowns sadly. "Fine." I nibble at the raw meat I brought from the coffee table. I close my eyes as I chew, tasting the meat, imagining it tastes of animal sweat and life and...

Fear.

"I remember being born—no, not born. I was coming into being off what you'd call the Caspian Sea. It was land, it had to be. Because I didn't claw up through the waves, I crawled up from the earth. I coughed sand up out of me. In me. From me?" I shake my head, gasping at the memory, like I'm choking. How ridiculous. I don't have to breathe, but I want to. I want...

Byron pauses. When I open my eyes, I see he's staring intently at me. "Are all Sirens born in sand?"

"I don't know. Tricky, trying to get a woman's age. That's a private matter for immortals, isn't it?" I stuff the rest of the food in my mouth and swallow the chunk of blood and flesh. I wash my hands clean in the sink, shake them dry, and head back to the kitchen. "Did you get enough for your book?"

"Yeah, Lil. Yeah."

"Good." I nod and Byron hovers at my side, calm as can be. We reenter the living room. Detective Ikiaq nudges the plate of raw meat toward me. "Here, Lili, I saved you the heartier bits."

"Thank you." I take the platter from his larger hands and place another chunk into my mouth. The Sweeneys have already finished their soup and sandwiches. Jo is busy polishing her sawed-off shotgun. The rest of our weapons lie at her feet. Waiting. Hushed.

"So—"

A knock startles us all out of our cloud of anxiety. We go for the weapons, passing over the crossbow to Patty and the spell vials to Jason. He was working on them for hours, chanting spells for disease, for stopping blood and ending life and all its twisted imitations. Quick deaths and ends. Jo gets her shotgun, easy as can be, stretching out.

"I'll get the door. It's my house," she announces.

Ikiaq and I scrabble at her heels like puppies, but the look she sends us is cold enough to stop us in our tracks.

She looks through the aperture in the door while we peer past her through slits in the window screens.

A young woman taps her foot impatiently. She dons a black leather jacket and jeans, a sword strapped across her back like she's a goddamned warrior. An undercut with hair slicked back, emerald eyes and tattoos peering off her neck and hands. "Hello?" she asks. "You letting me in or what?" Each word trots out faster than the last. A New Yorker's snark in her voice. She sighs, rolling her eyes. "I don't know, Dax. Maybe they don't need our help."

She has a van parked casually in the street. I squint closer at it. Aside from the graffiti and tags, I can make out one thing in the center in punk-rawk red.

MÜNSTER HÜNTER(S)

"If you pronounced the Üs, it'd be 'mew-nsters hew-nters', you know." Patty tsks at that. "Punk rockers. No respect for linguistics."

Jason snorts. "I think that's the point, sis."

A man leaves the van, the woman's partner in crime. He also has a sword strapped to his back. Not to mention, yes, I can see the faint outlines and smell the chemicals. Iron knives strapped beneath a gray bomber jacket. A cap pulled low over his head. There's something familiar about his face, but I can't quite place it...

The man rings the doorbell and folds his arms politely over his barrel chest as he waits for an answer. "Good evening." He speaks like a New England scholar, a proper university clip where each word is enunciated to a *t*. "My name is Dakari Borden. This is my partner, Alethea Styx."

"Retired rock stars?" Jason mumbles the suggestion.

"No, sir," Dakari sighs. "We're monster hunters."

Impressive, how he can hear that through the door. I peer closer at his ears and see he has two flashing earring-like implants. *Ah, advanced tech.*

"Munster hunters, yeah!" Alethea crows.

"Who brought along the hot Van Helsing?" Patty nods to Alethea, and Alethea seems to swagger a little more with pride.

Dakari lifts his chin slightly. "We can hear you, you know." He taps the implants I spotted before. Alethea's come in the form of constellation piercings.

"Oh shit!" Byron crows. "I knew he looked familiar. That's why he's got the cool tech. He's Erik Borden's dad."

Erik? As in, Byron's Erik? He's Byron's *Erik's dad?*

Dakari lifts the cap, revealing a faint burn of the Eye crest in his forehead. "Yes, Erik's my son. He sent me out here after you. Said he was risking his nice internship with the coven to help out some friends with a specific infestation."

I look to the others, sans the clearly smitten Byron. "Your call, Sweeneys? Detective? Jo?" They look back at me and nod slightly.

"We need the help." Patty demurs, waving at Alethea.

Strike that. Patty's smitten too.

Ikiaq bites his lower lip. "We don't know who they are."

Jo holds up her shotgun with a shrug. "Let them in. I'll blow them out of the water if they try anything."

Jason looks hesitantly between the detective and Jo. "We might as well give them a shot. Erik's one of the good guys at the Eye, right? He wouldn't betray us."

With that not-so-rousing confidence booster, Jo unlocks the door the rest of the way. Alethea strides in and gives Jo a little salute. "Sweet, appetizers!" She runs over to the coffee table and starts eating leftover grilled cheese crusts.

Dakari walks in afterward with a slight nod to Jason's bag of spells and Patty's crossbow. The shotgun's in full view, pointed directly at his chest by an unblinking Jo. "Nice place you got here. And looks like you're ready for an invasion." He pauses, taking a closer look at me and the detective. "Maybe it's too late and the monsters came in already."

Ikiaq growls. "We're not a sideshow, human."

Dakari looks over the detective. He's a tall man, but still hovers a few inches shorter than Ikiaq's regular form.

"Sure, you aren't. An *Ijiraq* and a Siren. All according to plan, huh? But I wouldn't expect a ghoul to mind." Jo bristles at the insult. It's incredible, like the man doesn't even comprehend he's on the receiving end of a shotgun. Dakari glances at Byron, wrinkling his nose. "I don't know about dead people. Sure, you're still human, but I don't mess with that."

Damn, there goes Byron's shot at impressing the parents.

"Who told you what we are?" I ask, subtly nudging Jo's gun aside. No point in her hair-trigger reaction before we find out what Erik's dad is all about.

"That would be me!" The other monster hunter swaggers over, licking her fingers clean of melted cheese. She does a little wave, and her forest eyes glow an even more intense green. Like a piece of jade hit by direct sunlight. "I'm Alethea. I'm a new Seer for the team."

"A Seer?" Jo scoffs.

"Yup. I see the truth behind what monsters try to pass as." She taps her fingers against her forehead, sticking her tongue out a little as she beams. A flicker of a tongue ring. "Seer. It's in the name. See. And it's also in my name, metaphorically speaking. Alethea, it's Greek for truth."

Patty nods enthusiastically at every word. "Styx. That's the river in Greek mythology, right? Do you speak Greek, Alethea?"

Alethea nods. "Θέλεις να χορέψεις μαζί μου. *Thélis na horépsis mazí mu?* Would you dance with me?" She laughs, flexing one arm to massage her neck. The jacket slides up her wrist, revealing more tattoos. A pattern of ink so twisted I can't even tell what each design is supposed to be. "Whenever I go to Athens to visit, it's the one line I always use. I'm a sucker for the nightlife."

Patty would propose marriage right there if I didn't protectively insert myself between them. Jason has the same idea. *Dammit, maybe I really am the Sweeneys' guard dog.* "Well, now that we're all cozy. What did you have to say to us, Borden? Styx? How are you going to help us deal with our infestation?"

"Yeah," Jason crosses his arms. "Erik's a part of the coven. The Franks that keep attacking us were sent by Sabrina. Couldn't he just have sent a magical message up to HR instead of sending a bunch of monster haters?"

Alethea and Dakari remain suddenly silent. The quiet's so palpable, it's almost like we're going to snap and hurt somebody. It's near-unbearable until Dakari finally sighs and says, "Yeah, things aren't going so well at the coven. This isn't a hunt so much as it is a rescue mission. And we aren't helping you." He coughs into his sleeve. "You're helping us."

Chapter Twenty-Two

Still Jo Kim's House, but Now with Even More Punks

"Oh, how the tables have turned..." Jo mutters, leaning back on one foot, using her shotgun like it's a cane.

"Yeah, I, uh, I guess they have." Dakari sighs, staring at nobody in particular. His gaze always shifts between us, lingering on the so-called "monsters." "Sabrina has the Eye Coven on some sort of lockdown. Doesn't trust anybody in the building or out of it. Only her Franks, and they're busy rampaging against, well, everything."

"Why?" Jason's turn this time.

Dakari looks more at ease when he speaks to the human necromancers. "Erik's hiding in one of the bathrooms. He messages me every few hours, saying I could trust you all. Someone named Byron was texting him, sent your guys' location."

We all turn to Byron, glaring. He shrivels under our gazes, throwing up an awkward *save-me* wave. "Sorry."

"Let Sabrina wreck the place." The detective huffs, ignoring Byron as he hugs his journal holding Erik's number protectively to his chest. *The ghost clearly disagrees.* "They're humans. We're monsters, right? What do we care?"

Alethea inserts herself between the two. Like us, she probably senses the obvious animosity between the two aggro males. "Hi. Just gonna pop right in for a second." She claps her hands together. "We saw your place, nice place. The inn, right, Sweeneys?" She makes a wipeout gesture, her hands sliding across an invisible flat surface. "Gone to a zombie horde. All it takes is Sabrina sending one reanimated out there with a summoning spell and that place is extinct. Gamin is going to be *gone* if you don't do something."

"Forget about being the town's heroes." Dakari points around us, nodding at Patty's bow and Jo's shotgun. "How many can you kill before you run out of arrows? Or you with the bullets? And who becomes food for who, huh? I doubt you lot are all vegetarian. You might hold out for a battle, but there's no way to withstand a siege."

I snicker at that. Dakari raises an eyebrow.

"Ah, the..."

Alethea tilts her head, pauses, and then smiles. She stares into my eyes for a beat. *What the hell does this Seer like so much about what she can read of me?* "Siren." She finally spits out, all self-satisfied. I'm not sure if I like how long it took her to say that.

"The Siren." Dakari rolls his neck along his shoulders to work out the knots. "You've been silent for quite some time, haven't you?"

"My name's Lili. And this is Jo and Detective Ikiaq. Patty and Jason Sweeney. Our ghost friend Byron. We all have names, funnily enough." I look the man over, walking a slow circle around him. I examine the sword, the blade not cleaned perfectly. A missing edge that's crusted over slightly with old red. He spins around like a dog that doesn't want me to see its tail. "So, Sabrina's finally lost it, huh? And nobody's going to escape her wrath, what a pity." I laugh as Dakari finally faces me. Alethea even cracks a smile just because he looks so unnerved. Like I've suddenly sprouted rabbit ears which, I'm fairly sure, I don't do.

"I'm sorry." Dakari nods. "I should have asked your names. That was rude of me. But can we get to the point?" He whacks his hand against his thigh. "My *son* is in that building." His mask finally slips a bit. The calm and stoic coolness. It goes away as he shows just how much he's worried about the situation. "I don't know what Sabrina has against you people or what you've done for her to start a damn zombie apocalypse, but Erik didn't take part in this. How could he? He's a goddamn intern!"

Jo takes them in for a moment, licks her lips, and then shrugs. "Okay."

Dakari blinks a few times. We all stare at her in disbelief. "Just like that? You'll really help me?"

Jo nods. "Sure thing, sweetheart." She cocks the gun and aims it directly at his face. "Right after you apologize for insulting us."

"You're monsters."

"We still have feelings."

Alethea scowls, reaching for the stakes at her hips. But Detective Ikiaq already has her in a sort of bear hug grip.

Patty shoves her way between Jo and Dax. "Please, Jo, don't!"

Jo shakes her head. "How can we just trust them? My brother trusted every pretty face with a sob story. Look where that got him."

Patty blushes, unsure how to answer that one.

"All right, all right. No need to defend my honor, Red." Dax goes, slowly, to his knees. He holds his hands far away from his swords and other weaponry. "I'm sorry for calling your lot monsters. Now, will you *please* save my son."

Jo snarls, "Not good enough."

"Wait. There's another way to make sure we can trust them." Jason flips through his damned spell book and stops at a picture of two interlocking hands and an Eye symbol drawn on their wrists, etched right above their veins. "Blood oath."

Dakari blanches. "The break it and you die kind?" He looks at all of us again. "You can't be that crazy."

Jason holds up the book with his phantom hand. The book floats in midair, and part of Jason's shirtsleeve rises with it. "I have a ghost hand, and I've been to the Dead Realms. It's not *as* scary of a consequence as you'd think for me."

Jason holds out his arm, and Dakari glances at it for a moment. "No, Dax!" Alethea bites Ikiaq's wrist and he releases her slightly. She lunges at him, but the detective's caught her up again. "Let me take it instead."

"Alethea. You've done enough just leading me here. I'll take the oath, but you leave her out of this, you hear? I can't have anyone else getting hurt because of me." He glares at me, his eyes burning a hole through me. "Before Alethea, I had another partner in this line of work. Let's just say there's a reason I hate monsters."

I'm about to reply, maybe mumbling a half-assed apology, but Jo beats me to it. "Don't worry. We hate you back. Now take the nice necro-boy's good hand and shake."

Dax grunts and takes Jason's outstretched, fleshy hand. The Eye burns its way into their wrists. Jason sweats and bites his lower lip, hissing in pain. Dakari yelps. The stench of burning mortal flesh, I'm ashamed to say, makes my stomach growl. Detective Ikiaq also looks uncomfortable, and Jo licks her dry lips.

"Betray us," a noticeably paler Jason squeaks, "and you die."

Dakari takes his hand back and rubs at his sore wrist. The Eye burn is already blistering over. Jason nods at Patty and she takes a poultice from her bag and rubs it over both their wounds. Dakari takes a pair of black gloves from his pocket and pulls them on, hiding the new mark.

"We go. Soon as possible," Dakari croaks, and everyone re-sheathes their weapons. Patty and Jason gather their things from the kitchen. A few more poultices. Jason with his books and spell-holders, Patty with her crossbow, and Jo with her shotgun.

Alethea looks at me, hovering near the door. Her arms are crossed, biceps bulging with a nest of tattoos. Serpents from mythology. Hydras, Minotaurs, and webs of blue symbolizing rivers. "You aren't grabbing anything? Now, I understand the big guy because he's jacked. But you're kinda petite, you know. As far as monsters go, Sirens don't strike as much fear in one's heart as a zombie."

I glance over the sword strapped to her back. "I prefer brute force to tin toys."

She unsheathes the sword and holds out its padded hilt to me. "Would you like to hold it?"

I look her over for another moment, the punk rock monster hunter with burning eyes beneath the jagged hair, and take it from her hands. I twist the sword around, seeing symbols etched into the blade. The hilt tapers off into a crucifix, padded for comfort.

"Like I said"—I hand it back to her—"a pretty toy."

Alethea looks at me from the edges of her vision, a slow smile spreading over her face. "Oh yeah? Well I like pretty things. See ya around, Siren. Gotta set up the van for Dax."

She takes a set of skeleton keys, and by skeleton keys, I mean keys carved out of bone and metal, and flounces over to the van. Unsure of what to make of the flirtatious monster-killer, I wait until Dakari and Ikiaq catch up with me. Dakari glides by me, but Ikiaq stays at my shoulder, munching on uncooked meatballs, fresh from the freezer.

"We should kill them," Ikiaq says. It's not so much a threat as a fact.

I clap him on the shoulders, a real feat since he's so tall. He's only ever seemed to grow taller since our fight in the woods. "He shook on a blood oath."

"She didn't."

I swallow the disappointment, snagging a meatball off Ikiaq's hands. "Yeah, I know." I lick my fingers clean of the dried blood, striding over slowly to the car once Patty and Jason go past. "Keep close."

When I clamber into the van, Byron is floating cross-legged near the back of the driver's seat. The back seats have been cleared out, and the bottoms and sides of the van space are peppered with flyers and band posters. I check out one of the flyers and see a creatively designed face of a vampire glaring back at me. The creature looks like they were drawn in the style of abstract expressionism with all the harsh colors of cut lines.

"A ten-thousand-dollar reward for a single vamp." I crush the paper beneath my foot, sighing. "I should go into this business. You hiring, Grim and Grimmer?"

Jason wrinkles his nose. "Yet they still live in a van."

"We've taken a break from all that," Dakari calls back. I can't help but notice his sword is wedged halfway beneath his seat. That puts the monsters at a distinct advantage if we were to, say, try to murder him.

"Yeah." Alethea buckles herself in. Funny, the punk rock monster hunters still using seat belts. "We're into revenge now."

Dakari glares at his partner in crime, lips pursed thin.

"Revenge?" Byron perks up this time, ready to jot some more notes down.

Dakari sighs as we swing into the main road, his knuckles tensed round the wheel. "Before Alethea, I fought monsters with my wife. Kinda like date night, with Erik at home with the youngest monster hunters as babysitters. She died when we took on a job too big for either of us. And Erik's hated me ever since. Would rather become some techno-wizard."

A monster hunter judging his son for his job choices in life. That's rich.

I press my forehead against the glass as the car settles into an uncomfortable silence. Jo finally mumbles, "I lost my brother. These Sweeney kids lost their parents. We all know how it feels."

Dakari bites his lower lip, glancing at our weird, motley crew sprawled out over the back. "Nobody stays long in this world of ours. Least of all those involved with the darkness."

With that cryptic message, he drives on. To face zombie hordes at the Eye Coven.

"As I said before," Ikiaq whispers to me, just low enough nobody else can hear. "We should pin down the bullet records at the Eye. Find out who tried to shoot me, who got the Siren outside my office."

"Bag 'em and tag 'em," I reply.

Ikiaq stares at me, miffed. "What the hell's that supposed to mean?"

"I thought it sounded cool. Look, let's just put an end to this. I'm tired of running."

Ikiaq digs dried blood out from underneath his fingernails. "What are you going to do when the dust settles down?"

"Sleep," I reply. "Until the world finally ends."

Chapter Twenty-Three

Your House (just kidding)

The Eye Coven Corporation doesn't look so bad, considering it's under zombie siege. A group of screaming necromancers huddle in their car as four Franks rock their vehicle from side to side. Dakari nods to Alethea and, in one smooth movement, she's decapitated two of them. The other two, Patty takes out with an exploding arrow.

"Ichor of the gods," Patty informs us, hefting the modified bow over one shoulder. "Like fireworks when connecting with the undead, but bloodier."

The necromancers veer off before we can even get thanked properly. "Ungrateful," Byron tsks. We turn to the automatic doors near the lobby, seeing how a bunch of undead hands have wedged the doors shut with their sheer weight.

We look to Byron, who pockets his journal with a sigh. Another moment and he's floating above our heads, piercing lights emanating from blank eyes as he goes poltergeist. "Got it. Let the destruction...*begin.*"

A few rattling moans and the doors blow entirely from their doorways. We step over a pile of corpses. But

Byron's gone. A few unlucky necromancers litter the floor alongside the Franks. We hear a distinct scream from far-off.

Byron?

We follow the sound to a bathroom that's sealed off. "Move," Ikiaq mutters, ramming his shoulder against the door. Antlers peer through his dark hair, dark *Ijiraq* veins showing. A quarter transformation, but enough to take the reinforced door down.

We step through, see necros screaming and crying. Erik's leaned against one of the stalls, head bleeding and wrapped up in someone else's shirt. Byron wails, cradling him in his arms. "Help him!" he cries. Still mostly in poltergeist form, he's able to hold Erik like he's still physical and alive. It might be my imagination, but Erik nuzzles in closer.

Patty falls to administer witchy First Aid. Dakari is at his son's side, soothing him. "It's all right. Just like that time when I picked you up from summer camp, right?"

Erik peels open one eye, glaring at his father. The glare softens after he sees the concern. "Sure, Dad. Like deadly summer camp."

Joke's on him. Those money pits are all deadly.

"This might take a while. You should leave me behind." Patty chews on her lower lip. "He's been hexed. I don't know how I know exactly. I just do."

"Yeah, I'll stay behind too," Jo pipes up. A Frank gets too close to the doorway and she delivers a quick head shot to end it. "If there are any more survivors on this floor, I want to get them safely out."

"Hold on a moment. My son's been hexed?" Dakari leaps to his feet, anger incarnate. "Who did this?"

"Sabrina..." Erik gasps. "She's lost control."

We all make for the door, leaving Byron and Patty to tend to Erik. Jo is ushering a young mother and her child to their car out near the parking lot. Ikiaq sets the door back on its hinges. Taking one of his spell vials, Jason throws it against the door. It erupts into flames for a moment, welding the door back onto its frame.

"Come on." Jason's already down the hall, not even glancing back to see the spell through. Surprisingly focused. He nods back to me. "Where's Sabrina's office?"

"Corporate level. B9," Alethea replies.

How did she know that? Her powers?

She holds up a flimsy map. "They had these at the welcome desk."

Her partner's less focused. "Sabrina? Erik's boss really has lost it? I thought Erik meant in a metaphorical way," Dakari mumbles, tagging along at a furious distance, sword drawn. But unlike Alethea's old-school version, his has a shotgun embedded into it.

"How would you explain the rabid Franks?" I shoot back.

"Employee development."

We head toward the elevators, but those are no good. In a smoking, electrical-wire-hissing heap, the elevator's been permanently discontinued. Franks moan from inside its trapped interior, struggling to break out.

"Guess it's leg day, champs." Dakari heads toward the stairs, glancing down at the map in Alethea's hands. "Get ready to sweat."

A new group of Franks amble down the halls. Unfortunately, these are particularly mobile. They rush at us once they see us coming, arms itching for our necks. Alethea has her sword at the ready and Dakari starts firing. Jason throws another vial that erupts into an acid spray further down the hall. The shining matter adheres quickly to the Franks, eating away at their skin. Ikiaq just slams a few against the walls, smearing them everywhere.

One manages to sneak up on me and wrap its arms around my neck.

"Not this time."

I sink my sharpened teeth deep into its flesh, not stopping until I crunch through bone. It howls and releases me, but I've already torn near-through its wrist. I alight on it, bringing it tumbling down as I straddle it. Clawing at its face until, with a final shudder, it stops moving.

"Huh." Alethea helps me up, reanimated, sticky-sheen blood on her sword. I clasp her gloved hand, wiping blood from my mouth. "Attractive."

"Enough," I growl, "let's get to B9."

We slam into the stairwell and rush down the steps quick as we can. Ikiaq leaps over the railing to skip a couple of flights. Jason trips and falls when he loses his footing. I help him back up. He's so tired, he doesn't even mind the bloodstains.

"You holding in there, kid?" I hoist him up.

"So much running. And fighting." He's breathing hard. Panting. "I can't keep up with you guys."

I wait a beat before carrying him bridal style the rest of the way. "Then come along for the ride." He slumps against me, embarrassed but not about to refuse the royal treatment.

I put him down before we exit at B9. The others have already gone through the door since we lagged behind. Jason places his hand on my shoulder. "Thanks, Lil. I'm sorry for being shitty to you early on."

"You too," I reply. "Now let's get out there."

We exit through the B9 doors where the rest of the squad's gathered. A sea of ghostly silent office cubicles and white walls now stained with unspeakable substances. Most of the office has been cleared out, except for an unlucky few still hunched over their desks or sprawled out from trying to run. I inhale, smelling something burning. And something else.

The scent of antiseptic.

To top it all off, the harsh fluorescent lights are flickering. I lean down to check out the red stains. My fingers come away with a powdery coating. "Candlewax," I repeat. Jason gets out his cell phone light and wheels it around the room. The light illuminates summoning spells, peppered all over the walls.

No, not summoning spells.

"Containment spells," Jason mumbles, shaking his head. Sweat plasters his blond locks to his forehead, stress acne breaking out along his jaw. "What's she keeping in here?"

"Hello, children."

A cubicle flies toward us, and we barely roll out of its way in time. Behind it, a door is drawn in wet paint, dripping on the wall.

"Isn't that—?" Alethea begins.

"Yes," Jason mutters, running his good arm against the phantom one. "I can feel it. A door to the Dead Realms."

"I said hello!"

A ghost with a bald head and a smartly trimmed beard floats above our head. He wears joggers and a sports coat, all in dark gray, with a giant Rolex watch on his wrist. His eyes are just gaping holes of red flashing light.

"Poltergeist," Alethea spits.

Dakari turns to his partner, wide-eyed. "I told you that's why I don't mess with that."

Jason yelps as he's carried into the air by his neck. The poltergeist is holding him up as Jason kicks and flaps his arms around. Ikiaq tries to pull him back down, but the poltergeist throws another cubicle at him. The detective dodges just in time but ends up getting another desk thrown at his head for his efforts.

Alethea screams and hits at him with her sword while Dakari fires bullets. The ghost laughs, pointing at the missiles that just plunge through him. *"I'm dead, you idiots."*

I move to crouch behind a desk. He hasn't seen me yet. I'm the only one who hasn't rushed into the fray. I watch as the spirit lifts Jason further into the air. *"Who are you? No, don't tell me. I know a Sweeney when I smell one. Your mommy and daddy killed me, you know."*

Jason slumps in his grip, defeated. "You were going to kill them first."

I'm about to creep forward when something slams into me from behind, pushing me out into the open. "Hello there, Lili." Sabrina's form rises over me, wielding just the arm of a paper-cutter machine in her grasp. It looks kind of like a machete. She slashes at me. The blade digs into my bicep, and I twist just in time to avoid getting decapitated. Sabrina pauses long enough to fix her hair, waving up at the spirit. "Hello, Daddy."

I grimace. "Please, never say that again."

She scowls and lunges at me again. I turn back, see Alethea and Dakari behind some chairs. *Hide,* I mouth at them. They disappear behind a still-standing cubicle. I barely have time to let loose a sigh of relief before Sabrina stabs the paper-cutter into my shoulder blade, lodging it so deep she can't even take out the blade.

"You witch!" I spit at her.

She smirks. "Yeah, duh." She twists the blade out of spite, and I grit my teeth to avoid giving her the satisfaction of screaming. "Lili, meet Clarence Bender. Murdered by the Sweeneys. Leaving *me* an orphan."

"Get in line!" Jason spits, surprisingly heroic in the face of death. "We've all lost parents. It's in the goddamned Chosen One contract."

"Mm, brave. Nothing like your backstabbing parents." Clarence sighs, peering closer at Jason, helpless in his grip. "It shouldn't have been this way, kid. It should've been easy. I was just going to poison you and your sister in your sleep. Your parents, too, until they got violent. I didn't even have to do anything. In the end, their own spell backfired on them. And to think I was just going to stab them, but the irony was delicious!"

"Poison them for what? A goddamned sign over a door? A fancy Eye logo?"

"My little girl did her father proud, bringing you Sweeneys over to me so I could exact my revenge. We were going to take you off to a side room and kill you once you'd signed the contract for the business, but you lot took the hard way out. Brought over your little buddies. Ah, but in the end, it's just business. Like this."

Jason chokes as the poltergeist narrows in on his windpipe. I claw toward him, but Sabrina steps on the blade end, digging it deeper into my shoulder. Fire and so much blood. I wasn't aware I could bleed that much.

"No..." I gasp. "No."

Jason snarls, baring his teeth like a little wolf. Another flicker of fluorescent lighting and I see an arm fashioned of pure light. He squeezes it around Clarence's neck and starts choking the poltergeist. "No!" Clarence coughs. "You're not supposed to be able to hurt me."

"Guess again, you son of a bitch."

As Jason chokes Clarence with his phantom arm, the pair dip lower. The poltergeist loses control, spinning rapidly in midair. "No, Daddy!" Sabrina screams.

"Hey, witch."

She swivels over to me, her black bob swaying. I kick at the back of her knees, and Alethea's there to catch her in her arms.

"Sleepy time," Alethea tells her, pressing a point at Sabrina's neck. The deranged witch slumps in her arms, unconscious.

Meanwhile, Jason twirls in midair, still fighting Clarence. He gets thrown off, hitting the wall with an audible smack. A row of chairs and plastic tables fall in on him. "Jason!" I scream. Dakari goes to clear the debris off him.

"Take that, Sweeney spawn," Clarence snarls.

A shudder passes through the rubble. Suddenly, it all just melts away. A shattered spell vial, and Jason has another one in his grip. His Eye is flaring on his forehead, and he has another sheet of paper in his hands.

The containment spell for a poltergeist. More specifically, an Eye Coven.

"Delete..." he whispers, holding it up to the flame emanating from the vial, "...history."

He could've gone with something more badass like "your contract's expired" or "see you in Hell" but he goes with a computer reference. Fine, that's fine. You know what, I have a paper-cutter in my arm; I shouldn't be complaining about catchphrases.

Jason slumps to his knees, spent, as the poltergeist screams, erupting into thousands of splinters of white light. What's left of him reaches out toward Sabrina. "Goodbye, pumpkin," he murmurs, "I'm sorry."

When Clarence Bender vanishes, all the fluorescent lights in the building go off at once, exploding in a shower of glass. Dakari shields Jason while I shield Alethea.

A beat and the monster hunters pull out glowsticks while Jason reaches for his cell phone light. A hunk of toppled cubicles and desks shifts in the corner.

"Over here..."

It's the detective, trapped under sidelined debris.

He pushes his way out of the dust, hands balled into fists, antlers scraping the ceiling. "Where is he? I'll get him!"

"Fight's over, buddy." Alethea claps his shoulder, her tiny frame like a ragdoll compared to the *Ijiraq*. "Good try."

Sabrina comes to, blinking blearily in the light. "Where's my father?"

"Dead. Again," I reply, grimacing at the blade that's still sunk into my side. "Ikiaq, I can't move much. But while we're down here, get the bullet records."

"Oh, come on." Alethea rolls her eyes. "It's obvious the crazy witch is behind all this."

"You just got here." I narrow my eyes at her. "What could you possibly know about those records?"

"You were blabbering in our van. News flash, not the best way to handle sensitive information." She pushes up in my space, hands on her hips.

"Alethea, enough." Dakari nods to Ikiaq. "If you want the records, go ahead and get the records. You saved my son, Erik. That's enough." With that, he pushes back his sleeve and reveals the Eye burn mark disappearing. "We've repaid a debt," he tells us. "Maybe you monsters aren't all bad after all."

I stare into his eyes, so like Erik's despite Erik trying to magically modify his. The components are still there. I see what Byron sees in them. The emotion. The vulnerability. The monster hunters just trying to make sense of a world that's both good and bad.

"You too," I reply. "Now, um, hate to bother y'all. But can someone get this paper-cutter out of my arm?" I wince as it shifts slightly. "I'm starting to lose consciousness."

Chapter Twenty-Four

Just Outside the Evil Corporation

We're waiting outside for Ikiaq's buddies from the police station further in town to show up. They're human, mostly, except for one of them who's part werewolf on his mother's side. Only grows the tail during a full moon. It's awkward for everyone.

I scream as Patty pulls out the blade and packs the wound with herbs, mumbling magical spells to knit the flesh back together faster.

Fire and blood.

"You're being overdramatic." Jo rolls her eyes.

"Try me, ghoul," I reply, gritting my teeth.

"I'm just happy to have you back." It's Dakari this time, escorting his son Erik, all wrapped up in a shock blanket. "After your mother..."

"Dad." Erik pauses, shaking his head. "I know you wanted me to go to a regular graduate school for engineering. Or join you in monster hunting. But this is what I want to do with my life. Necromancy." He takes Byron's ghostly hand in his. To everyone's surprise, he grasps it firmly—that is, until we see the modified tech glove he's wearing, run through with golden ichor and wires. "And this is who I want to spend it with."

Dakari nods, clasping his son and Byron in a hug. "After what you did for my son, you're welcome in the family."

We all whoop and cheer. Even I crack a reluctant smile.

"Lili." A grim-faced Detective Ikiaq pulls me out of the premature celebrations. Patty finishes rolling a bandage over my shoulder, run through with jagged stitches. "I found the records."

"And?" The smile disappears from my face. "Who bought them?"

"The ones that match the correct date and model…" He finally just hands me the case file in a manila envelope once Patty goes to check on Erik's head wound. "Just read it for yourself."

I peel open the file to reveal a flutter of images. A name in typeface. A cap pulled low over his head. A gray bomber jacket. A van.

"No, this can't be possible." I shuffle the papers and hand them, crooked, back to Ikiaq. "It says here that Dakari Borden bought those."

"Think about it. Aside from Anna Snow and a couple of the other humans, most of the victims lately have been monsters. And he said he wanted revenge for his wife…" Seeing the stubbornness in my face, the detective lets up. "Look, Lili. I've taken a shine to the grouchy old geezer too. But we have to face the facts. It all lines up."

"What about Alethea?" I challenge, glancing at the little punk with her undercut and sword. "She didn't want us looking at the files either."

"Yeah, and she's his partner in crime. Makes sense she'd want to protect him, right?"

"No, it's too neat. It's too—"

"What are you lot talking about?"

It's Dakari Borden, grinning like a fool. He stops grinning when he sees the envelope.

Erik, catching his father's disappointment, looks between the three of us. "Dad, what's wrong?"

"It's nothing, champ. Just old news." He leans his head down toward me. "Come on, not in front of my kid."

"Oh my, look at those bandages. They're loose. Erik, back to Patty. Let's get that head wrapped properly, okay?" Erik goes, still glancing over his shoulder as the detective ushers him away. Leaving just me and the old monster hunter.

Dakari holds out his hands helplessly. "I know it looks bad. Alethea and I saw the wanted posters once we hit Gamin's town hall. But trust me when I say I had nothing to do with those other murders. How could I? I only arrived a while ago."

I show him the images of the Siren the detective took, stamped with a date. "Just in time to kill the Siren and try to kill Detective Ikiaq."

He shakes his head, moaning low in his throat. "No, no, no. You've got me all wrong. Fine, I'll admit to the Siren and the detective. But that was because I mistook them for someone else. Something else." He wrings his hands together, almost pleading. "What Alethea told you in that van, that I was chasing down the monster that killed my wife. We think it's here. Here in Gamin. But it's in hiding, pretending it's something else. I don't know what exactly, but..."

"You don't know what it looks like, so you just go shooting every single monster in sight?" I'm furious this time, clenching my fists in retaliation.

"Come now," he tells me, nodding to himself. "Look at me. You think I don't know what that's like? Being mistaken for someone else based on looks? Being shot for another's crimes when shooting them wasn't the goddamned way to protect people? I made a mistake out of grief for my wife. I learned better."

"I know," I tell him, knowing exactly what he's talking about. "Humans can be monsters too." I swallow. "Look, I don't think it adds up either. But the detective's going to want to arrest you. One of the earlier victims who died, Anatol. A vampire who was close to a lot of people in this town. They're going to want blood. Yours." I nod to the tree line, pasting an easygoing smile on my face. "Get in the car with me now. I'll tell them I drove you into the station in town. But you're actually going to get off just outside Gamin. Run, don't look back. You hear me?"

"How will you convince the station that I'm there?"

I smile flirtatiously at one of the cops, unleashing my hair from any restraints and shaking my loose, dark locks over one shoulder. "I'm a Siren, darling. I won't like it, but I'll manage."

Dakari looks sadly between me, the detective, and Erik. "My boy, Erik. You and the ghost keep him safe, all right?"

I fold my hands over his. "I promise, Dax. I promise."

*

Jo's Place

"Do you think I'm some kinda idiot?" We're back in the kitchen at Jo's house. Alethea's playing card games with the Sweeneys. Byron's cuddling Erik on the couch. Jo's putting what's left of our weaponry in the cellar.

"If this is about Alethea and Erik crashing at the house again, I won't hear a word of it." I cross my arms, staring up at Detective Ikiaq. He's dressed back in his regular detective's outfit, even clutching his telltale cup of hot chocolate that we swung through a café for. He wears a thick black jacket with a caribou patch on the shoulder. Dark hair loose and curling past his shoulders. He's kept a bit of scruff around his jaw, to cover up the bruises he got from the fight. We all have pretty bad scrapes from infiltrating Sabrina's lair. "Come on, detective. We took out the bad guys. The Sweeneys get what's left of Eye Coven when they choose to sign for it. It's a good day."

"You know what I'm saying. Just because Sabrina's in jail, doesn't mean our story is over." The detective downs the last of the hot chocolate and crushes the Styrofoam cup in his grip.

"That's just wasteful. Styrofoam? Really?"

He snarls and throws the remnants in the trash. "Stop playing around, Lili. You know that you let a possible murderer free. Dakari's skipped town. I checked out the station myself. You might've fooled the humans and that part werewolf, but you can't fool me." He leans in closer, glancing back at Erik. "What will we tell Erik? Or Alethea when we tell her that her partner's gone missing?"

"Erik cannot know. And Alethea..." I look over at her, and see her glance over, winking flirtatiously at me. I shake my head. "I don't trust her."

"She helped us fight the Franks. Maybe it's not her you don't trust."

"What's *that* supposed to mean?"

The detective shrugs. "She's suave. She's attractive. She's *cool*. Maybe you're jealous."

"I'm *not* jealous. Stop pitting women against each other. I don't hate her out of jealousy. She's hiding something."

"So are you."

He looks into my eyes like Alethea did. Like he sees something. I shudder, wrapping my arms around myself. "I don't do that anymore. I'm not who I once was."

"Then who are you, *Lili*?" He unleashes a shaky breath. "I can't say I haven't thought about the possibility that you're the one behind this."

"Ikiaq..."

"Lili?" Alethea's leaning on the doorframe. She's shrugged off the layers of weapons and weapon holsters, leaving her in a black tank. Her arms and face are scrubbed relatively clean of blood, hair damp from a shower. "Can I speak to you?"

Ikiaq watches me expectantly. I swallow my words, trying to make my face as stoic as possible. "Sure, what's up?"

Alethea turns around and walks in the other direction. I turn back uncertainly to the detective, but he's already clearing up and washing spilled hot chocolate off his hands. Alethea reaches one of the tables and snags her bone-and-metal keys off one of the counters before stuffing her gloves in her back pocket. She slings her sword around one of her arms.

"Uh, care to tell me where we're going?"

She turns back, casting a toothy smile my way. "On an adventure."

I grab her sword and yank her back with it. "I'm done with surprises."

"I know you arrested Dakari or took him somewhere. Look, I could care less. I don't need him here for what needs to be done."

"And what needs to be done, pray tell?"

"God damn, you're too much sometimes. *Pray tell?* Prithee, Shakespeare, get with the twenty-first century." She snickers, her green eyes glinting, sharp as a cat's. "Dakari told me we were hunting a demon, a big one. One that could put wanted posters on city hall if you catch my meaning."

I flush, half with rage and half with embarrassment. "Go on."

"Well, I think I've got a lead on a demon. Something raising hell in Gamin. The same monster that murdered Dax's wife."

"And why aren't we bringing anyone else along to fight this...mega monster?"

She tugs at my peacoat, revealing the jagged line of scars that are healing over themselves from where Sabrina dug her blade in. "I know your type, Lili. No matter how many hits you take, you're still better off working alone." Her fingers dance along the stitches. I shudder at her touch. "You got this because you were liable for someone else. How much faster could you work without the little humans bogging you down?" She leans back, leaving a vacuum where she once was. "I love Dax, but vengeance is a hell of a drug."

"Why do you care about catching a demon?"

"I'm a monster hunter, baby. It's what I do." She reaches for the door. "What do you say, you want to take a ride with me?"

I tear free of her grip, her strange flirtation. "No."

"Why?"

"Because I don't trust you, Seer."

Something flickers in her eyes. Not anger, just bemusement. A sparkle. "A challenge? Hm." She shrugs and swings the door open anyway. "I like you, Lili. You're interesting."

How much faster could *I work if I worked alone?*

I see it then, solving the entire case. Saving a town. And then...

Leaving. Alone at last.

As the door swings shut behind Alethea, I snap out of my daydream. But her words never leave me. Or those eyes. That strange glint in them. The challenge.

Chapter Twenty-Five

A Police Station

"Why are we back here, Lil?" Ikiaq grumbles as we enter the station where Sabrina's currently housed.

Arson and a bombing, that's what covered up the whole magical-zombie affair. Sabrina isn't getting free any time soon, no matter how much she tries to bribe them with.

"Hey there, Ick." One guard greets him, raising a hairy hand. His face disappears behind a thick beard and big teeth.

"Hey, Shaggy," Ikiaq replies, waving at him. Shaggy hands him a cup of hot cocoa. "Ah, you shouldn't have."

"Anything for Gamin's top detective."

The detective's laugh is big and jovial, expanding in the room. His laugh's almost as imposing as him, but it's pleasant. Full of happiness. "You're making me blush."

"Is that the werewolf?" I ask once we're further down the hallway.

"Nope, he is." He nods at an acne-covered rookie, hiding behind a choppy haircut. Weighs maybe one-thirty when soaking wet. "Hey, Toothpick."

"Ick," he squeaks. "She's in the interrogation room."

"Perfect." I can't help but insert a bit of glee into my voice.

The detective raises an eyebrow at me as Toothpick fumbles with the keys. "Personal vendetta?"

"Nearly took off my arm and ripped out my spinal cord. But I'm just here for answers, same as anybody else. *Ick*."

The metal door swings open into a darkened room covered in mirrored walls. Sabrina glares at us from beneath her lashes, her chin sagging forward, her hair a mess. She's cuffed to a metal chair, a lamp staring harshly into her face. A desk sits in front of her, more metal chairs on the other side of it.

"Hey there, bitch," Sabrina spits. "Your arm still sore?"

"Your face still Botoxed?" I reply, droll as ever. I swing a chair around to sit on it and prop my chin on the backrest. Ikiaq takes a seat gingerly besides me. "Tell me why you sold Dakari bullets to try and kill us."

"That's one way to start questioning," Ikiaq grumbles.

"We sell to tons of monster hunters, prick," Sabrina tells us.

"But you know the name of Dakari Borden?" Ikiaq counters.

"Of course, he's the best hunter in the country. Or he was before his wife died." Sabrina's eyes go hungrily toward the hot chocolate in Ikiaq's hands. Smirking, I get pleasure from taking the drink and wafting it beneath her nose.

"I haven't eaten since I got here." Her face pales. "Just one sip. One."

"No, no, no." I pull the drink back in slow, agonizing circles. "Not until you tell us why you killed so many people and released a poltergeist on your own offices."

"They never were my offices, were they?" Her eyes glaze over. Eye makeup smeared, bloodshot gaze. People get drunk when they're tired, and Sabrina looks positively exhausted. The words trickle forth like she's under truth serum. "They were always the Sweeneys'. Thought they were doing me a favor, poor little orphan. Allowing me to run the business until the kids were of age. But what good's that? Like letting the valet babysit your Lamborghini. It's never *really* your car, is it?" She laughs, throwing her head back. "But my father came to me in my dreams. Showed me the truth."

"What do you mean?" I lean in closer, and her eyes suddenly latch onto mine. Mad.

"I'm not the first Eye necromancer to summon something terrible. You can blame Todd and Beatrice Sweeney for that."

I think back to Alethea's earlier proposition. *I think I've got a lead on a demon. Something raising hell in Gamin. The same monster that murdered Dax's wife.*

And then, there were Clarence Bender's words. *In the end, their own spell backfired on them. And to think I was just going to stab them, but the irony was delicious!*

Could it...could Todd and Beatrice Sweeney have summoned something beyond even their combined powers? Something that broke out of its containment spell?

"Why did they summon it?" I place my hands against Sabrina's shoulders. She winces.

"Lili..." Ikiaq warns.

"Why else? My father was die-hard loyal to them. But the Sweeneys wanted the old ways, and everyone else wanted to join the modern world. Even my father got sick of it when it put his livelihood in danger." Sabrina laughs, tossing her head back. Her laughter ends in dry, raspy coughing. I give her a sip of hot cocoa. She sighs, calming down. "If the Sweeneys were going down, then they needed to bring down others with them. But they overcalculated their ability to handle the thing, so it got loose. Killed my father and them."

"You're saying a demon's been unleashed on Gamin?"

"I'll admit, I went too far. But you caught me." Sabrina looks up to me, veins in her neck showing through with the strain. "Can you catch *it*?"

I hand her the hot cocoa and she goes for it greedily. I restrain myself from smacking it out of her hand and watching her as it all dribbles to the floor. Watching as she falls to her animalistic instincts. Not so clever then.

Instead, I turn and let her finish the cup as I walk out of the room.

*

A Parking Lot (Fascinating, did we run out of money in the budget for scene changes?)

Back in the car, just me and Detective Ikiaq. I'm sipping at a canteen of Patty's specially prepared blood stew, same as Ikiaq.

"The old Sweeneys messed up. Bad," I tell him between sips.

Ikiaq shrugs out of his thick down jacket, the one with the caribou patch. He wears a button-down and khakis with combat boots. I'm in my regular peacoat that's been with me pretty much since they became a fashion item around the 1800s. It should be in a museum. Hell, I should be too. But not yet. Not until we...

"Why are you still on this case, Lili?" Ikiaq turns to me. "I know I asked you this before, sort of. But amuse me."

"Why are you still a detective in this deadbeat town?"

"Fair enough." He licks at the edge of the canteen as a drop of scarlet dribbles down the side. "I said before it's because of the energy. The magical vibes that keep humans and monsters from absolutely killing each other any more than necessary. But honestly? It might be more about the peace. The quiet and anonymity. People mind their own business in their town, and when they can't, I mind their business for them." His eyes go back. When I look at him from the corner of my eyes, I see the darkened antlers scraping the car ceiling and the dark hair sprouting from a lengthened snout and razor-sharp maw. The cloven hooves tenderly balancing a canteen with the ease of years of practice playing at human. "It beats roaming the frozen wastes and stealing children, doesn't it? Nothing more than a bogeyman."

"You ever miss it?"

His grin shifts, and when I turn to look at him head-on, I only see the man with a soft smile and melting eyes, the crow's feet at the edges telling of shared laughter. I see sadness, too, sadness of times long gone. Moments lost. "Nuh-uh. You aren't going to turn this questioning on me, Siren. Answer the question. Why are you still in this town, still on this case?"

"The Sweeneys, the ghost, the ghoul. Sounds like a bad joke, huh? Even had a bar in it." I chuckle at it, the thought of all of us sitting round at the inn's bar before it got destroyed. "I was wandering the frozen wastes, too, but instead of ice on the outside, it was inside."

It's okay if you're feeling a bit, well, sick today. I understand episodes. I have them, myself. Get some rest, love.

Your story's coming along nicely. A real hero's tale.

Thanks, Lil. I'm sorry for being shitty to you early on...

It's good luck to kiss a Siren.

"They've tamed you," the detective says with a slight smile.

"Persuaded me of my better nature. No." I shake my head. "Persuaded me I had a better nature to begin with. Healing and..." Feeling awkward, I reach over and snag the rest of his canteen from his hand. "You finished with that?"

Baffled, he turns the key in the ignition, and we spin out of the parking lot. "Sure, we're finished. For now." I help him struggle with his seatbelt. "Gotta avoid those fines." He jokes. "But, Lili. Now that we know there might be a demon in Gamin, how do we go from here?"

"This thing killed those kids' parents. Do you think it's *we* anymore?"

We roll to a stop at the stoplight. The red lighting flares along our skin, illuminating the detective's dark eyes. "So, what, after all this you're going to cut us out of this? I'm the detective here, Lili. I can't have you playing Batman and going vigilante on this."

Even in times of crisis, the detective is fond of his nerd references.

"Would you really try and fight me, Ikiaq? Is that one battle you're going to win easy?" He bristles, drumming his fingers against the wheel, jaw tensing. "I want the kids to be safe, that's all. Jo's still frail, still turning from what was left of her human form. And I want her to have extra muscle if need be."

"Fine then, but you bring Alethea with you." The light turns green and he steps on the pedal, the engine groaning back to life. "And Byron, if you're so concerned about casualties. He can't die again, right?"

"Aw, detective, it's almost like you don't trust me."

"None of us trust each other," he replies. "It's how we survive."

Chapter Twenty-Six

Jo's Place (It could always be worse)

"Alethea, we need to—" I enter the house to see Patty lounging across the sofa with her crossbow aimed at Jo. The ghoul has her hands up and Alethea's watching it all, bemused, while Jason panics. "What the hell?"

"I need aspirin. Lots of it. And chocolate." Patty growls. "I don't want that vampire anywhere near me."

"*Gangshi.*" Jo fights an eye-roll. "I told you before. I go for souls, not blood."

"Then why were you licking your lips earlier?"

"They were *dry.*"

Byron floats in, and Erik's wielding a basket of chocolates and various aspirin brands. "We got your stuff, Patty."

"See?" Patty groans, ditching the shotgun to tear open an aspirin packet with her teeth. "Was that so hard?"

"Chocolate." The detective gapes at the scene. "You nearly shot Jo because of that?"

"Endometriosis pain, actually," Patty replies, dry as can be and twice as irritated. "Take a bunch of knives and stab them all along your back, stomach, and even parts of your ribs. That's the pain we're talking here." She prods along her stomach. "It's when there are growths outside your uterus. It gets worse during my period—" and here she grins cheekily. "Even necromancers aren't exempt. Sorry for nearly shooting you, Jo."

Jo shrugs, dropping a knife she had behind her back. "I would've done the same."

I fight the anxiety growing within me, making me sick, by taking a deep breath and exhaling. I make a beeline for Alethea. She smirks, all self-satisfied as she takes in my desperation. "Hello, hello. Look who came back. Lili!"

"Your earlier offer, I'm taking it." I don't know if that's astonishment or self-congratulations I'm reading in her face. I don't care. "You were right, okay? Some kind of demon has been summoned in Gamin. If you know anything of it..."

Alethea nods, waggling a set of keys in front of her. "Then let's go."

"Whoa." I grip her forearm which, I note, is very muscular. "Not without Byron."

"A babysitter? I didn't realize we were going to get up to no good."

"We aren't," I reprimand, lips pursed thin. "It's a case."

"All right." She unleashes a low whistle, pushing her loose hair behind one ear. "Oy, Byron, right? Come along. We're taking a ride."

Patty pushes herself into a sitting position. Byron apologetically leaves Erik's side. "Where are you going?" Patty asks.

"Following a lead. We'll be back soon, don't worry." I nod to Patty, who's grimacing from the cramps. Her eyes are already drooping from the medicine. "Jason, take care of your sister. And Erik, I'm sorry, but you're wounded. Jo and Ikiaq can keep you all safe."

Jason looks up at me, kneeling dutifully at his sister's side. I'm proud of the little quarterback. He used to want nothing more than to have flings with girls in the back of bars. Now, he cares for his sister. He understands responsibility doesn't always equal heroics.

Not playing hero like you are, huh?

"Keep safe," Jason tells me.

"Of course." I nod at him as we head out of the door. "Always."

"You're a bad liar." Alethea tells me once we're near the van.

I glance back, thinking on the Sweeneys. Funnily enough, they aren't just stupid humans anymore to me. To me, they're something closer. Something, dare I say it, akin to family.

"Who said I was lying?" I reply, but Alethea has no answer.

*

A River that Never Ends. Nor Does It Begin

We're back at the river, with Gamin's usual, telltale fog enveloping the marshy ground. The sky's covered in clouds like ink, tendrils of red mud seeping into the icy riverbank. All along its edge, there's staticky crackling as the larger ice chunks break up. The river flows with newfound ferocity.

"*For men may come and men may go, but I go on forever*," Byron whispers, staring out at the gray expanse of rushing water.

"Frost?" I venture.

"Alfred, Lord Tennyson," Byron responds, still lost in the scene. "Frost is more along the lines of...if I had to perish twice, I think I know enough of hate that it would be...ice. Or, something like that."

"Byron, are you quite all right?" I lean closer to the poor ghost, still stuck staring at the drifting ice, the screaming water. "You know, ever since you came back from the Dead Realms, I've been worried. You don't scribble as much in that little book of yours."

"Ah, yes." Byron shakes his head, offering a weak smile. He pushes his glasses up the bridge of his nose. "I've been happier lately. With Erik. Sometimes, I forget about it all, about being dead. Then I think of that red crayon door and how everything just went on forever in the Dead Realms. And yet, nothing did."

Alethea is still trying to find the perfect hiding spot for the van, throwing dead branches and fallen leaves over it. "You never told me how you ended up in Gamin."

"You try being gay, Catholic, and a first-gen with parents from Oaxaca," Byron says with a sad smile. "I ran away from home. Took a break from college, reading to special education kids out in the sticks. I figured it would be fine enough work; I hung out with my little cousins all the time, one autistic and sweet as hell and the other deaf and would still kick your ass any day of the week. My parents had mental illnesses that went undiagnosed, and insisted I was just making shit up when I told them about mine. I didn't grow up in a place where everything was fine and dandy. But moving out here? I did it for all the wrong reasons, thought that helping others would help me be less angry and sad at the world. Then Anna Snow went missing, and I couldn't live with that. Here I am, feeling bad for myself, and they lost their beautiful little kid to some asshole on a power trip."

"So, you knew about Anna Snow before you even got involved with me."

"Of course, *bruja,*" he whispers, hovering close enough for me to sling my arm around him. He nuzzles closer even if he just goes through me. The closeness seems to soothe him. "I saw her every night in my living dreams."

"Just because others suffer, doesn't make your suffering any less, Byron." I watch as Alethea jogs toward us, really letting the cold of Byron's touch and the icy river spray soak in through my bones. "And you want in on a secret?"

"What?"

"One night, I met this little asshole of a ghost in my hotel room. He asked me for help, and I humored him. Did it for all the wrong reasons, thought that helping him would help me be less angry and sad at the world."

"Do you regret it?" he asks me.

"Never," I reply. "Because, in the end, I loved that little ectoplasmic shit. And I learned to love myself, or at least, I'm getting there."

Alethea claps her hands a couple of times, bouncing from foot to foot. "Hey, I don't know what you weirdos are talking about, but we have a demon to track!"

Byron and I exchange a look. I shrug. "All right, lead the way, huntress."

"You shrug a lot," Alethea tells me, matter of fact, as she walks down to the riverbank. We pass a copse of trees, all hanging suspiciously low to the earth.

"I have a lot of apathy inside me," I reply, watching as the punk huntress bends the branches back to reveal a cellar door.

How did we miss that giant trapdoor?

She taps her emerald eyes. "Perks of being a Seer," she replies. "Little help?"

I bend down to lug the cellar door open. Thanks to Patty's expert healing, my arm stays mostly attached. It's still sore, though, and my strength isn't what it once was. The cellar opens down into a maw of shadows. In one quick movement, Alethea has fallen back and slid herself into the darkness, disappearing as though it's thick as mud.

"After you," I tell Byron, who obliges, his eyes illuminating the cavern's soft glow. From what I can see of it, the space looks mostly nature-hewn, with only a few artificial touches to widen the structure out and flatten other ends.

I have to go further to see any more.

I dip down onto my back, sliding down past the door as though it's a chute. Mud seeps into my poor peacoat and cakes beneath my bootheels as I work my way down. I finally reach the bottom and take Alethea's hand as I get to my feet.

"You've got a worm in your hair," she teases, plucking out a dead leaf and shaking it in front of my face. "Just kidding."

I grimace, glad to have braided my hair back. I don't care much for worms. Remind me too much of bodies decomposing.

Byron twirls around, his eyes further illuminating the expanse.

"Care to tell me how you found this creepy crawlspace?" I ask, wiping mud from my jacket.

"Pleasure," Alethea replies, reaching for a light switch. A bunch of bulbs hanging from a single beam swing into action, spilling light onto the space. Wooden boards sink into the mud to keep most of our feet out from it. The dirt gives way to stone-cobbled walls, like in a well. "Clarence Bender used to work with the Münster Hünters crew until the late Sweeneys found out and killed him for it. This is his main office, so to speak."

"Why would a necromancer businessman work with monster hunters?" Byron's voice sinks with irritation, absolutely frazzled at the thought.

"Because immortals tend to be stodgier in their ways. Don't like change." I think of Anatol, complaining about young vampires. "Old humans are much the same. But Clarence was a forward thinker. He wanted humans to know that magic and monsters existed. No more hiding behind disguises or glamour. No more clandestine meetings in fairy circles or the dead of night. All in records, digital. Join the internet, not a cult." She nods to the racks of weaponry and shelves of rotting spell books near the edges of the cellar. "To do that, the competition had to be eliminated. Any monsters against the new ways had to die with the old."

"Bender was an insane, greedy murderer," I snarl.

"So are monsters," Alethea counters. "Like the one the late Sweeneys summoned to do away with Clarence Bender and his supporters." She holds up her hands as she goes to one of the doors. I stay at Byron's side. "No need to get mad at me. I have no quarrel with you. Bender did, and he's dead." She peeks her head out of the side room and steps over a silver-spiked chain that's blackened with garlic oil. "Come on, don't you want to see what he was working on? What Dakari and I found when checking out the Gamin Münster Hünters HQ?"

"And you didn't tell us earlier because?" Byron looks unnerved as he scans the room. I feel much the same to see all the monster-hunting metal torture devices lingering beside rotting spell books and full-length diagrams of lethal stab wounds for various fiends.

"Because I thought Dakari and I would be working alone. But Dax is gone, so now I have you two stooges. So, come on."

Her dirty-blonde hair disappears again as she reenters the side room. "You first this time," Byron tells me. I mumble a curse as thanks, slipping through the door to see the lights have already been turned on for this room.

This one has a friendlier layout as far as underground lairs go. There are sun lamps heated over a few chairs that were clearly dragged down here to be assembled. A few throw cushions and blankets pad the chairs, and a larger box serves as a makeshift bed tucked away beneath a desk with even more pillows. An open book presses into the pillows, the title in smeared cursive. "*Book of Beasts*," Alethea informs us, "stodgy thing written in Latin. I googled it before my final. Monster hunters are so scarce these days, they just put me through." She doesn't break eye contact with me as she continues. "I scored *brilliantly* on the athletics portion."

"His bedroom?" I kick the book over, unimpressed. "Quaint."

Alethea points to another wall, a corkboard that spans it in length, stuffed through with pins and lines of connecting red thread. "A murder-clue board. Just like on the shows," Byron mumbles, mildly impressed. I still try to maintain my stoic façade.

I walk closer, at an even pace, and peer at more diagrams. A paper peppered with question marks, asking for WEAK SPOTS? in desperate letters. A few more spells in Latin, a couple in older tongues.

"Is that Sumerian?" I squint at the glyphs scrawled across a different page.

Alethea smiles as she points to another diagram. "And here's one in Greek. And over here are various star charts pertaining to the summoning spell. And look at how absolutely metal this is." She nearly tears down a charcoal sketch of sharp eyes gazing out from a shadowy fog. A smiling mouth. Too beautiful and horrible. "Bender had visions of its coming for him before it did. Then it got him. Real bummer."

"That's all great, but how do we stop it from killing any more people?" Bender snaps us out of our fawning. Ashamed, I step back from the diagrams, no matter how much longer I could stare at that terrible beauty.

"Bender couldn't," Alethea replies, hands in her pockets. "That's what Dax and I were trying to figure out."

We all stare at the corkboard, the seeping cold and eerie quiet descending on us all.

Eventually, I break the silence, looking back at the makeshift box bed. "I can take that bestiary back with us. If it was near his bed, then he had fallen asleep reading it. Must have been awfully important to study it for so long." I look briefly around the room. "Alethea can take stuff down from the corkboard and..."

"I'll keep watch?" Byron offers.

"Yes," I reply, already reaching for the *Book of Beasts*, yearning to hear the pages sing. "And Byron will keep watch."

Chapter Twenty-Seven

Jo's Place (It gets worse)

We come back when the sun's gone down. Patty, on many pain meds, is fast asleep. Erik, also on a stunning amount of pain medication for his head, snuggles on the sleeper-chair across from her. Jason's picking at cinnamon oatmeal in the kitchen while Ikiaq microwaves savory duck.

"You know," Ikiaq mumbles, staring at the tiny, rotating glass dish until the microwave alarm beeps. "I'm getting really sick of this savory duck business."

I wave it away. "I understand whole-heartedly."

"Whole-heartedly? Was that a pun?"

Jason looks up. "Find anything neat on your outing?"

I hold up the *Book of Beasts* and Alethea dumps a bag full of papers on the countertop. Jason flips through it, his eyes disappearing into his noticeably longer hair. One of us should see to it he gets a decent haircut; he's starting to remind me of the 1960s. "Demonic rituals. Oh, Latin. It's never written in Mandarin, is it? What a shame."

I glance around the kitchen. "Is Jo asleep?"

"Why, miss her already?" Detective Ikiaq this time, and I can't help but notice the teasing in his voice.

I shake my head, blushing. It's miraculous, really. I wasn't aware I could properly blush until recently. "It's nothing like...I can't be..." I think back on how I hated any attempt at seduction, only going through the motions. Disinterested in sex, not even wanting to *hug* another person unless the other person felt like family to me, or I had to kill them.

"You could be gray ace or demisexual, you know," Jason informs me between bites of soggy oatmeal and cinnamon-flavored milk. "Not attracted to anyone until you have an emotional connection with them. I had an ex-girlfriend like that. Super sweet. We just weren't right for each other at the time is all."

"I...I..."

"You're welcome." Jason tells me, turning directly back to his oatmeal. "And, if you're wondering, Jo is in the bathroom closest to her room. She's been there for a while now." He casts me a knowing glance. "You should check on her."

I mumble my thanks as I exit the kitchen, suddenly feeling the space is too small for me.

Could I really have feelings for Jo? An emotional attachment?

No, I can't... She's a gangshi and I'm...

It couldn't be. I couldn't have.

"Jo?" I knock hesitantly on the door, pressing my ear against it. A slam as the toilet seat cover hits the porcelain. The slap of bare footsteps against tile, and all at once, the door wrenches open. I can only see a peek of Jo's eyes beneath her silver-blue wisps of hair, a shaggier version of the pixie cut I originally saw her with. Her gaze doesn't really focus on any one thing at once.

"No, you can't see me like this." She gasps, trying to wrench the door shut again.

"Jo, please, I'm sure you look fine. Why? Have you hurt yourself?"

"Go away!" The *gangshi* bares her fangs at me, her lips flaring up to rouge red, skin going paler as she shifts. I can see the letters on her forehead, the traditional paper talisman sealing spell. Just, instead of actual parchment, it's been inked into her skin.

A final present from Anatol. Undying life.

The door slams, nearly taking my fingers with it. I bang my fists against the door, and the wood creaks against my force.

"Jo, come on. You're a grown woman. You shouldn't be embarrassed about whatever happened." I lay my forehead against the door, waiting. "Please."

A beat. The clatter of glass spilling over into the sink. Running water and hands against skin. Another moment. More muttering.

"Don't laugh," Jo says, but her voice sounds...lighter this time. The traditional smoker's rasp is replaced by a voice that's smoother, almost unsure. She's wrapped her body in a robe, but what peeks through is firm flesh. Not ravaged by cancer or chemo or drugs. No needle points, just the ghost of old bruises and scars you can only see if you knew what she looked like originally.

Like I did.

She reaches a hand up, smoothed out from wrinkles with nails shaped into crescent moons, and pushes the silver-blue hair behind her ears and out of her face.

"Holy shit." I place one hand over my mouth, not trusting my own body to react. "You look hardly older than the Sweeneys.... You're what? Somewhere in your twenties?"

I take her head between my hands, staring into her face. The sharp eyes still hold all the years of pain within them, but they're set in a face that would, otherwise, be described as "dewy" and "carefree." Her lips turn pale again when her *gangshi* form calms. Her canines are still sharp even when retracted, peeking over her lower lip.

She stays for another moment in my grip before pulling away. "Yeah, I know I look like some kid," she mumbles, wrapping her arms around herself. "I took too many of the anti-aging potions. Just a little sip, and your wounds heal. But I'd gotten a few scrapes from the zombie scum, and they weren't healing quick enough..." She looks down at herself, slumping over. "But this, this is ridiculous. Any younger and I'd be drinking whiskey out of a goddamn sippy cup." She sniffs, rubbing her hand beneath her nose. "I dumped the rest of that shit down the toilet. Magic's not all cookies and gumdrop fairies, huh?"

"It's a hell of a facelift."

"Lili." She stares me down, all the intensity of the liquor-and-pill-swilling-and-gunshot-toting firecracker I knew before. Just with somewhat oily skin, her silver-blue-hair still intact, and pointier fangs. "I look like a joke now. A couple years is fine, but this? I could star in one of those goddamn sparkly vampire movies that Anatol hated so much."

I cross my arms, smirking at her. "Come on, look in the mirror."

"Why?"

"Just do it."

She goes over to the mirror and I join at her side, clasping her shoulders. I note, somewhat uncomfortably, that the robe's slipped down a bit and her shoulders are bare. I fix the robe for her, my fingertips receiving a little shock as they brush the nape of her neck. "What do you see?"

"A couple of kids."

"But *who* do you see?"

"Lili and me, Jo."

"That's right." I grin and she grins, too, peeling her lips back into a fanged smile. "Lili and motherfucking Jo Kim. An immortal and a reanimated *gangshi,* ready to take names and kick ass."

"I guess it's got its perks," she says, a slight tilt to her head.

"Why's that?"

She leans back suddenly, and my arms fall over her as she repositions herself. I end up holding her in a half embrace. Her eyes meet mine in the mirror, her silver-blue hair caught up beneath my chin. "Because now I feel like we'll get less judgment when I do this." She stands on tiptoe and whirls around with her lips inches from mine. "Lili, may I kiss you?"

"I...um...I..."

She waits, staring at me with such sincerity there's a twinge inside my chest. Anxiousness, a deep sense of unease as her attention zeroes in on me. *Gods, I hate this.* "Yes?" She waits, ever so damnably patient.

She's so patient.

I can't believe I'm doing this.

I hold a moment, shakily continuing. "Wait. I wanted to...if we're going to. If we're going to *continue* this, there are boundaries that I think I need to set. Especially when it comes to what counts as intimacy for both of us."

Jo considers this for a second before nodding, a large smile making her the most wonderfully warm and kind being I've ever seen. *In all my years of existing, I never knew people like her existed. What is this, happiness?*

Jo waits, not moving any closer than necessary. "Okay, what about kissing then? Do you mind if I kiss you?"

I think on it, on all the other times I was compelled to kiss her. Initially, she was a stranger to me, and I had no compulsion to kiss her. But now, knowing her and being known by her, feeling such a deep emotional connection, makes it all so wonderfully inexplicably new to me. "I would like a kiss. But I *am* older than you, you know."

"Shut up, you old hag."

She kisses me then, pulling me close. I don't draw away.

"So..." She pauses. "Do I kiss best in all your thousands of years' experience?"

I shrug at that. "I'd still prefer drinking the blood of my enemies to making out." She shoves at me playfully. "But still. I'm just happy being with you." A pause. "Jo. You should know that I'm..."

"Demisexual?" Her face, that beautiful face, remains unchanged. Doesn't shift to incredulity or boredom. Just understanding. Beautiful understanding and acceptance. "I know. I won't press you into anything you don't want. I love *you,* Lili. All of you and all of how you think and live and breathe. Demisexual just means loving differently, and there's nothing wrong with that. It's your everything I love. Not bits and pieces."

"My everything?"

She nuzzles her forehead beneath my chin. "Yes, your everything. Silly Siren."

Chapter Twenty-Eight

Awkward

Patty's eyes widen as she catches us kissing. Then her freckled face erupts into mad-happy beaming. "Oh, um, sorry," she says.

She's not.

"Uh, thanks." Jo breaks apart first, stepping back and fiddling with the knot at her robe's waist. "We should get some sleep."

"Yes. Separate rooms," I emphasize, seeing Patty's sheer glee. "I have a case to work on."

"Mhm, and nosy witches to babysit." Jo offers severe side-eye to Patty, who has her hands wrung together to avoid bursting into applause.

"Babysit? Hey, you're my age now," Patty says, her eyes raking over the empty anti-aging spell vials. Then, on seeing Jo's obvious discomfort, changes the subject with, "I have to pee." She shoos us out of the room, casting a knowing wink before shutting the door on us.

"Well, the secret's out," Jo tells me, scanning my face with her eyes, like a starless night.

I kiss her forehead. "So?" Both of us beaming, happy as can be now, I head back to my room, sliding the *Book of Beasts* out from under my peacoat. "Big day tomorrow. Demons to summon. Monster criminals to catch."

Jo leans against the wall, arms crossed, hair fresh with the scent of shampoo and lavender. "You do that, killer. I'll keep an eye on Borden and the Sweeneys. Detective Hotshot too," she teases, turning around to slam the door to her room. But the look in her eyes, the intensity of a woman who's lived a lifetime, all caught up in a body that has aged none the wiser.

I feel the intense urge to drop the book and join her, to hold her in my arms and never let go. But that's stupid. I'm not a guard dog, and Jo can take good care of herself.

But it doesn't let the irrational fear go. *I can't protect them all.*

I never could.

*

Opening the Book of Beasts

I lie on my belly, splayed across the floor. It's easier to think when you avoid beds and chairs. Comfort never properly suited me. I prefer being closer to the earth, to feel its steady hum beneath me. Feels realer that way. Something close to being alive.

Not that I ever knew what that was like.

I crack open the cover, biting back my squeamishness as a worm sits, squirming pathetically between the front cover and the first few, damp pages. I chuck the poor thing out of a hole in the window screen and go back to the book. It's bound in leather, with a set of velvet ribbons marking certain spots. Little pinpricks of ink, too blotted to read, serve as notes in Clarence Bender's long-dead hand. The pages feel thicker, not the wisps of parchment like current paper's made from. These pages are stretched and bent out of shape from something that was once living. Skin. The book is written on skin.

I ignore the sensation, like maggots crawling on my skin, as I thumb through more pages. The bookmarked ones are all related to some demon that feasts on the various organs of their victims. Another page and a diagram of figures cloaked in black hoods, eyes glowing and skeletal figures clutching candles in their grasps. Jars containing human organs and decapitated animal heads on the ground around it. Another diagram and I see an hourglass, brimming near to the top with dripping, red-soaked sand.

This feels too much. Like an imitation meant to inscribe fear.

Uncomfortable with the too detailed and over-the-top diagrams, I try to quell my biases.

The person who wrote this book didn't know what immortals and reanimated are really like. These images are by the hand of someone who saw the darkness, but never knew what it really was.

This is a parody, pure and simple. Drawn up by necromancers who only saw twisted freaks, labeling our kind monsters without knowing the half of it.

I turn another page, wondering if this is how Beatrice and Todd Sweeney saw us. Wondering if, perhaps, they saw us in a different light. Something worth saving from humanity's wrath. Toward the back of the book, there are a couple of pages that look halfway torn out. A sheet of blood on the spot. The half-torn page appears to have bit back.

A hex?

When I turn the page, the script has changed. The paper's given way to modern typeface and regular, reedy thinness. A photograph of the authors, grinning at us. Beatrice and Todd Sweeney, Eye Coven Corporation. Data logs transcribed by Clarence Bender. NOTE: CLASSIFIED. NEVER TO LEAVE THIS BUILDING.

The pages fall out of the book. A protection hex? They've avoided the damp and the blood. Were they inserted in this book to be hidden?

Stolen?

LOG—1985.

We've consulted with a tarot reader on the side of the road. Beatrice thought they were the usual quack, but Todd paid her an exorbitant sum to get a reading. Said it was for charity. She said she sees eyes wrapped in shadow. A future battle. Fire and blood.

I charged her a fee for practicing magic without a license.

I skip ahead a few pages, seeing most of the notes are on the exact fees for licensing and how many days each license is good for.

LOG—1991.

We pooled together our resources and bought a building. The Eye Coven has a real logo now and everything.

I sense great things.

LOG—1999.

Beatrice is pregnant with her first child.

Todd is losing sight of PROJECT EIGHT.

I pause. Project Eight?

I turn back a few pages, landing on a few pasted images of various summoning circle set-ups. Each has a red X slashed through it.

PROJECT FIVE—failure.

PROJECT SIX—improvement, but participant suffered aneurysm...

PROJECT SEVEN—disagreement. Todd and Beatrice suggest the test subjects need rest. I say we get more before fear immobilizes them.

PROJECT EIGHT—abandoned.

No, that seems too fast. Whatever this PROJECT EIGHT is, it wasn't abandoned.

Unless...Clarence Bender didn't get the whole story.

Another page falls from the book, this one in storybook style. It has a large illustration of a figure with wings, like an angel. But the angel is drifting past the stars and planets. Falling.

It holds something in its hands, cradling a belly that's swollen.

It's pregnant.

Story by Beatrice Sweeney. Illustrations by Todd Sweeney.

Excerpt from A Storybook for Magically Inclined Children.

Long ago on this land there was a battle. On one side, a mother pregnant with child.

On the other there were men ready to tear her apart.

The woman died and from her womb all this was born. The men turned into monsters and spread their seed across the earth: these monsters were called humans.

The men who repented became the Chosen. But still the mother loves her children. Ugly as they are, they are hers. So, her children come back to her. From the human men came violence. From the mother, life.

A riddle as old as time. In the end, which was the greater gift?

Feeling that I've read enough for today, I slam the book shut and place the strange hodgepodge of Clarence Bender's maddening notes and stolen documents on my bedside table. I lay my head back, focusing on healing as much as I can.

As an immortal, you don't sleep. Sleep becomes a routine of resting within the darkness. We enter the dark space between waking and dreams, the space no mortals can enter without cursed magic. We roam a plane of endless wandering, the space where the horizon stretches for infinity. These are our Dead Realms. The curse to walk on and on forever until what counts as our bodies return to the dust that bore us. Never allowed to rest. Never allowed to die unless we are destroyed until the point that we fall into this plane for good.

As I wander, I imagine the pregnant woman, falling from the sky. Spilling forth monsters of all sizes and creations, watching as men cut them down because they fear her power.

I wander as I dwell on this. The power of monstrous creation. It is then I recognize that the number eight, when turned on its side, becomes ∞, the lemniscate. A mathematical concept representing the eternal reaches of infinity.

I wonder if it is planned that Project Eight looks that way.

Or maybe, like the birth of monsters, it was a happy accident.

Chapter Twenty-Nine

I Think I Heard Something

I wander downstairs at four in the morning before anybody else is up. Or so I think. Alethea's in the kitchen, polishing her sword with salt.

"Is that good for the metal?" I ask her.

She shrugs. "Burn the villages and salt the fields. It's an old monster-hunting superstition." She lifts the sword and straps it to her back, settling in. "If you're meant to wield the blade, it won't quit on you until you die."

"Sounds like hocus to me."

She raises a thin brow, tugging her sleeves back. A serpent winds around one of her arms, the tattoo bleeding ink like night. "So is our whole world." She jangles her usual set of skeleton keys, waving them in front of me like I'm a dog. "Well, since we're both up early, how would you like to take a ride?"

"What, no monologue? No, we're one and the same, you and I. Lone wolves, ready to take the open road in our grasp." I reach past her into the fridge and scoop up fistfuls of raw meat.

She wrinkles her nose at that. "Do you ever have to shit that back out?"

I wipe my mouth, annoyed. "We can do anything we set our minds to."

Alethea fiddles with her earlobe piercing, a chain of interconnected safety pins dangling so low it nearly brushes her collarbone. "I get vibes that you don't like me much."

"I don't."

"Why?"

"Sometimes, us monsters get irrational like that. Same with people."

She points to the road outside, trailing off in the distance. "Doesn't mean you can't take a ride. Admit it, your skin's itching to get out of here."

I don't know how she knows that. Maybe it's the way I walk, like I can outpace the murders if I go fast enough. Maybe it's the edge in my voice, like a tamed wolf that's been caged too long. Like I'll bite my master's hand that feeds me at any moment. Make their hand become my food. Turn feral. Mad.

"You drive," she tells me. "If you hate me so much."

I watch the keys; see how they catch the light. The bone and the metal.

"Whose bone is it?"

She smiles. "Dead monsters."

I suppress a shudder. I've met worse than the unnerving Alethea Styx. At the end of the day, she's just a punk. She knows nothing.

I take the keys and head for the door. Still with that infuriating smile, Alethea trails after me. She smells like too much fake leather holding in too much rage.

A human smell. Compensating.

*

Highway to Hell

"Why do you chase after me?" I place my hands on the wheel, feel the engine thrumming beneath me. When I press the gas, the van spins forward, nearly crashing into a tree.

Dammit, haven't driven since the Model T. Stole some cars since then, but speed chases don't really count as civilian driving.

I ease back into it, steadying my breathing, letting the car tread along the road instead of fighting it. "I said before, I like pretty things. And I like you," Alethea replies, opening the window all the way and sticking her head out of it to feel the scant wind against her face.

"Sexually?" I venture.

She laughs at that. "Of course, I have a type. And darling, you fill it out nicely." I bristle at that, the way she casually lays claim to me. Anyone else would probably melt, but as I said before, I don't much like Alethea Styx. "But I see the way you look at that shotgun-toting badass, Jo Kim. I don't move in on people who don't want me. Doesn't seem fun, does it?" She sighs, nudging her head further out as I turn onto the main highway. It's empty, save for a few lost truckers and bleary-eyed travelers. I start driving, nowhere in particular to go. "But I like the Sweeneys. Especially that Patty. Fire, that one."

"Don't talk about her like that," I growl.

She laughs. "Oh, come on. I told you before, I only want people who want me. And she wants me. Admit it." Her laugh sounds youthful and vibrant. Even aggressive—if a laugh can be aggressive. "I'm her type, yeah?" She kicks her feet up on the dash, combat boots shining. She must have wiped those down alongside her sword.

Strutting like a peacock. "Besides, you're not her protector. Or are you?"

She takes my silence in. I see her staring at me in the mirror, her eyes studying my face. She deflates, taking her feet off the dash, wringing her hands together. "I'm not all bad, you know. This persona"—here, she waves at herself—"I put this on because, otherwise, I'd get hurt. You saw how Dax was, put everything out there for love. And what happened when his love died? Part of him did too. If you never love, you never settle. If you never settle, then you have nothing to lose."

And nothing to continue existing for.

But I don't say it. The nosy Seer sees far too much already. She doesn't have to know about my mental state or history.

We keep on driving. Alethea cranks on some college station alt-rock, headbanging until she's sweaty. She drums her hands along the dash with abandon, overtaken like she's been possessed by a rock god. She croons tune after tune, with a voice that's not perfect, but it's not bad either. We settle into this rhythm until I pull over at the side of the road.

Gamin's sign blinks down at us. The population number's crooked, probably because it's been updated far too much as of late.

Alethea steps out of the car and leans against the hood. I join her, pocketing the keys in one smooth movement.

"Vape?" She hands me an e-cigarette, blowing out cotton candy scented plumes.

"That's bad for you," I tell her.

"So is monster hunting," she counters.

"You're aggressive," I mutter.

"Is that what you don't like about me?" She twists around to face me, staring at me to the point I have to turn away. "Or do I make you uncomfortable because I can *see* you?"

"That has nothing to do with it."

"It has *everything* to do with it." She puts the e-cigarette away and waves her hands in front of my face. "Earth to Lili, your cover's blown, and you're scared I'm going to tell everyone."

I shake my head. "No, it's not. They're...they're my friends." My voice sounds pathetic, even to my own ears.

She can't be threatening to take them away from me. To take it all away from me.

"You're throwing away a gift here, Lili. I see the power inside you. You're dampening it down, so you don't scare them. Hell, I could lop off your head right now and sell it for millions in the monster-hunting underground." My talons extend, ready for a fight. "But I won't," she continues. "I see you. I see who you've been, what you are, and what you can be."

"That's why I hate Seers."

"Stop it, Lili. I'm not going to betray your secret. I want to help you keep it." She takes my head between her hands. Everything within me recoils. "As long as you promise to free yourself."

"Why would a monster hunter want that?"

"Because I like you, Lili. And I can see how it's killing you, huddling within this G-rated form. All cuddly and cute with those human kids and that deer detective. My mother..." She pauses, biting her lower lip. "My mother gave me this power, the ability to See. We hid in a town just like this one. She started to hate it, the Seeing. So, she took drugs to hide it. I left her behind in rehab soon as I turned eighteen."

"I'm sorry. But it's not the same. I'm hiding to protect—"

"To protect everyone? Funny, that's what my mother said every time she snorted. Or smoked. Or pressed the plunger." She laughs, rubbing her knuckles against her forehead. Little swords in various positions are tattooed on her knuckles, pointing north, south, east, and west. Even getting the places in between. "Promise me you'll stop hiding, Lili. Power makes people scared, but they shouldn't be. You can control it, Lili. You just have to embrace it. Stop making yourself small. Make yourself big." She holds her hands out to the Gamin sign, stretching her arms out as the sun rises over the letters, darkening them in shadow. "Make yourself so fucking big that the world sees you as who you should be."

She's crazy, but she does have a point. Perhaps I shouldn't lie to everyone. Perhaps I should figure out a way to stop playing pretend.

"I'll try," I tell her.

She nods. "Good." Alethea reaches for the driver's side and opens the door for me. I slide in, ready to take the wheel and turn back toward home. "That's what I wanted to hear."

*

Jo's

I fumble with the keys before we reach the door. Jo made copies for everyone, even Alethea. The detective wanted to make sure we all had a safe house.

Even if it's not much safe with this punk psycho around.

I end up dropping the house key, groaning as I bend over to pick it up. But Alethea's ahead of me, reaching down to press the key into my palm, brushing my hand with her fingers as she does.

"Careful," she tells me.

But I'm already gone.

*

Hell

Memories. Chasing down the girl in the woods. Unable to see anything but flesh, bones, and a beating heart.

Children of men.

I reach for her back. She screams, kicking out. Wailing.

Anna Snow?

Pathetic.

I scoop out her flesh, reaching for the heart I can pop between my giant claws like a cherry. I lick my lips.

"Bon appétit," I growl.

The girl does not respond. How can she? She's gone for good.

*

Help

"Lili, you okay there?"

"I'm fine." I take the keys, the wave of vertigo washing over me. Roiling my belly. Making my head spin with nervous anxiety. Blackness clouds in over my vision.

I make it to the couch before I sink into myself. I cuddle in on the sofa, my hands clamped over my ears, willing my hands to wring out my horrid memories.

"Lili?" It's Patty's cool hand, pressing against my forehead. I remember the girl in the woods. Fighting against me, the feeble, tiny thing.

"Leave me alone," I growl.

Only then do I allow myself to secede to something like sleep.

The wandering planes calm me. Calm me enough to think.

Dear gods, what have I done?

Chapter Thirty

Around a Kitchen Table

"And that's why I think—" Alethea dips her veggie burger into a liberal amount of ketchup before cramming it, with a heap of sweet potato fries, into her mouth. "That's why I think the demon causing the deaths died beneath the rubble of the coven building."

Patty reaches over for some lentils. The humans have banded together to go vegetarian, saving the meat for the rest of us monsters. Jo just sips at her glass, winking at me as she reaches for my free hand beneath the table. I still don't know what Jo eats. I should ask her about it someday.

"But that doesn't make sense." Jason this time, fingers steepled. "We would've seen it in the building somewhere. Only parts of it collapsed. And we already have builders fixing those parts up. They should've come across some massive, hulking demon carcass by now."

"Well, think about it," Alethea mumbles, working around another helping of fries. "There haven't been any more murders since the zombie hordes, right? Whatever your parents summoned"—Jason bristles at the accusatory insinuation—"it must be gone. Dead. Buried."

"Lili?" Patty turns to me. I can hardly look at her, not remembering what I've remembered. "What do you think?"

A flood of images. The sheer joy as I tore into that puny human girl, plucking out her heart. And that's only one murder I can remember.

Stop hiding it.

Control it. Protect them.

I turn to Ikiaq, who's hardly touched his pile of raw meat. Strange, he always eats as much as a bro trying to bulk up at the gym. I remember what he said the last time we met for investigation reasons in the kitchen. *I can't say I haven't thought about the possibility that you're the one behind this.*

And how would that look? Me telling him to lay off the investigation, that I had it handled. It would look like I was purposefully trying to cover it up, wouldn't it? That I changed teams for good? I mean. I didn't *know* the girl I saw in that memory was Anna Snow, did I? I mean, sure I tore out her heart and had great pleasure doing it. But it could've been years ago.

I can't have been the murderer. Can I?

"I think we'll keep looking, but for now, I'm glad there aren't any more killings." I turn to the detective as I say this. "I want Gamin safe. For all of you."

The detective huffs, turning back to his plate. He starts to eat, chewing slowly, still glancing up from time to time at me. "What did you read in that Beast Book?" he asks me, not turning away from his plate.

"Fairy tales. Stuff about summoning demons. Project Eight, it was called. The summoning spell that brought whatever's causing the murders to Gamin." I eat my own food, noticing how much it tastes like dust. "We'll catch them or kill them, detective. Don't worry."

"Bag them and tag them, right?" Ikiaq chuckles at that. "How convenient that you're on the front lines."

"Enough. This is my house and you're all acting like pigs." Jo this time, pouring herself a glass of ice water. She downs it, silver-blue hair whipping back as she tilts her chair to glare at us all. "Lili says she has it under control, then she has it under control."

"You've got it, Lili," Erik says, smiling. "And then it'll be safe for my dad to come home too."

"Yeah." I look at Byron, who's smiling at Erik. But mostly, he stares off into space. I remember what he said, staring off at the freezing river. I wonder if he's thinking about the Dead Realms, how much he'd like to be back with them. Erik's sweet smile hurts me more than anything. "We'll bring him home." The lie tastes even worse than the meat.

"So." Patty winks at Alethea, who beams right back. "Alethea, tell us about your adventures." She leans in closer, laughter caught up in those eyes of hers. "And while we're on the subject, are you single?"

Half groans and half laughter erupt from the table. Alethea hams it up, tapping Patty on the nose so that her freckled face lights up, red as the deepest of strong Bordeaux wine. "Oh, Patty. You lady-killer you."

Feeling sick, I push back from the table. "Sorry. I have some studying to do."

"Nerd," Jason jokes. More laughter. Jo gets up in response.

"No, please, enjoy yourself. I'm just drained is all."

The detective's eyes never leave me as I exit to my room. The rest settle into a comfortable enough pattern. Except for Jo.

Jo's eyes are pierced with worry.

*

My Room

"I knew you weren't studying shit." Jo bumps the door open with her hip, clutching two glasses. One is red, the other clear as glass. "I brought drinks."

"I don't think now's the time..."

Jo closes the door behind her, eyes sparkling dangerously. "Don't worry. I know I'm underage now, so I made the cocktails virgin." She laughs at the confusion in my face. "Bloody Mary made with real blood and ginger ale with a squeeze of lime."

"Thank you," I sigh and drink the spiced beverage, the blood trickling down my throat. "You have a gift."

"You do too." She laughs, sinking into the covers beside me. "For finding trouble."

If only you knew.

"I get you probably don't want to talk that much about the investigation. I get it. You struck me as the quiet type. Not really interjecting all that much. You never wanted to play hero. I'm much the same way. A whole lot of hurt but not much sense."

"How can you call yourself that? You're a hero to me."

"Am I? Or are you just blindsided by what you feel?" She quirks an eyebrow at me, sighing when I remain silent. "I'm sorry. I'm tired is all. Of keeping a secret..." My senses rise, on high alert. My skin tingling, antiseptic stinging.

"You can trust me."

Can you, really?

"All right." Her tongue darts out, licking nervously along her lower lip. She pushes her silver hair back, the obsidian studs pinching against her ear. Her face looks so different when you ignore her eyes. The incorruptibility. "You asked me, a while ago, how I manage to feed off souls as a *gangshi.*" I reach out and rub slow circles along her shoulder, trying to comfort her. She leans into my touch. "Well, you know how I died, right?"

I think back to the dusty wheelchair stuffed in the closet. The piled-up IV drips and oxygen tanks. The endless doctor receipts and notices.

She peels up her shirt, showcasing her soft belly. "You can still kind of see the scars, despite the de-aging." She points along a paler thread of skin, like moonlight cutting through the gold. "My little lumps. I'd almost grown fond of them. Drew sketches of them at the hospital. With big, grinning faces to make me less afraid." She swallows, a black tear trickling down her cheek.

I wipe it away. "That's over."

"It isn't." She shakes her head, gripping my sheets so tightly that I fear she'll pierce through the fabric with her nails. "Because I went back there, to the hospice they put me and all the other cancer-hopeless."

I can already sense where this is going. The dread builds up inside me. "You swallowed their souls."

"Don't say it like that, like I'm..." She turns away. "Like I'm some monster."

"Hey now. *Hey.*" I pinch her chin, tilting her face up to look at me. I stare at her eyes, feeling like she's reverted to a child. Terrified. But those eyes, they tell me otherwise. She's lived too much. Too much hurt, still pent up within her. "You're the bravest person I know."

"They tell you that a lot. When you're dying. Stay strong. Stay brave." She fights to hang her head down low, but I want her to look at me. To face the world. To face her fears. She senses that, she stays strong, her neck stretching up. Her eyes burning into mine. "I only took the ones who asked me to." She pauses, pushing back her violet-tinged bangs to showcase the scroll tattoo. Her *gangshi* form peeks through slightly. The perfect, porcelain skin. The red lips. Brightly dark eyes. The smiling mouth, like a prayer. "They thought I was their deliverer."

"Where do they go when you take them?"

At that, she hugs her arms around herself. In turn, I hug my arms around her. "When I take someone, I absorb parts of them. Those parts keep living inside me, but the other halves. The husks, I call them. What really makes them people..." She takes out a tiny leaf, one side coated a healthy green, the other run through with blood-red veins. "I whisper their names to Tae, the mandrake tree. He carries them to the Dead Realms, or so he says."

These words are true. This much I know.

"I'm not a bad person," she whispers, trembling.

"No," I tell her, wrapping her in my arms, keeping her close. And then, so soft that only I can hear it, I confess. "I am."

Chapter Thirty-One

I Definitely Heard Something

A clatter. Something slams into the wall. Glass crashes against the floor.

"Jo?" I hear her voice, screaming through the corridors. I slam the door open, sliding down the halls. "Jo!"

Jo screams, "You traitor!" I narrowly avoid getting a glass thrown at me.

The cup splinters at the wall beside me, leading to the open kitchen. Alethea holds her sword in front of her like a shield. At the other end, there's Jo. In the crook of her elbow is Tae's tree, noticeably diminished and plucked bare. She keeps picking up glasses to chuck at Alethea's head. The monster hunter keeps cutting the missiles down in single strokes, but Jo doesn't care.

She's fury incarnate.

"Whoa, hold on." I press my hands into the empty air. Alethea and Jo swivel toward me in the dim light. Patty, Erik, and Byron trickle out of their rooms. The detective is trying to soothe Jo on her end, and Jason tries, unsuccessfully, to wrestle the sword from Alethea's grip. "What's this about?"

Alethea pushes the sword into Jason's hands, nearly knocking the poor boy onto his ass from the impact. "She started throwing."

"Yeah," Jo snarls, holding Tae's tree aloft, "because I found you with a pair of clippers beside Tae."

"A mandrake has intensive anesthetic properties and can act as a narcotic for dangerous creatures. You shouldn't be hiding it away when we could use it," Alethea counters, nonplussed.

"Jo, it's just a tree..." Ikiaq soothes.

"It's *just* a tree?" Jo swivels to me. After what she told me earlier, I know how much more this means to her than that. "Lili, tell them."

I turn around to stare Alethea down. A moment later, and I hold my hand out. "You shouldn't wield a sword in the house. Give me all your weapons," I say. "You won't stay in here with them on. You'll get them back in the morning."

"I'd rather sleep outside," Alethea tells me, arms crossed.

"Then do that!" Jo lunges, but Ikiaq plucks her easily off her feet. The *gangshi* bares her fangs but, unwilling to strike a friend, she quiets.

Alethea shrugs, picking up her sword and tugging her jacket further round herself. "Gladly." Whistling softly, she slams the door behind her. Jo slumps to the ground again, and Ikiaq runs one large hand across his stubble, thinking.

"Show's over, folks. Get some sleep." Ikiaq glares at me with a look that tells me somehow, this is all my fault. I don't much blame him. I don't trust myself either. "Jo, take your plant back to your room."

"It's not over for good, detective," Jo spits back, hugging her arms around Tae. She presses the tree into my hands. "Guard this with your life," she informs me.

I press my lips to her forehead. She calms beneath my touch, still angry, but somewhat soothed. "I will," I promise. "Do you want me to stay with you?" A murmur, a question.

Jo shakes her head. "I'm too angry. Not like this." She presses my hair behind my ears, the dark locks curling around her thumb. "Another night."

With that, we all filter back to our rooms. The kitchen, quiet again, aches around me. I hold Tae's tree tight. When I go to bed, the tree sleeps beside me. I shove Bender's cursed book into one of the drawers, letting Tae's tree take up all the room on the tabletop.

"Goodnight, Tae," I tell the tree. "Guide them well," I mumble, imagining I see the tree glow with a bluish light as I close my eyes to drift into oblivion.

Chapter Thirty-Two

Insert Fight Sequence Here

I enter the kitchen to see the shattered glass from last night's been swept up. Patty's sipping hot cocoa with Ikiaq, both of their cups sporting tons of whipped cream. Jason's picking at burnt scrambled eggs and Alethea's sipping from a giant mug of coffee with honey. Erik's tossing pieces of buttery waffle to Byron who catches them in midair in his mouth before they drop to the floor.

No magical hunter swords in sight.

"Nice, dude," Erik mumbles as Byron hovers into a sort of backflip to catch the last piece. "Morning, Lili." He does a little wave as he plucks the waffle crumbs off the ground.

I look around. "Has anyone seen Jo?"

Erik shakes his head. "Nah. Not in the bathroom." He grins, running one hand against his head. "Which probably explains why I got to take my sweet time this morning in the shower." He shudders a bit. "She intimidates me."

I grin. "Yeah? She intimidates me too."

Erik swivels around on a spinning chair while Byron perches on the countertop. "Did you check her room?" He tilts his head to the side. I can see that Byron's sitting on some sort of half-built gadget board, the open wires fizzling. A glimmering gem sits at the center. A touch of magic fueling a tech wonderland.

"I will."

Catching me staring at his invention, Erik holds it up with a grin. "It's a circuit board for a monster tracker. Like what Alethea does, but more tech and less inherent ability type thing. See?" He reaches for one of the wires extending from the gem and presses it against a set of metallic arrows propped on top of a rigged watch-face. The arrow spins for a bit before landing on me. "Got you."

He takes away the wires and the arrows return to their original position. "Clever," I tell him. "Really clever." Erik positively glows with the compliment.

"Then take this one, it's all finished." He hands me a watch that fits more like an armband. I slide it up beneath my peacoat, tucking it safely away from prying eyes. "Cool, right? Magic for when you're on the go."

"Isn't he great?" Byron drifts down to press his ghostly lips to Erik's cheek. "He's my absolutely wonderful genius."

Erik's face heats up, and he presses his thumb to the spot where Byron was. "Aw, stop."

Absolutely warmed by their relationship, I head back to the hall. I knock on Jo's door, waiting for her to get up. "Let's go, sleepyhead," I murmur. But there's no answer. Cautiously, I turn the knob. No resistance. The door creaks open.

"Jo?"

Her bed is still neatly made, save for a slight indentation where she sat down. There's a breeze, a chilly draft from an open space somewhere. I move quickly to check her window, feeling the latch give. The screen's been torn through. I look closer at the windowsill, see jagged claw marks where Jo's fingernails must've clawed at it.

She'd been dragged out.

*

Witch Hunt

"Go on." I shove Alethea into the room. The rest gather behind me, peering curiously into the space. "Use your tracking skills, monster hunter. Find out what took her."

Alethea nearly falls onto her knees. I wrestle the sword from her hand before she can wield it. Ikiaq presses a warning hand to my bicep and tugs me back with Alethea's sword in my grip. "Calm down, Lili. I know you two fought it out yesterday, but that's not how you get people to help you."

I turn on him, snarling until I feel the words scratch their way out of my throat. "Good cop, bad cop. But I'm always the bad cop, right? Unhinged?" I press a finger into the detective's chest, poking and prodding and wanting *something* to happen. Wanting to get hit. Wanting to have a reason, to be justified in being so angry.

A reason other than being blindsided by grief and worry.

"Lili..." Patty this time, hugging her soft arms around me. I relent, slumping over in her grip. "We'll find her."

I watch, helpless, as Alethea brushes herself off. "You're welcome." She snorts, stretching her arms overhead like she can touch the sky. "Now, let's see what we got here." She runs a finger along the windowsill, rubbing her thumb against her index. "Interesting. No dust. That's surprising. For an old woman."

I bristle, but Patty holds me tighter.

"Excuse me." Alethea takes out the window screen and shoves the glass window upward until it digs into the sill. She claws out of the hole and drops down into the dirt. The rest of us take the long way outside, watching as Alethea bends to her knees in the mud. She claws her fingers into the soil, checking out the footprints. The slash marks against the ground.

Alethea's smirk dies down into lips pursed thin. Brow furrowed. She gazes off. "A struggle. Then the struggle calms as the *gangshi*, for some reason, loses the ability to fight." I sink at those words. "The mud leaves off once the creature drags her to the cement, the main road."

"What took her?" Ikiaq this time, examining the tracks from the garden path.

"Ordinarily, this is where we'd be stumped." Alethea reaches down and tenderly plucks a shimmering green scale from the dirt. "But the creature was shedding that night before it changed back into its disguise to fight her off."

"A snake?"

"A serpent." Alethea pockets the scale, inhaling a bit. "If my hunch is correct, then we don't have much time." She makes toward the van and we trail after her. "It'll be at the river. Jo's struggling, assuming she's already been poisoned."

Poison...

Jo's been poisoned?

"Come on, Lili. Fight later, run now." The detective and Jason bundle me up into the van. I clench my fists, waiting for the time to strike.

This serpent being won't stand a chance.

Chapter Thirty-Three

The River That Snakes

We drive the car along the riverbank, the wheels digging into mud. The fog rising to leave only a scant patch of window space clear. But the seamless ground gives way to seeming craters dug into the earth. Patches of twigs scattered amongst shed scales. Entire sheets of silver-and-green-scaled skin accompanied by dull, lifeless bloodstains.

We pull over at the worst of it. I tumble from the car, hardly able to wait for the doors to unlock.

"Lili?" The detective comes after me, but I tear from his grasp.

"Jo!" I scream, standing at the riverbank with my fists balled at my sides. I pick up a rock the length of my forearm and toss it in the river. Watch it sink.

Like a body.

"Jo..." I scream and scream my throat raw. Jason walks hesitantly beside me. Patty grasps my shoulder.

Alethea picks up the shed skin and examines it, pinching it between her fingers like she has all the time in the world. And Byron floats desperately close to the water, hovering at its edge. Erik reaches out for him, tossing pebbles, waiting for Byron to come back to him.

"Byron, get away from there. You're fading. I read about this in Eye training, that rivers are close to the Dead Realms. Liminal gateways or something." Erik pleads. "If we lose you too..." He swallows, head swiveling guiltily in my direction. "Sorry, Lili." He winces.

Byron hovers a moment longer, his eyes turned to the ice floes. Eventually, he gives way, turning back into Erik's open arms.

For now.

"I should go in," I tell them, pacing and turning at the riverbank. "What if she's down there? She can't exactly drown."

"...unless she was torn apart," Alethea replies, popping her lips.

I want to kill you.

I dampen down the thoughts. *Control it. Control whatever it is inside you.*

Come to the river.

"There!" Patty points to the east where two figures break the endless monotony of the river current. A scaly hide slithers to the surface, a smooth, naked back. Two arms taut around a smaller form, biting into the creature's bare skin.

A naga. Half human. Half water snake.

Green blood seeps into the river, and Jo releases her jaw, choking out, "Lili!"

I rear back, ready to hurl myself into the river after her. Alethea beats me to it. Her weapons and holsters are piled on the riverbank to avoid weighing her down. Smooth strokes take her across the river to where the pair is fighting. I beat back at whoever was holding me, following her in.

"Let her go." Detective Ikiaq this time. "It's her existence."

The river is cold, so cold I feel it in my center. Funny, I can hardly feel anything, yet I feel this. The desperation. The fear.

The creature disappears beneath the water again, worming down toward the riverbed with Jo in its grasp. Alethea catches its tail, the final thing to go beneath the water, and holds on tight as she, too, vanishes beneath the foaming river.

"Ale!" I manage to blurt out, my talons extending, useless to help. What does it matter if my teeth are sharp or my nails? What does it matter if my eyes turn red? I can't help her, not like this.

Not unless you fully turned.

"Lil!" Alethea coughs up water as the serpent twists back, this time directly underneath me. I wrap my arms tight around it, digging my claws in beneath the scales. "The thing's scales are too tough! You have to go for the soft bits!"

The soft bits?

I climb upward, but the creature screams. Jo claws at its cheek and the human half disappears once more beneath the waves, howling. This time, unarmed by Jo, it turns at a crooked angle. Digging my claws in like picks into a mountain, I clamber along its scales. In water, in air. The beast turns, its muscles undulating beneath me. I keep clawing, watching as its green skin sheds into the water for every scale I pry loose.

I make my way toward the human half, the *soft bits* as Alethea put it. I'm near what would be its waist now. Jo is still wrapped up in the howling creature's arms. A twisted death embrace, refusing to let go. Like a dog with a garden snake in its jaws. The naga has beautiful long hair, shimmering over a thickly muscled human body. The human half has a well-developed back, a round chest. The shimmering, violet hair a curtain plastered round its thicker neck. "Lili..." Jo whispers, still clawing at the creature, trying to break free.

I'm clutching onto its back now, wrestling with my legs around its serpentine scales, digging my claws beneath its arms. "Pull with me," I tell her.

Jo nods, exhausted, dark eyes glassy. We both tug at the creature's impossibly strong arms. *Turn. Turn. Turn.*

The voice inside my head battles against the endless lullaby of the river. *Sleep. Sleep. Sleep.* The water begs me.

Jo bucks against the creature's grasp as I slash at its arms. The naga whimpers, its forked tongue flicking out.

In the last moment before it finally releases Jo, I see its eyes. Pleading forgiveness.

The eyes of an animal led to slaughter.

"Kill it!" Alethea cries.

The creature releases a final yowl, a death cry, as it goes for Jo's neck.

I slit its throat before it can go any farther. The creature, silenced, slips beneath the waves. Returning to the same river it guarded. Alethea kicks away, avoiding the heavy downward tow. I go for Jo and cradle her in my arms as I swim back to land. The others are in the van, driving along the riverbank, following us.

When I finally slump my way to land, dripping wet, my skin cold, I can hardly hold myself up. Jo slips against me. I turn her around, shaking her. "Jo? Jo?"

Her eyelids flicker, not gone. But for all intents and purposes, not with us either.

Alethea follows, gasping and choking. She pulls herself to her knees, tearing off her signature leather jacket. "Well, that's ruined," she mumbles, throwing it in the open back seat.

Jason and Patty lean over Jo. "Jo is still with us. As much as a reanimated can be," Patty informs me. The detective helps heave Jo's body into the van, carefully arranging some jackets like blankets over her.

"I need to go get my weapons," Alethea says, shuffling her feet as she turns away from us. "Let you guys catch up or whatever."

"Thank you." I reach for her hand and take it in mine before she goes. "Thank you for helping us find Jo."

She smiles somewhat, her lips upturned into that teasing smirk. "It's whatever," she tells me with a mocking shrug. But I catch a flicker of pride in her eyes. "All in a day's work."

She leaves with her hands in her ruined jean pockets.

I turn back to Jo, whose lips are even paler than usual. I look out at the river, no trace of the spirit that stole Jo away. "A naga. How the hell did one get so far inland?"

The detective sniffs, blowing his nose in a tissue. He acts surprisingly human sometimes, with his hot cocoa and caribou-patch jacket. "Maybe our murderer isn't through with us yet."

"Maybe," I reply, unable to shake the horrible voice that says...

Maybe it wasn't after Jo at all. Maybe, somehow, the other creatures can sense it. Can sense who killed Anna Snow and all the other mortals.

Maybe the only true *murderer around here is you.*

Chapter Thirty-Four

Jo, Not Jo

"You should rest," Patty informs me. Jason nods his agreement, carrying a tray of mushy blood-pudding to spoon into Jo's mouth. "We've got her."

"I'll stay if it's all the same for you," I reply, holding Jo's hand in mine. I'm too tired to correct them, telling them Jo drinks souls, not blood. But let them feel like they're helping. It won't hurt her, after all. Nothing much will in this state.

Patty nods, and Jason helps lift Jo into a sitting position on her bed. Jo, still with her eyes closed, manages to take in some food.

I watch over her even after the Sweeneys clean her up and shut the door behind them. I watch over her and Tae's tree, which I've moved back into her room for the time being.

"Find her, Tae," I whisper, watching the leaves flutter softly in response.

I can't help but feel that perhaps the mandrake is just a plant after all. I watch a single leaf fall as I close my eyes, and enter the endless, wandering plane.

*

Subliminal Messaging

I made my way toward the Tigris. But they didn't call it the Tigris then. It was Idigna. Idiqlat. Water rushing everywhere when I walked into the city. My feet were bare. They covered me with wool. When they learned what I was, it changed. Linen. Silk. Thread spun from royal human hair for my accessories. Padding my cushions.

"I was actually born somewhere in the Caspian Sea, a Siren born of ash and clay."

The humans lie at my feet. My enemies do, too, but they're not in one piece. They lay gold at my feet, battered swords. Beautiful virgins. It's always the virgins. I don't take pleasure in their company, only in their delicious flesh.

"I'm so old I saw the sun rise and set on what *you'd* consider to be humanity's ancient empires. I'm so old I was there at the beginning."

I raze the cities my followers despise. Reward their loyalty and blind adoration with destruction. Bloodshed. I am the destroyer, standing so much taller than even the tallest man. The one they called a giant, the one that shepherd boy killed with a stone. He hardly comes to my knee. They sing songs and write stories about me. None of them come close to the terror that is my truth. None of them can know.

"I'll be there at the end."

Laughing. Laughing. My reign will never end. Even as the years go by and new kingdoms replace the old, they know my name. They all know my name, no matter how far I wander along the endless stretches of the world.

For I am the great mother who fell from the sky.
I am the most fearsome of all the immortals.
I am the First. The birther of chaos.
I...am...
I am...
Who am I?

*

Who's There?

I open my eyes to catch Alethea leaning in the doorway, watching me.

"You're remembering," she informs me.

"Did I..." I swallow, hard. "Did I kill Anna Snow? All those people?"

Alethea shrugs. I'm starting to see why she found it so irritating. She dangles her metal-bone keys out in front of me. "Want to catch a ride? I'll help you figure it out."

I shake my head before turning back to Jo and kissing her palm. "No, I don't think I want to know. Not yet." I shudder, my hands nervously going to my hair. Releasing it and re-braiding it over and over again, just so my shaking hands have something to do. "I don't want them to know if I did the murders. I don't want them to hate me."

Alethea laughs. "You could leave them before they find out. Run away with me."

I shake my head. "Why would I?"

But Alethea's already gone. Her emerald eyes flashing in the night, driving a car with nowhere to go but away from here.

Chapter Thirty-Five

Where Am I Going?

I don't know how long I wait there, but something twists within me. Curiosity. That cursed curiosity that makes me more human than anything.

I pad toward the door. "Ale?" I call, my eyes scanning the darkness for the monster hunter's usual van.

"Going somewhere?" It's Patty, staring at me with her arms crossed. Her retainer in place and her auburn hair piled over her head in a messy bun.

"No."

She quirks a brow at me, but both of her eyebrows go with the movement, making her look more surprised than anything. "With Alethea? At this ungodly hour?"

I close the door as quietly as I can behind me, wringing my hands behind my back. "I'm sorry. I know you like her. Trust me when I say it's not like that between us."

She shakes her head, clicking her tongue against her teeth. Like a parent disappointed with their rebellious teenage kid. It's funny, how Patty acts sometimes. Like she's even older than the oldest immortals. "I'm not mad about you moving in on Alethea. Hell, I can't judge who Alethea gets with. Ultimately, who she likes is her decision. Even though I thought you were with Jo, and I disapprove of you skipping out on her. Unless Jo's in on this, too, somehow." She pauses, taking my hands in hers. "I'm mad that you're just going to leave us like this. You're just going to run away from us." And here, she gives my hands a gentle squeeze. "Your *friends*."

I have no heart to beat. I have no mortal blood in my veins. I have no right to the acts of living, their humdrum traditions or follies. But here, something dwells within me. A sense of dread. Of loss. Of hurt.

I'm scared of losing them.

"Trust me when I say Alethea and me, we're not like that." I bite my tongue, wondering if I can chew right through it and just end this comment prematurely. No. No, that's cowardly. "I wanted to solve the murders." A half-truth. "I wanted to find the murderer and restrain them so that none of you would have to get hurt." Better.

"You wanted to solve this all by yourself?" Patty chews on her lower lip, her metal retainer glinting. "We can help."

"No, this thing... I'm afraid you can't." *I'm afraid it's me.*

"Wow. I never took you for one to underestimate your friends, Lili." Patty shakes her head, that one movement nearly enough to break me. "We're here for you. Are you here for us?"

She treads back to her room, her soft footsteps disappearing as she closes her bedroom door behind her. It leaves me with that sick feeling inside. The worry. The fear.

I should just leave them. If I weren't so selfish, I'd just leave. If I really am the murderer, and I fully turn one day, I might end up killing them all. Revert to that maddening bloodlust. The power trips.

Friendship has limits, and I'm pretty sure certain death is one of them.

*

Who Am I?

Jo sleeps for a week. Alethea disappears more and more often, taking joyrides. Detective Ikiaq even has to bring her back one time for speeding. But she's not the only one who feels restless. Our silverware clatters too loudly against our plates. At the dinner table, Jo's noticeably absent.

"So...what?" Jason shouts one night, his brow pulled low over his eyes. "Are we just going to wait for someone to die?" He throws a fork against the table. "That asshole sent a snake demon to kidnap Jo. Are we not going to retaliate?"

"We don't have any leads," Erik replies.

"Bullshit!" Jason pushes back from the table, craning his neck up to glare at Detective Ikiaq. His phantom arm is so strong that the entire table lifts from the ground, the plates and dishes spilling all over the cloth. "What about the logs in the Beast Book? What about searching through the rubble of the Eye Coven? Interrogating Sabrina until she talks. Looking over the autopsies of the victims. You're a detective. *Do something!*"

"As I told you before, Lili's in charge of the investigation." The detective glances blandly at Jason, acting like the young necromancer is just another little kid throwing a tantrum. "You'd do well to remember that." A warning.

"I..." I pick at my words just like I pick at my food. "I just want to keep you all safe."

Jason rolls his eyes. "No, you want to keep us all imprisoned. Face it, Lili..."

Patty turns to her brother, trying to quiet him. "Jason, stop being an ass."

"No!" Jason continues his tirade, getting to his feet for emphasis, his plate only halfway clean. "Ever since Jo dropped into that river, Lili's been scared." I flinch at his words. Ironic, that I'm brought down by a little mortal boy. "So what? You just gonna fall into one of your *moods,* Lili? Moods! Don't bullshit me. You're depressed, you're depressed. What kind of big, bad monster gets *depressed*?"

Erik goes quickly to Jason's side, trying to get him to sit down. His soft voice, pleading. "Come on, man. Don't do this." His words slur slightly.

I drop my fork, getting to my feet, as well. Patty moans and drops her head in her hands. "There haven't been any murders. We don't even know if Jo's kidnapping was connected. There's been too many injuries already. Dakari gone, Jo unconscious, Erik's concussion. Patty's poultices can only heal so much. Maybe..." I swallow. "Maybe we should forget about the case."

"*Forget* about the case?" Jason laughs, the sound grating to my ears. "All right, humor me, Lil. Say we forget about the case and that, wonder of wonder and miracle of miracles, there are no more murders. What do we all do, huh? Ikiaq goes back to his detective agency. Alethea returns to New York to hunt monsters. Byron writes poetry on napkins. Me and Patty run our parents' business. Erik invents the next magical fad. And you? Where do you fit in for all this?"

"Stop it, you little brat," I hiss.

"Better a brat than a coward." Jason lunges at me, breaking free from Erik's grip, and I hit back out of instinct.

"Jay!" Patty falls to her knees at her brother's side and checks his face. A bruise is already blooming on his cheek, a puffiness below his eye.

"Lili, back up," Ikiaq warns, kneeling beside Patty.

"I'm sorry..." Everyone's eyes turn to me. "I...I'm sorry."

I'm a monster.

I'm losing control.

"I'm sorry," I repeat, stumbling toward the door. Taking the shock of air against my skin. Alethea doesn't really join us at dinners any longer. I see why after tonight's episode. She often just vapes outside, leaning against her van.

She raises an eyebrow at me. "Oh, Lili, wanna smoke?"

I wave it off. "Wouldn't work on me anyways."

She purses her lips, seeing me bouncing nervously from foot to foot. She reaches behind her in the van's open interior. She reveals a paper bag with grease dripping down the edges. "French fry?" she offers.

I take the food, and though it tastes like fried, dead earth to me, I work through swallowing it. "Thanks."

"Don't mention it." She crams more of the food into her mouth and tosses the wrapper behind her in the van. "So, how about that ride?"

I turn back to the house. *They don't want me there.* "Sure," I mutter, heading into the passenger's seat.

We drive for a bit as Alethea turns the college alt-rock station on low. She croons along to one of the ballads. It suits her voice better, the lower pitch soaring to a medium-smooth solo. The drums kick in. The wail of a lonely guitar.

"In another life, I might've gone for someone like you. Made you fall for me, for the power," I tell her. "Before I devoured your flesh, that is."

"Uh, thanks." She glances over from the corner of her eyes, long lashes framing the darker green of night. "You sure you okay?"

"No. I hit them. I hit them and don't even know why. Maybe I was upset about Jo... Maybe..."

"You weren't meant to be around people." Alethea sighs, shifting in her seat.

"Maybe."

We drive along the open road. Alethea guns it. We even pass Gamin's welcome sign, and my words catch in my throat as she asks. "Do you want me to tell you what I see when I look at you? As a Seer, that is."

Be free. Unleash. Devour.

"Yes." The word sounds like a snarl despite how I try to keep my power tame.

"All those notes on the wall that Bender stole. Dakari Borden's revenge. Even the containment spells in the Eye." Alethea turns to me. "All that was for you."

I knew it. I didn't want to, but I knew it. I knew it. I knew it. I knew it.

"And the murders...?"

"Oh." She shifts in her seat again, grimacing a little as she stretches out her legs. "I don't think I should tell you that."

"Don't play games, Alethea. I hate those."

She drums her fingers against the wheel. "But you know the answer already. You just want to hear me say it.

To fill the air with empty words." She grins. "Figure it out yet?"

Oh gods.

"Who was it?" I take her in. The casual grin as she discusses it all. The long fingers that splay against her undercut. The fake leather jacket that smells of river water. "Tell me!" My voice is raw, no longer my own. No longer pretending.

"I'm sorry, Lili." Her dark lashes brush along her upper cheeks. Miraculously, she still maintains control of the car. Her voice falters. Whatever chasm passes as my heart drops into the pit of my stomach. "But your hunch was right. That dangerous monster the late Sweeneys were so afraid of? The creature that killed Dakari Borden's wife? The reason Sabrina pasted all those containment spells..." Just as quickly, she drops the false sorrow, springing to life, clasping my limp hand in hers. "Feel those hands? These are the fingers that tore Anna Snow to bits. Fuzzy memory? I don't blame you. If I did what you did, to so many people, I'd try and forget too. With whatever it took, really. Hiding. Pills. Simple memory cantrips." She flexes her fingers against my knuckles, brushing her thumb over the veins. I flinch but feel too weak to draw away. Too numbed to learn that...

All along. It was me...all along, I've been chasing clues. Playing detective. Just a dumb dog chasing after its own tail. A cat leaping at its shadow.

"Why are you telling me this?" The van speeds up. I could jump out, but I might be torn to shreds by the cement. The speed. "What's to stop me from just ending myself right now? Keep them all safe. This town. The people within it."

"I'm sorry you found out this way, really, I am. You won't tell anyone. You can't. But you won't end yourself either. No, Lili. I *know* you, remember? I'm a Seer." She stops the car, the brakes screeching. The van spins in the middle of the road, crossing into one lane and then spinning back. Luckily, nobody's out this far. My forehead slams against the dash, trickling blood before, inevitably, it slowly heals. "You're too important to die nobly. To die easily. Worthlessly." Breathing hard, panting, her hands still on the wheel. She grins with ferocity, like she wants every single tooth to show. "I never told you what I see when I look at you, huh?"

End it.

End it.

No. Stay. Stay with the darkness. Surrender to your urge.

"What am I to a Seer?" I tilt my head, watching those green eyes light up. Reminding me of broken glass against concrete, shining in overhead lights.

This is Alethea—if I can even call her that anymore. Anything, really, but a deranged Seer. She takes my hand and presses it to her brow. I think she's mocking me, but with her voice absolutely saturated with sincerity, she says, "You are everything, my Queen." And she kisses my palm, lips cool against my skin.

Queen?

Seeing my confusion, she continues. "You've been remembering, haven't you? The thrill of the hunt. Your old power. How they worshipped you. No, I shouldn't have said *my* queen. I'm from a different story. But you are the queen of many who reside on this earth. Monsters. Immortals. Reanimated." She smiles, running a single finger down my cheek. "The mother who fell from the heavens and gave birth to all anathema."

I turn away, leaving her hand in midair. Her face still tilted toward mine, a strange obsession. "I don't know what you're talking about."

"You'll remember." She frowns, staring into my eyes. "Do you want me to take you back to them? To the necros, the ghost, and that brooding detective? That insignificant ghoul?"

"Don't call her that. Insignificant. And no." I stare at my hands, wondering what power would surge from within. If I just unleashed. Took up my crown, the crown of a stranger. This obsessive murderer beside me, ready to serve. "Not until I figure this out."

"It's not a puzzle." She sighs, turning the ignition again. "But I'm here to *save* you, your Highness. Where to?"

"Away." I tell her, turning back to see the Gamin welcome sign blinking behind us. A tiny light. *Insignificant.* I move my hand to the watch. The arrows are spinning uncontrollably in Alethea's presence. *What are you?* I press a tiny button on it, one Erik didn't explain to me. One I haven't seen. Something starts blinking.

"A tracker." Alethea tuts. "They stuck you with a tracker. Some friends." She unbuckles it from my wrist and tosses it carelessly from the window. Drives over it until it's nothing. "We'll get you far away from here," she tells me.

"Yeah." I stare, numb, at the remnants of the watch, crushed on the road. Its reflection all distorted in the rearview mirror. "Away."

Chapter Thirty-Six

Why Am I?

We pull to a stop at a gas station just outside town. A rusted metal arch hangs over tilted gas pumps and a carwash that groans when the wind shoves against it. Snow drifts toward the asphalt, spinning in slow, lazy circles like fat lightning bugs on a summer's day.

Alethea pulls up to one of the pumps, takes a drag of an e-cigarette, and then pockets it as she releases the plume of smoke. "Aw shit," she teases, "wrong side for the gas."

I fold my hands beneath my armpits, staring at the swirling snow. The cloudy gray sky that releases the little bits of heaven. "Global warming?" I ask, pointing at the snowfall.

"The only truly unnatural thing about this world is how easily humans mess it up," Alethea replies, and then she smirks so I can't tell if she's kidding. She always smirks at the worst of times. "And no. The god of weather took an early sabbatical. Her daughter was pregnant. Again." She laughs, coughing a little at the end of it. I can't see her telltale emerald eyes. She's chosen to cover them with aviator glasses she dug out of the dash. "Some gods don't do birth control, apparently. Too arrogant to use a mortal creation. No matter how much it'd help them. Still think they're the shit."

"Aren't we?" I venture, leaning against the car. She joins me, her shoulder digging into mine. Igniting at its touch. Something I shouldn't do. Something dangerous.

To connect with whatever this Seer truly is. This... creature.

"I don't know." She stares down at her fingernails, more interested in digging invisible dirt out of them than continuing this. Perhaps she suspects me. How, even with this supposed trust we've built up, I still want more information. "I personally think you'd kick Percy's ass."

At that, we're both drawn out of the conversation because a busted yellowish-gold Cadillac pulls up to the abandoned gas station. Funny. Gamin's probably lost half its population, and this gas station is doing the best it has in years.

The door cracks open, and none other than Dakari Borden comes striding out of the driver's seat. He wears a short coat with deep pockets, and from those pockets, he pulls out a host of paperwork. Licenses, a row of global passports, and a host of other identification. I think I even see a few high-tech student IDs. Barcodes and everything.

"Congratulations. You're five hundred different people all at once." Dakari tells me and then turns to Alethea. "You? Less so. Not that you need help in that department."

"I thought you were on the good side," I tell Dakari, still hurting. Not knowing if there is any good side left in this battle.

"Good doesn't necessarily mean legal. And besides, I got these forgeries from a little goblin who made a deal with me in the '90s," Dakari replies, stone-faced. But a twitch at the edge of his lips gives him away. He pulls in closer to me. "Don't trust her," he whispers. "She threatened my son. I had to pretend she was just a Seer. Just a..."

Dakari's getting coerced?

Who is *Alethea?*

"You had a way out of here," I tell him, seeing the panic in his face. Hearing the fear trembling in every shaking word. "I *got you* out of here."

Dakari leans back, takes a deep breath, and looks Alethea in the eyes. "My son?"

"Safe, if he doesn't chase us." Dakari exhales, a brief moment of respite. But Alethea plows on. "But you, on the other hand. Such a quick betrayal of your friends." She raises a gun, a sleek brand with *Excalibur* on its side. A monster hunter's weapon. "You broke a blood oath."

Dakari snarls and springs at me, hands aimed for my eyes. I scream as the nails break skin, and fall to the ground.

A gunshot. My eyes.

Nothing but stars and aimless sheets of painful color.

"Lili!" Alethea gathers me in her arms. I hear rasping breathing. Mine? Dakari's? "A little blood and that'll heal. Eat." She forces open my jaw, sloshing blood toward it. "I know it's not a meal fit for a queen, but it'll do."

She cradles me to her so that my ear is pressed against her beating heart. I hear it.

I want to tear it out of her.

But there's no time. Alethea's already hauling me into the passenger's seat. My vision returns, blurry. I see my reflection in the side mirrors, a smear of blood over my lips.

Dakari's body is gone, just a puddle where he was. Alethea reaches for a coil of metallic rope and a hook in the backseat.

"Dakari...where's..."

Alethea nods to the trunk of the busted yellow Cadillac. "Taking a ride in the back. Nasty things, blood oaths. I'll have to sink the body off along the way. Car too. *Psycho* style." She stuffs the documents poor Dakari gave us in the dashboard. "I can't believe he'd attack you like that."

"He was fighting for his life."

"So, you'd just let him kill you? What are you, suicidal? Don't answer that." I glare at her from beneath my lashes, hoping she feels every ounce of hatred. She throws her hands up, backing off with the metallic cord in her arms. She moves to the Cadillac, drives it behind our car, and starts to hook it up, tying it like a makeshift trailer.

"You threatened his son. You threatened Erik. Murdered Dakari."

Alethea runs over to me, so quick I hardly process it. She runs a thumb beneath my chin, to where the dried blood is. "And you drank his blood to get your eyesight back. How innocent are you in this, angel?" I wish I could retch, but that's not what I was created to be. Truth is, I missed the taste of human flesh. I'd been living off animal substitutes for so long.

A hunter.

A queen.

A monster to rule them all.

"Powerful, the kill, huh?" Alethea laughs, dropping her hand from my face. I miss it. The pressure. The exhilaration of the hunt. "Tell me, did you miss it?"

Her heart. I want to rip her heart out and devour it.

Her eyes fall to my hands, the talons growing out of them. She tosses a pair of wool mittens at me. "Put those on. I know you want more, but I'm not putting my head on a plate, your Highness."

I lean one arm outside the open window, the metal cool against my skin. The snow not melting against my unfeeling flesh. "Where are we headed?"

"New York City. Home of a thousand-thousand monsters. Only half of them human. Easiest place in the world for a ghoul or a creep to disappear."

"And is that what I'm going to do, disappear?"

"What, were you enjoying the small-town hick lifestyle? Waking up to a rooster every morning, with Aunt Susie from down the street being hopelessly involved in your business?" Alethea gets back into the driver's seat with a slam. I blanch, staring at the trunk with poor Dakari in it, following us like a makeshift hearse. "And no, to answer your question. You're going to change into a real person. Not this Lili of the Valley bullshit. You're going to be the *real* you." She taps my nose with her fingernail at that. I fight a sneeze.

"You want me to murder again?"

"Yes. And to threaten. Lie. Make allies with the biggest monsters in the city. Destroy those who would destroy you. To see a new empire rise, one to replace the one that's fallen. Monsters shouldn't have an underworld. They should live in the light. Not be tortured when the sun goes down." She pauses at a stoplight. One tired old car beats past us at the barren intersection, trapped between a cornfield and a single, lonely farmhouse. Alethea smiles, her entire face twisting upward. As she leans to the side to kiss me, the glasses slide down her nose making her appear as stunning as she does deadly. "With me by your side to make sure nobody hurts you again." Lips run over mine, down my jaw in a whispering trace. "Gods, how beautiful you are now that you're remembering again. Not that any other gods can beat you."

"Beautiful. Beautiful." *You think you're the first to tell me?* But I watch her, restraining myself from killing her, trying to catch a glimpse of her eyes beneath the sunglasses. But she's already turned back to the road. "You're obsessed with me. But you still haven't answered what I am. What you are."

"You're a god, and I'm your servant."

"Alethea..."

The light turns green, and she's zooming off again. Racing down labyrinthine rows of corn and bales of hay and horses that are hardly standing. Gamin's just a memory now, a hazy, hazy memory. Running, but from what? Not just a small town.

The monsters there, are they less worthy because they chose to hide in the odd town's magical peace rather than fight in a bigger city's underworld?

"The mother of anathema. Like Lucifer, but if you tried to bring down heaven, you'd succeed." A chill runs down my spine as she hands me a book. I open it to Genesis, the Creation story; every other chapter is torn out. "Torah. Bible. Quran. In each version, you are the Abrahamic equivalent of Lady Macbeth, except a hundred times worse."

"A monster?"

"Stop using that mortal terminology. You are Malka, מלכה. Malika. Eresh. Vasílissa. Raja. Regina, dammit. A queen!" She hits the steering wheel, hiding her bruised knuckles from me. The gun tucked near her abdomen where the lines near her stomach disappear toward her waist. Death and life. "The one to bring about the end of the world from your womb because, according to legend, you rejected Adam for not loving you right. Naughty girl."

"If that's right, I should've killed Eve."

A shrug, a dangerous slit of a smile. "You tried. You sent the serpent. You played the long game, and I'd argue you won." I'm reminded of the naga I killed in the river, the tumble as it bared its throat to me. The amount of control I had over it, like total domination.

Another half-bred serpent, obeying its Malka.

"Lucifer tried to take down God in heaven. You were smarter than that, saw that you needed reinforcements. Hacked into Creation to serve your own needs. The anti-Eve. Bringer of corruption into the world of men."

"The world of men did that just fine without me."

"Lucifer took credit for that. But you planted the seeds of all the things men wanted. People call Eve a seductress, what a lark. You promised things greater than just sex. Empires. Worship. But you never followed through. Just took their desire and created creations of your own. The reanimated were what your admiring creations spawned. But you...?"

I connect it. The strange carvings in the wall of Clarence Bender's den. The diagrams and maps in the Book of Beasts. The mother with her belly swollen, giving birth to the first...

"True immortals," I gasp, as if taking in first air, like a newborn. "I created the first true immortals."

Alethea pulls into a parking lot. A motel whose front sign is slightly tilted. She pulls a wad of cash from the documents Dakari gave us, fanning out the hundred-dollar bills and waving them at herself to cool off. She plucks one between her fingernails, places the rest in the dash. "Bingo. You discovered you're the maker of anti-Creation. Every single monster in New York should bow down at your feet if they know what's good for them. Sure, some of the other ones, the snobby Fae, for example. The badly behaved Reanimated. They aren't quite so grateful. Don't respect their mothers or grandmothers, you know. Don't see the connection, and who can blame them? You've been gone so long, hiding as a *Siren*, they started to think you never existed." Alethea pauses, chewing on her lower lip. "Can't really blame the monsters that come from non-Abrahamic religions, you know. You're not in their books. But power tends to recognize power. It's hit or miss."

"But you never lost faith."

"How could I when I first fell in love reading about you in the Library of Alexandria? But things were in transition then, so to speak. I was changing my name. Something you can relate to, of course."

The Library of Alexandria... How the hell old are you?

But the time for questions is over. She's already booking a room in the motel. Groaning, I lean back in the seat, delving into this new information. Still hungry for more. I glance at my eyes, bloodshot, in the mirror. Or perhaps just bloody from when Dakari had tried gouging them out but failed.

"She's obsessed with you, you know."

I turn to the driver's seat. Dakari's sitting there, a tissue to his head. He removes it, blood soaked through. A bullet still lodged in his skull.

"You look good for a ghost," I tell him.

He rolls his head over to me. "Don't remind me." He looks back, grimacing. "Don't let Erik find me like this, please."

"He's a necromancer, he could..."

"Turn me into one of those frankfurters?" He snorts. "No thank you."

"But he can still *see* you even if you get rid of the body."

"Lili, I know I tried to gouge out your eyes. I was desperate to get away. And the only thing Alethea cares about in this world is you. You would've healed anyways with a little blood." He looks at my lips, frowning. "Mine, apparently."

"Point taken." I sigh, pushing out of the car and heading toward the busted Cadillac. "Where would you like to have your final resting place?"

"New Orleans."

"Dakari..."

He sighs, twiddling his thumbs. When he bends his skull, I get a really good look at what's inside his head. Lots of brain there. Smart guy. "Take me to the river. They're good liminal places. Maybe...maybe I can see my wife again."

I turn back toward where we left the Gamin welcome sign behind us in the dust. "That's back in town. The river is best back in town."

"I know."

"You want me to just leave?"

He stares at me from beneath bushy brows. He looks odd without his usual cap. Almost like he's vulnerable.

"You're good at running. But fine. Hey, it's only my final resting place."

Touché and retouché.

"Just answer this. I'm sick of getting the runaround for all my questions, ghost or no." I step closer, peering into his eyes, filled with the most life I've seen since meeting him. More dead than alive because he can finally tell the truth. "Who is Alethea Styx?"

"Go to the river," Dakari Borden replies. "And find out."

Chapter Thirty-Seven

Holding Out for an Antihero

The drive back to Gamin feels shorter than the drive fleeing it. Something about defeat. It makes time pass quicker when you have so much dread souring the pit of your stomach. My ghostly companion is in the passenger's seat of the busted yellow Cadillac. It drives well enough, despite its looks. Can't judge a book by its cover, or a car by its ugly-ass exterior.

I took some of Alethea's flashing money, stuck it in the dash. No point keeping it all in one place. Besides, I want to piss Alethea off a little. It feels good, even with just that pettiest bit of revenge. Dakari sticks his head out of the window.

"Airing out the bullet hole?" I laugh as he sticks his tongue back out at me. I drive on for a little while longer. We pass Gamin's welcome sign. The population's stayed the same, I notice. They really ought to change that. "How long do you think we have before Alethea chases us?"

Dakari checks the rearview mirror. I could swear I hear the sound of her car revving after us. The monster hunter who's not really a monster hunter. Whose identity I plan to discover at the churning of the river. "Soon."

With that, I go even faster. So quick that the speedometer can't even keep up. The car's engine makes it sound like the thing's going to pieces around us. All crackling gears and grinding and gnashing parts. I skid past the remnants of the Sweeney Inn. No summoning spells or bodies. Just pits in the dirt, a sad sign, and a bar roof that's caved in. For all we know, a storm hit it. Just the inn. And it was a hurricane.

We drive past Ikiaq's office. No dead Sirens lying outside it.

We drive past the town hall. The posters sit there, slightly damp since first I saw them. Curling at the edges. The faces peering out and watching us as we zoom down the street.

And, finally, we skid along the empty woods. The snow hasn't touched the river. It seems nothing much has. It just cuts its way through the earth, arrogant as a queen with her bridal train. The ice floes scatter. No nagas break the surface. No mer-people or kelpies or Anahita, Yam, or Sinann. No naiads or kappas or ahuizotl.

Just water, shifting endlessly through. Looping through the earth and giving life. Taking it, sometimes, but that's not its concern. It just continues, on and on. The story that never began. The story that never ends until the current dares to stop.

Dakari stares out at it with me, his hands stuck in those deep pockets. His eyes glazed over, watching the river run faster than a hundred horses.

"Come on, Dakari. Time to go." I clap his shoulder, which only partially works because touching a ghost is a real moving target, you know? Mother of anathema, or no.

He nods. "Uh-huh." And he wades further into the river. I see he doesn't have much time left. The aura of his soul is fading to the magic of the liminal place. I push the Cadillac closer to the water. The ground's tilted and slippery, and the car gives relatively easily. Or maybe it's just how fed up with it all I am. Ready to fight or die trying.

I press my shoulder against it and shove. My eyes water, probably still remnants of blood. My body burns from everything it's been through. I'm pretty sure my spine still aches from when a Frank ripped it out. But still, I push that car into the river. Because if I wronged Dakari Borden so much, hell, if I killed his wife and endangered his child, then I'll be damned unless I give him his perfect final resting place.

Damned either way, actually.

"My wife..." Dakari speaks, as though lost in a dream. Staring out at the river, I wonder if he sees the lands of the dead. Where Jason lost his arm and Tae Kim still waits to be reunited with Todd and Beatrice Sweeney. The elder Sweeneys, the ones who dared to bring me into Gamin. If only they knew what they summoned. For what? Love for the old ways?

Should the old ways have died with me?

"My wife passed away, but the first face I saw wasn't hers. It was Erik's. Because Erik was still alive, I had to be alive too. For him." Dakari speaks and the car gives a little more away. I ram my shoulder into the taillight, and the trunk bounces a bit. A thud as part of corpse Dakari's skull hits the edge. "But Erik doesn't need me."

"He still needs you. I think the words you're looking for are that he'll always have you." I laugh and the tip of the car hits the water. "You're a part of him, after all. Kind of hard to forget when he looks in the mirror and sees you in his eyes. His smile."

"Now, that's kind of you to say, Lili." Dakari chuckles, waist-deep in the water now. "But he'll get by just fine. He's always been terribly clever. Terribly, terribly clever." He turns back, and for just a moment, his eyes light up again. "But you, Lili. You're taking so damn long to figure it all out."

"Figure what out?" The car's halfway in now. One more push and it should...

The car turns over. Bubbling, frothing as the river hits up against it, pulling it in with the tow of a relentless current like a child wanting to play. The wheels float above the surface, the river opening wider. Pulling the car into its fathomless depths. Funny, I didn't think the river could be so deep. Yet the car keeps sinking, sinking.

Dakari fades as his body goes along with it. Soon, it's just his voice I hear saying:

"Her name is Alethea Styx."

Alethea Styx.

Styx...

Styx! Like the river.

I shake my head, grimacing now, though it turns out somewhat like a smile.

And I'm not the only one smiling. Alethea's left the car on the near-empty highway. A wonder, really, that anybody manages to ship in food and snacks and processed alcoholic beverages into this place with just how empty the roads are.

Must be on account of all the monster-hiding magic.

"You left me. Stole money, too, but who gives a shit about that." Alethea springs quickly down the hill, not even bothering to brush away the ferns, nettles, or razor-edge branches. She comes down with gashes on her arms. An ankle that swells past her low-cut sneakers. "Why?"

"You lied to me. You're a river goddess. The name Styx. The Library of Alexandria comment. Erik's watch spinning out of control beside you. How you mentioned Persephone and Hades as casually as you would your Aunt Susie." I hold my arms out to my side, still grinning like a fool. "Why?"

She holds out a single finger, her smile fading as quickly as poor Dakari. "You're close. Rivers, sure. But it's not Styx you should be fixated on. It's Alethea. Or rather..." She moves closer to me and clasps my head between her hands. Her face shifts into a little girl. The one I saw, and thought was the detective's daughter. It shifts again, this time to a young woman, the one I saw who pretended to be Alice, Patricia's ex-girlfriend.

Finally, she shifts to her final form. A powerful woman, standing nine feet tall. Thick brows that draw over dark eyes, hair pulled back into coils that drape down her back. A dress that's laden with multiple gold and silver threaded fabrics over her chest and waist. Arms thickly corded with muscle, a tanned neck that tilts at an odd angle. A wreath of laurels as her crown. She moves like river water. Fast. Unforgiving. Incensed. "My real name is Lethe."

"Wow, Alice then Alethea. Really out to break Patty's heart, weren't you, shapeshifter?"

Lethe shrugs. "I don't think you recognize the name."

"What can I say? Too many Lethes in my repertoire."

She goes to the river and runs her hands into the water. It bubbles up along her skin, resting in droplets that move and shimmer like beads of diamond-glass. "Lethe. The goddess of forgetting." She points to the river, the liminal space shimmering. Shifting to a curtain that overtakes the land like silk. "My river is the one that keeps this town in the shadows. It's the magical energy that draws monsters to it. The ability to be forgotten by the world that tried to kill us."

I stare at it, unimpressed. She lets the frozen water droplets fall and shatter against the earth. "Is that where you dumped the bodies of Anna Snow and the rest of those victims too?"

She shrugs. "I see why you like shrugging. Distances you from actually stepping up to the plate. Am I coming clean now? Finally, being baptized in my own river." She laughs, hands tucked into her waistband, revealing blue veins like tiny rivers in her skin. "I set that naga on Jo when Jo wanted to get rid of me. I brought Clarence Bender back to drive Sabrina insane so she'd stop bugging you. I convinced Dakari Borden I was a hapless Seer who just wanted to help his revenge quest to kill you. Hell"— she leans her head back—"I even killed that special ed girl. What did you call her, Anya Bow?"

"Anna Snow." I look her over again, the sparkling green eyes. Still so carefree. Discussing the weather.

"Oh, don't look at me like that, Lil." She chuckles, singing slightly to the tune. "You've done so much worse than me, haven't you?"

"You tried to make me think it was all me, that *I* had murdered Anna Snow."

"Get over it. I wanted to reveal the real you. To draw you here. I didn't think you'd lose every ounce of courage you had left."

How can I have more humanity than she does?

"Why the murders then?" I fire back. "You couldn't have known that I'd try to solve the case."

Her carefree demeanor breaks then, ever so slightly. "No, you're right. I didn't predict that you'd befriend those idiots. Try to play Sherlock." She exhales again, closing her eyes for a moment. She snaps her eyes open, moving toward me. "I thought I'd leave the entrails as gifts. But you've been in hiding too long, haven't you, Lil? You think you have a conscience." She snorts. "Isn't that just dandy? But, luckily, you drove them away all by yourself."

Jason on the ground. The bruise blooming against his face.

He had just gotten angry. Emotional, as most young boys do. It wasn't his fault. I should've known better, but I couldn't control myself.

I could've killed him. Easily.

"How did nobody recognize you? Nobody notice?"

She winks at me, leaning her head back. Shifting form again. Alice. Alethea. Lethe.

"Fine, you're good at changing who you are."

"Yes, Alice never left Gamin." She snickers. "Instead, she went on a crime spree. And when people started to notice, she killed those too. Or..." Another moment, another form. This time, she's a little girl with a spray bottle at her hip. In that sickly sweet, little girl voice, she continues. "I followed the detective around directly." She wiggles her hips, the spray bottle bouncing. "It's not window wiper. No, this stuff is much stronger." She giggles. "It's a memory wiper. Right from my own river. Neat, huh?"

"Great, you explained how you got away with it. But *why*?"

Alethea wrings her hands together, shifting back to the punk rock monster hunter I knew her as. It's not all that different from her Lethe form, really. Just more eyeliner. A little shorter. Which is strange to see Alethea Styx wringing her hands together. "Being forgotten might be my strength. Best way to get away with murder." She turns her face to the clouded sky, searching for something there. "But I was tired of it. Why do you think I'm telling you everything now? Because I'm stupid?" She shakes her head, laughing, taking my hands in hers. "It's because eternity gets so lonely. So, so fucking lonely. But everyone forgets me. Admit it, you can hardly keep your eyes on me, even now."

I shake my head awake, snapping back to attention. "I don't understand why. You were so clearly in focus when we were on the road. It must be because you're so close to your river."

"No. *No.*" She still has my hands in hers, rubbing her thumbs along the backs of my palms. Little shivers run down my spine. I try three times to stare into her eyes, but even with my growing power, I can hardly latch onto her gaze. I keep forgetting the exact geometry of her face, unable to keep it from slipping past my mind. Sand through fingers. "It's what I am. How I am. I was *made* to be forgotten. But if I left a trail behind me? A trail of...of death." She laughs, her teeth so sharp. So bright. "People can get famous for dying, right? Serial killers, they have that morbid fanbase all the time. Horrible people. I've seen them in history. Some even get called *heroes*. Legends. Killed millions in one foul swoop, and still they were on the right side of history, so they're fine!"

"Alethea... Lethe... You're trying to get remembered in the obituaries."

"No, listen. I won't be ignored now. Not when I'm telling you everything, begging you to remember me." She licks her lips, the circles on my hands. Tracing my flesh, what passes as my blood and body. "I just want *you* to remember me. Because...because I read about you. I followed you. Your empire. How it...how it all fell so, so quickly." I blink a couple times at that. I hardly remember the time they worshipped me, and now she's telling me to remember how it vanished? "You should know, shouldn't you? You were replaced by Eve. The first woman ever to be forgotten, to be villainized because you wanted more."

I smile a bit at that, still seeing fuzzy remnants of it.

*

Memories

I made my way toward the Tigris. But they didn't call it the Tigris then. It was Idigna. Idiqlat. Water rushing everywhere when I walked into the city. My feet were bare.

But the Tigris was where I always ended up. The water where I rose from sand. The same sand they made Adam from until they decided that I asked for too much.

I would have eaten every apple in that garden to become god. To make my own creations.

I would have to start again. To make my own creations from the sand beneath the Tigris.

To become mother of anathema, I'd have to harness power. And power came from bloodshed and glory. I couldn't make souls on my own. God didn't let me steal that, not really. But I could insert them into my own creations, the sand closest to where they first dropped me from Eden. The place where Eden's power was strongest.

The Seraphim threw me from the Garden because they sensed how I wanted more. How Adam was an afterthought in my grand plan. How I laughed in the gardens and took apart the creatures, nearly killing a few, except they couldn't die. None of us could originally.

I was too curious. Knowledge, too dangerously close to grasping it without the help of fruit. So, they made a pretty woman in my stead who would bear all the punishment. Have children torn out of her who killed each other. Watched her husband blister in the desert until he brought forth life from bleeding hands. In some ways, I pitied her.

If only she had the knowledge I did. Then I could make her something.

Chapter Thirty-Eight

Past the Point of No Return

"What was that? You remembered again." One hand drifts upward and comes to rest on my face. "Gods, if only you could return to your true form. Show them all what you truly are. Raise hell."

"Raise hell? One could only lower that cesspit." I step backward, intoxicated now. Walking toward the river. It's no Tigris...

But it could be.

"I had an empire." The words die giddy on my lips. "Wars were won. Cities ransacked. I brought out potential in my immortal creations. Sphinxes. Three-headed serpents. Jinn."

Alethea slinks up behind me, her monster-hunting sword still at her hip. Running her arms around my neck, kissing the back of it. "All could be yours again."

I flinch. "Don't touch me."

"Why?" She blinks, face still slipping like a mask of water in my mind's eye. "Do you want me to pretend to be her?"

"Who?" And I ask while knowing, in my miserable state, who.

"Your little reanimated. Jo Kim."

I see her start to shift. The silver-blue wisps of hair. The fatal eyes. I clasp her by her collar and lift her nearly off her feet. "Do it and I drown you in your own river."

She pecks my skin with her lips, staying Alethea. I stumble away from her, wiping my mouth with the back of my hand. She still looks pleased. "At least I made you forget her for a little while. Forget your little Scooby gang."

"It's in your DNA. If we have that." I sigh, running my arms around myself. Exhausted, I can't help but laugh a little. The sun doesn't show in this town, but it feels like it's been forever since I left the Sweeneys. Long enough that evening bled into night and then day again. My eyes are crusted over from all they've been through, my hair braided and then braided again into greasy coils, and I left my favorite peacoat back at the Kim house. "I've worn the same shirt for six days. And I haven't been put together since Chanel died."

"Six days? And on the seventh, God rested, so we could get in some real trouble then. Besides, you look sexy to me." I step into the river, the water lapping at my toes, soaking through my shoes. Alethea pulls me back in alarm. "What are you doing? You'll forget *everything*. You can't do that. Not now."

"Sexy. Beautiful. I might as well have stayed a Siren. That's all I am to you."

"Powerful." Alethea lets me go after spinning me around to face her. A wisp of dark hair. Looking up at me from beneath smudged eyeliner, and the jangle of black bangles along her arms like bones rattling in the wind. "Strong. Murderous. Vicious. Cunning. A goddess. A conqueror. A queen who will take down the world."

"Another obituary." I unsheathe her sword and hand the hilt to her. "Kill me and you'll be remembered still, won't you? The one who brought down the mother of anti-Creation."

"What?" Alethea's perfect triumph breaks then. The eyeliner smudges next to bared teeth. A snarl from the back of her throat. "That's not how this works. I'm supposed to rule beside you. We have to rebuild an empire. Together."

"No." I chuckle, stepping back toward the river again. She stops me, alarmed. Her hands digging into my flesh, hurting me to stop me from hurting myself. "No, I'm just a story you read about. And how can I live up to that legend? I peaked in the Garden. There's nothing more I can do."

"End the world with me." The desperate whine in her voice drums like the beating wings of a wasp.

I roll my eyes at that, embracing the look of pain on her face. "What are you, six? That's the plot of every supervillain movie ever. Christ, have some substance."

"But I did this all for you. To bring you to me."

"And so?" I step closer, satisfied to see her *finally* stumble back. Terrified to see me here before her. Terrified to see just how tamed I've become. "Am I everything you wanted? This alleged anti-Creation heroine who's little more than a Siren who doesn't even like sex. Sure, I once had power. I once murdered thousands just to feel the ghost of adrenaline. Then I got bored. Lonely. Sad. Dare I say it, depressed. What Malka, what monster, gets depressed?"

"You can be that again!"

I shake my head. "Oh no, Alethea. Alice. Lethe, whoever the hell you are. Well, this is who I am. Take it or leave it. I'm not your storybook. I'm not your evil superwoman. I am Lili. Not Lili. Lilit. Lilītu. ki-sikil-lil-la-ke. Lamia. The First. The Dark Maid. Maiden of Desolation. Mother of Anathema. Not whatever I once was."

Alethea laughs and laughs and laughs. I laugh with her. We're laughing so hard that Alethea has to stop to vomit. After another twenty minutes of this, I start freaking out. Because she's not stopping. In fact, she grows haggard. Stretching to a skeleton woman nine feet tall, with coils of hair and a laurel wreath that's rotting on her pretty, bleached head. Gaping holes where her eyes were, and lips curled into a permanent smile.

No wonder she wanted to be forgotten.

"Lili? *Lili?*" The laughter turns to sobs, tears of blood running down her cheeks, over her tilted neck. "After all I've done for you. Lili." Her voice even sounds distorted now, the cruelty of laughter turned to horrid, choking sorrow. "After all I've done..." I try to run, but I've seen it too late. The murder in her nonexistent eyes. *"Then die."*

She snatches me up, outpacing my meager attempt at running with her unnatural height. Grabs me by the back of my neck and forces my head beneath the river water.

I don't know how, but I can feel the cold as it soaks through the tiny holes in my skin. I can feel what it's like to lose breath. I can feel, after all this time, what it's like to die.

To put it most plainly, it is the absence of living. Existing.

But to put it in song?

If I had a million lives to live and a million deaths or to not go gently into that good night or have miles to go before I sleep. To take the road less traveled by or dying is an art that, like everything else, I do exceptionally well. Or walking in beauty like the night or fields of daffodils or still, I rise. But still, measuring my life out in coffee spoons, ours is but to do or die...and I didn't eat the plums.

But I like Oscar Wilde. He put it in this way.

"Yes, death. Death must be so beautiful. To lie in the soft brown earth, with the grasses waving above one's head, and listen to silence. To have no yesterday, and no tomorrow. To forget time, to forget life, to be at peace. You can help me. You can open for me the portals of death's house, for love is always with you, and love is stronger than death is."

But who knows if that's even what he said or wrote or dreamed of?

I got that one from the internet, after all. What a wonderful invention.

Chapter Thirty-Nine

(???)

"Who are you?"

The figure in front of me doesn't say much. It's not that they don't shift in and out of focus like Ikiaq as a shapeshifter or Lethe with her river. It's more this person occupies a space that isn't much of either. Neither here, nor there. Neither above, nor below.

They aren't really one to be confined much at all. Not unless you count that they're technically everything at once. Yet nothing because the maker cannot make oneself.

But, just to be certain, I ask.

"Who are you?"

"Iam."

"That's it? Just the three-lettered name? None of the other titles?"

"Iam."

"Ah, I see."

A brief pause here.

"So, will you be sending me back?"

A shrug, if you can call it that, from Iam.

"I don't know if you were mine to control."

"Free will." I snort a little at that. "Funny, isn't it?"

Iam doesn't laugh back.

"So...I can go now?"

"You're doing better."

For once, even in the face of all that power, of the one who threw me out like so much trash. The one who, in some ways, started it all and could end it all if they wanted...

I'm speechless.

Better? I'd hate to wonder what that entails.

*

The Minor Chord

I'm floating, soaring down a tunnel that consists of the reflections of a hundred versions of me, split up into a hundred stars. A comet races past a planet. A moon crashes near a solar system. And through it all...

I finally open my eyes and see myself. The real me hiding behind "just" Lili.

The one that, despite every fiber of my being fearing I can't control it, I need.

Hello there, Mama of anti-Creation.

How've you been?

*

The Major Lift

I rise at thirty feet, tall enough to snap trees between my hands. Loud enough to roar so loud in the ancient song that every living being trembles before me. Talons stretch like machete blades down from my fingernails, hands extended into claws. A face that yawns into a gaping mouth with two rows of teeth. When the mouth is closed, as triumphant as a battle goddess. Beautiful? Sure, if you ignore the blood.

Skin the same color as the earth my maker made me from. Eyes that reflect the souls of everyone I killed. Hair the color of night that drapes down my back like a cloak but is currently braided into the style of the serpents that worshipped me before all the rest did.

Lili. Lilit. Lilītu. ki-sikil-lil-la-ke. Lamia. The First. The Dark Maid. Maiden of Desolation. Mother of Anathema.

I don't have horns. That's Lucifer you're thinking of, sweetie. But my name, it's etched all over my body, inked in the burning blood of my enemies. In Hebrew. Sumerian. Aramaic. Greek. Latin. The Romance Languages. Austronesian. Hierogylphs. Sigils. Indigenous tongues. Languages dead, still living, or resurrected. Languages only the gods dared speak. A part of me. To remind myself that something might have made me, but *I* am the one who saved me.

"If the Sweeneys had successfully summoned me instead of you?" I laugh, the sound carrying over all of Gamin. *Let Lethe's river try to wash away that.* "Well, it's no wonder this town's still standing. Tsk, tsk, Lethe. You even had a head start."

I scoop her up, the skin and bones, and bring her to my face. Folding her between my hands, the talons encasing her like a second skin.

"You lied to me. Humiliated me. Killed those who were important to me."

"So, what? You're going to kill me for saving you?"

I raise a single, inked brow at that. "Darling, you tried to kill me first."

"We're monsters..." Lethe starts.

I immediately dunk her in the river. She can't drown in it, probably. It's her child, after all. But she can certainly be mildly inconvenienced. "Monsters. Oh dear, that's a foul word, isn't it?"

"What do you want?"

"What most deities want." I laugh, spinning her upside down so she hangs by her heels. "Revenge."

Tear out her heart.

Devour her flesh.

I peer at her closer. New plan. She doesn't really have much of a heart, not as rotted to Hades as she is. "No, I can't kill you. I'm kind of your mother, aren't I? Sort of? How wonderfully Ancient Grecian. You'd appreciate that." A pause then. I kneel, locating Clarence Bender's hidden cellar. I brush the leaves off it, lift the door. "No, I think I'll send you to visit Percy and Hades, the royalty of hell. You miss them, right? They're probably awfully worried wondering why one of their rivers of memory went rogue."

She splutters as I lift some chains from Clarence Bender's cellar and start wrapping them around her. A cage soon follows to place her in, nice and reinforced blessed iron. Necromancy charms included to even keep the undead civil. "What? You think I didn't figure it out, Lee, baby? The five marks you cut into every dead body. Clever. Just like the five rivers of the Underworld. And here we thought you'd stop at five murders."

"All serial killers have calling cards," she mutters.

"Not the smartest ones. And the good ones are cocky. You aren't good enough for that."

I lower her then, and finally, the worst part. I take her sword and start sawing off one of my talons, the one on my left pinky finger. It'll just grow again if I eat anyway.

"What's that for?" A note of worry in her voice.

I stab it through her heart. She inhales sharply, eyes go unfocused. But still, she continues to exist, even weakened as she is, scrabbling weakly at the five-foot, severed claw that's piercing her. Not much she can do, chained and caged and impaled as she is. "Funny." I laugh, closing my eyes and willing myself to fit back into the skin that's too small for me. Into *just* Lili. "I guess that proves there was nothing there in the first place."

I take a flyer from the floor of the cellar before closing it up for good.

I paste it on her cage, forcing her head to prop up and stare at it.

"Her name was Anna Snow," I tell her. "Remember that, you heartless bitch."

Chapter Forty

This Too Shall Pass

"Will you follow him?"

My eyes are glazed over. I'm soaked through with mud and river water, curled up on the floor and currently heavily staining one of the blankets I tore off the couch.

"*Bruja*?"

It's Byron and Erik, peering at me with anxious eyes. Eyes glittering with worry, unsaid emotions and just the barest hint of supernatural tears.

"Your father's dead. Promise me you won't follow him," I mumble weakly, every inch of my body itching. Wanting to go back to the monstrosity before, but I won't let it. As hungry as the thirty-foot version of me would be, but I refuse to feed. "Or I'll kill you," I finish weakly.

Erik slumps over, too shocked to cry. Byron hugs his arms around him.

"Lil, you can't just return like this!" Byron shouts, angry now. His eyes blinding, going semi-poltergeist. I'm too tired to care. "Dragged in from who knows where, saying you...you what? You killed Erik's dad?"

I shake my head. "It was Alethea. Lethe. Your father wanted to protect you, Erik. That's why he didn't want you to know who she was. She was going to kill you. All of you."

"Then what did she want with you?" Erik this time, his voice a moan, nuzzling as much as he can into Byron's nonexistent warmth.

"She wanted a ghost. Who she wanted died a long time ago."

"You should've brought us," Erik scolds.

I scoff at that, thinking at how weak I was before I went with Iam. Wherever *there* was. "I couldn't have protected you. I wanted to die alone, not dragging you with me."

"You damned idiot! Playing the big, bad lone wolf all the time. What are you, Harrison Ford?" Erik screeches. I flinch at the pain in his voice, deciding that's worth it compared to the pain of seeing him dead beneath Lethe's hands.

"No, I'm Lil."

"Chill, Byron. I knew." Erik hugs his arms around himself, even as Byron nuzzles him closer. "I just knew that idiot..." He says *idiot* in a way that sounds false. Like he's really trying to say every word he never got to say for his father, but it's coming out as anger instead of a broken heart. "I knew that idiot got himself killed."

"He's happy. He's with your mother." I inform him, remembering how Dakari Borden looked before entering the river. "He says he's always a part of you. You have his smile."

Byron just stares at me. And the bewilderment party doesn't let up.

He continues staring at me, running a freezing finger down my spine. "You're sweating. Chills everywhere. You're immortal. You don't get sick. No." His eyes adjust slightly. "You *look* different. Like two things at once, like Ikiaq."

Erik holds his wrist out. Dimly, I see one of his fixed-up watches on it. The needle spins out of control beside me. "Damn, Lili. Byron's right. What the hell are you?"

"Promise me," I repeat. "I can't lose anyone else tonight."

They exchange a look, dragging another pillow beneath my head so that I can ruin that too. The blanket wasn't enough, apparently. "Fine, fine. But you give us a full report in the morning." Byron places a ghostly, albeit confused, kiss on my cheek. Confused why I'm here. Why I ran in the first place. Why I made Jason take Ikiaq and drive out to a remote location in the woods to pick up a "package" left by our suspect. Ready to bare it all with some of Patty's ultra-high-tech truth serum. Why I'm so adamant nobody else *dies* tonight.

"Good night, *bruja,*" Byron whispers.

Erik kisses my other cheek, his eyes fixated on Byron above me. "Night, hun."

I pause, rolling over just as they hit the living room door.

"Guys, it's Lil." A deranged smile comes to my face, one I quell as quickly as possible. No more talons. No more teeth or impaling for a while. I want to eat waffles in the morning and drink warm tea with Patty and talk about how I'm feeling or what cute girl she has a crush on next. I want Jason to make burnt toast and talk excitedly about sports I'll never want to play, and then about how you can use physics to optimize the curve of the football. I want Ikiaq to tell me more about his journey with immortality. I want Byron to read poetry beside a fire as Erik works on a way to bring him back from the ghostly realms, kind of like Casper in that old, live-action Halloween movie.

And I want Jo to wake up.

Yes, that's it. I want Jo and every single facet of what makes Jo herself. I want the silver-blue hair alongside the whip-smart sarcasm. I want the dry sense of humor beside the tendency toward whiskey with straws. I want the skeletons in the closet alongside the dances we have in front of the bathroom mirror. I want her stupid plant that she believes delivers souls straight to Tae. I want her to tell me why she loves the little fox girl so much and why that's her favorite folktale her parents ever told her.

But most of all. I want my friends to say my name. My *real* name.

"You can call me Lili too."

About the Author

Sophie Whittemore is a Dartmouth Film/Digital Arts major with a mom from Indonesia and a dad from Minnesota. They're known for their *Gamin Immortals* series (*Catch Lili Too*) and *Legends of Rahasia* series, specifically, the viral publication *Priestess for the Blind God*. Their writing career kicked off with the whimsical *Impetus Rising* collection, published at age seventeen.

They grew up in Chicago and live a life of thoroughly unexpected adventures and a dash of mayhem: whether that's making video games or short films, scripting for a webcomic, or writing about all the punk-rock antiheroes we should give another chance (and subsequently blogging about them).

Sophie's been featured as a Standout in the *Daily Herald* and makes animated-live-action films on the side. Their queer-gamer film *IRL—In Real Life* won in the Freedom & Unity Young Filmmaker Contest (JAMIE KANZLER AWARDS Second Prize; ADULT: Personal Stories, Third Prize) and was a Semifinalist at the NYC Rainbow Cinema Film Festival.

Their prior works include *A Clock's Work* in a Handersen Publishing magazine, *Blind Man's Bluff* in Parallel Ink, a Staff Writer for AsAm News (covering the comic book convention was a dream), and numerous articles as an HXCampus Dartmouth Correspondent. Ultimately, Sophie lives life with these ideas: 1) live your truth unapologetically and 2) don't make bets with supernatural creatures.

Email: authorsophiawhittemore@gmail.com

Facebook: www.facebook.com/thesophiewhit

Twitter: @thesophiewhit

Website: www.sophiawhittemore.com

Also Available from NineStar Press

Connect with NineStar Press

www.ninestarpress.com

www.facebook.com/ninestarpress

www.facebook.com/groups/NineStarNiche

www.twitter.com/ninestarpress